# THE LAND WHERE LOST THINGS GO
## BY OLIVE WATSON

Novels by Richard Francis

*Blackpool Vanishes*
*Daggerman*
*The Enormous Dwarf*
*The Whispering Gallery*
*Swansong*

*To Helen —*

*with love*

# The Land Where Lost Things Go
## by Olive Watson

**Richard Francis**

*[signature]* 26 Sept 90

CARCANET

First published in Great Britain 1990 by
Carcanet Press Limited
208–212 Corn Exchange Buildings
Manchester M4 3BQ

The quotation from *The Enchanted Wood* by Enid Blyton
is included with the permission of Darrell Waters Ltd.

**British Library Cataloguing in Publication Data**

Francis, Richard, 1945 –
    The land where lost things go.
    I. Title
    823.914 [F]

    ISBN 0–85635–886–X


The publisher acknowledges financial assistance from
the Arts Council of Great Britain.

Typeset in 11pt Bembo by Bryan Williamson, Darwen
Printed and bound in England by SRP Ltd, Exeter

*for Jo, William & Helen*
*with love*

## Note

This is the first draft of a novel
for children by the late
Olive Watson (b.1900, d.1975)
and includes autobiographical
and journal material.

'He will not come down until he wants to,' said the biggest brownie. 'That is the oldest and most magic tree in the world. It is the Faraway Tree.'

'The Faraway Tree!' said Bessie, in wonder. 'What a strange name! Why do you call it that?'

'It's a very strange tree,' said another brownie. 'Its top reaches the far-away places in a way we don't understand. Sometimes its top branches may be in Witchland, sometimes in lovely countries, sometimes in peculiar places that no one has ever heard of. We never climb it because we never know what might be at the top!'

'How very strange!' said the children.

— Enid Blyton, *The Enchanted Wood*

# Chapter 1

## We meet Dot and her Family

There was once a little girl called Dot who lived with her family in a nice house quite near the sea, in a part of the country called Cornwall. Her family consisted of her mother, her father, her brother Harry, and her two uncles.

These uncles were her mother's brothers. The younger was called Arthur, and he was never referred to as Uncle, even though he was old enough and ugly enough, goodness knows. (In point of fact he was quite handsome, if you like a man to look as smoo-ooth and groomed as a goldfish; but he was *certainly* old enough.)

The other uncle was called Uncle Taylor and he was *always* known as Uncle, even by his own sister and her husband (Dot's parents). I suppose it was because there was something deeply uncle-ish about him.

Not that he was the sort of lovely uncle children hope to have, the sort with great big warm hands containing a tip for their nephews and nieces, like the coins in a Christmas pudding, the sort who has lived a life at sea and is chockfull of salty yarns. Uncle Taylor wasn't in the least an uncle in that sense of the word.

Though come to think of it he *had* once sailed to Africa. But surely no parrot had ever stood, or sat (whichever parrots do) on that dapper and dandruff-free shoulder. When you were with Uncle Taylor you did not remotely sense the swish and flicker of grass skirts. No *indeed*. There was no after-echo of tom-toms. You caught not a whiff of acrid leonine odours. Heavens, not the merest tiddly whiff of such things!

But blow and blast the uncles for now. Oh dear me, all Enid

9

Blyton has to say is Once upon a time there were Mick, Dick, Janet and a dog, and there you are, deliciously expectant. Mick has rumpled hair, Dick is greedy, Janet likes doing the washing up, and the dog woofs a lot and wags its plumy tail. Wonderful! We believe in them at once, Enid does too. While I can't even provide a rollcall of my characters without getting into a dreadful muddle, despite the fact that this batch doesn't have to be realistic, since they are, or were, real in the first place. My writing is like my cooking, with bits of character and story all thrown together any old how. I only hope it will have turned into something recognizable by the time it comes out of the oven.

## Dot's Mother

Dot's mother was a pale quiet lady who rarely seemed to *do* anything. She had a way of sweetly drifting round the house.

Have you ever noticed how a cloud makes its way about the sky?

If you look carefully at its very very edge you will see white round legs dangling and billowing along as it huffs and puffs across blue grass. Cloud legs look like hundreds of little white balloons.

Dot's mother got about in much the same way. Not that you could make out her soft, tumbly legs because they were hidden away under her clothing. You see, I have to admit that I am one of those writers of rather long ago. The sort who make you feel impatient because they use stiff and unhelpful words like infatuated and consumption. Even our words have dresses down to their ankles. When *I* say Once upon a time I mean it personally. I was born with the century, which was a grave mistake, since alas it means that I'm now seventy-five years old. I have to *keep up*, you see. Anyway, what I'm trying to make you understand is that children born in my era had mothers without legs. Even our mothers' ankles were only fleeting.

Despite this handicap, other children's mothers always seemed (to Dot) as busy as flies against a windowpane. They buzzily exchanged cuttings, or were 'at home', or chose curtains. Or sewed and knitted.

10

If you've ever watched a cloud knitting you'll understand quite a lot about Dot's mother. Cloud fingers are not at all suited to holding knitting-needles, even those nice fat helpful ones that children use. So clouds rarely try their luck with them. And when they do, oh my! They drop stitches at a quite dreadful rate.

Have you gone for a walk on a cold winter's day (wearing your hat and coat and muffler, I hope!) and discovered that the air is becoming full of fluffy white flakes? Now you know what they are. Dropped stitches, from the sky. Clouds only try their multitudinous bumbly hands at knitting in the winter-time, because that's when one feels the need for woollies.

Clouds are incapable of thinking ahead.

Listen to this. It is going to be of NO HELP whatsoever, I suspect.

> *Uncle Taylor:* Sis! Sis!
> *Mother:* Heavens, Uncle Taylor, is that you? You frightened the life out of me. I was miles away.
> *Uncle Taylor:* You're *always* miles away.
> *Mother:* Well, this afternoon I was further. It must have been the, you know...
> *Uncle Taylor:* Weather.
> *Mother:* Weather.

(Weather in our household was a term sometimes synonymous with sherry.)

> *Uncle Taylor:* Since you hardly ever go out, it's extraordinary how influenced you are by weather.
> *Mother:* I think that must be why I hardly ever go out.
> *Uncle Taylor:* You need one of those comprehensive umbrellas, like that thing Arthur's so terribly proud of.
> *Mother:* Arthur is terribly proud of all his things.

How true! Even now I can see his surprised and elated fish-like face, the eyes boggling with the wonder of it all. Look at

11

me, I'm Arthur! What a treat! Look at my umbrella! It's a great big one, keeps me dry as a bone. And my bicycle! Such a useful machine!

> *Mother:* In any case, I *have* a sturdy umbrella. I call it *home.*
> *Uncle Taylor:* I've brought you a present.
> *Mother:* You *are* a darling.

[And they look at each other significantly. Here is spindly Uncle Taylor in his finery, hat and cane in one hand, present clasped behind his back in the other. And there is mother, generous, lazy, in a long floaty dress. So different. But they share the same colouring, the same eyes. Sudden rich browns against their palish complexions, like splotches of soil. My eyes are brown, too, but then I'm brown generally, so it's not the same. I don't share the eyes, or the glance.]

> *Uncle Taylor:* A roll of drums, a tootle of wind, and voici!
> [He produces his present, much beflounced with ribbon]
> *Mother:* Sheer greed! Also, avarice. Not to mention *lust.* [Tears wrapping off]

And then

> *Mother:* [in sudden school-mistressy voice, two octaves lower than usual]: Uncle Taylor! What have you been up to?
> *Uncle Taylor:* [coyly]: There's a pattern-book also. And needles. I hoped you would do me some socks.
> *Mother:* Socks? My dearest bro, I can't knit at all, let alone round a corner.

[Her voice was cool and still as a pond, while comicalness darted about below the surface. A change came over Uncle Taylor. His insignificant cossetted features puckered in grief. His face, silly old-fashioned sideburns and all, that intricate little face of his, *ran*, much as a little boy's face might, having been left out all day in the rain.]

> *Uncle Taylor* [humbly]: A new knitting-wool shop has opened. Just by the bridge.
> *Mother:* And I suppose you queued with all the dears.
> *Uncle Taylor:* I suppose I did.

Really, hand on heart, I don't remember this scene at all. How could I? I was probably about eight. And yet I see the whole thing in my mind's eye, hear it with my mind's ear. That is the magic of fiction. In the real world, things either happen or they don't happen. In a book, though, you can steer a middle course. If your possibility is alive, it will bloom. Which is why a good book seems more true than real life. I might not be able to report what Uncle Taylor and my mother actually said in my presence when I was eight years old, but I remember their possibilities.

I also remember that Uncle Taylor would walk the streets of our town for hours at a time. I think he was always hoping that he would one day turn down a previously unremarked avenue, and find himself in a different place altogether. No doubt this was the side of his nature that had propelled him to Africa. Even a little woolshop could catch his attention, and give him a momentary hope.

[My mother looked at Uncle Taylor, her mouth pursed as though to hold the smile in. Uncle Taylor looked back, his features relaxing. Suddenly he laughed. He had a crude, ugly laugh for such a finely-chiselled individual. (It strikes me this is quite often the case.) My mother reciprocated by letting her lips twitch, and then poured out her lovely golden laughter, as one might pour Cornish cream on a bowl of turnips.]

The scene, as far as they were concerned, had come to its proper conclusion. I think that's the point – that must be why I've written it as a little play. Mother and Uncle Taylor seem almost to have organized such episodes, to have made sure they had a beginning, a middle, and an end. I'm convinced I can remember that much; I can remember feeling that I was a spectator at a series of small-scale domestic dramas. I was aware of their deliberateness. That must have been one of the reasons why these scenes seemed ominous to me.

Back to Dot, for heaven's sake.
Never mind. Why not rampage, if I feel like rampaging?

13

For years I made *up* children's stories, playing ninth or tenth fiddle to Enid in the thirties and forties. It was a way of earning an adequate income without having to leave the house (and in those days I had an ailing father to support). Then I ran out of steam, or perhaps the requirements changed, because I faded away in the fifties, if a person like me can be said to fade away. And all these years later I find myself putting pen to paper once again. But now, like other old folks, I want to get back to my roots. I remember the way my father, in his last illness, would study our family album. His gaze wasn't nostalgic or bitter-sweet: it was *searching*. He was exploring the browning photographs as if they contained some clue, some information that would help him manage his comfortless last days of life. It was rather like one of those children's puzzles, where you look at a drawing of mummy, daddy and the children going about their business and you have to find the secret treasure or the wicked witch that has been concealed somewhere in the crevices of the picture.

Anyway, back to Dot and her family.

Luckily it didn't matter too much that Dot's mother was so bad at doing things because the family was quite well-off and could afford servants.

They had a little housemaid for one, who was known as the general because she was employed to do nothing in particular.

(Years later, when the papers were full of generals of another sort, I found it hard to shake off a mental impression that the young men of Europe were being led to their deaths by a coterie of adolescent girls.)

They also had a weeping cook, rather as one might have a weeping willow.

And a gardener, who dug the garden, groomed the horses, and polished Arthur's bicycle.

And so Dot's mother had to do very little. She could drift around the house, her mind open to the weather.

14

One task she liked, however: she did the washing with nothing short of gusto. She would come in and seize it from the general's tiny grasp, kick off her shoes, discard her stockings, hoist up her skirts (lo and behold, legs!) and blissfully crank the mangle. Dot would watch admiringly as clods of wet material went into the rollers on one side and came out flat and firm, like a tongue poking out between lips, on the other.

And the water, spattering into and out of the basket, and pooling on the quarry tiles! You can bring me water in calabashes, by the river-load, swimming-pools, oceansful, and it will never sound as watery as her mother's mangle-water sounded to Dot.


(And yet my mother wasn't necessarily clean in herself. She had her own priorities. I've caught myself observing some mark on my dress and blaming it on her, as if grubby clothing could be inherited down the years.)


## Dot's Father

My father was a different kettle of fish altogether. He never stopped working.

Dot's father was a giant. He was a very small one, however, so in fact he wasn't any larger than an ordinary person. (He was large to *Dot*, of course, because she was just a little girl.) He was very strong, as you might expect, and he ran their family tin-mine. Dot only saw him when he came home (rather tired) in the evening.


## Dot Herself

Dot was an ordinary little girl. She had brown hair, brown eyes, brown freckles. What more is there to say? I didn't write much about Dot's father, but that was because, since he worked long hours at the tin-mine, he spent much of his time off, or under, the page. He might be burrowing about under this very sheet even now. I'm sure if you dig your way through the rest of this book you'll find him *some*where, toiling away.

But Dot, on the other hand, was just like you or me. She was one of those little girls who are not much more than a triangle. You know what I mean: △ . Dot isn't a bad name for her when you think about it.

Better than Olive anyway. I can still hear those horrid square-headed little boys with tufted hair, those nasty squeaking girls in pinafores, crying out in the playground: 'Eugh! I hate olives!'

And I, forlornly trying to keep my end up: 'Olive's what?'

But if Dot isn't much more than a △ , what are we going to make of her brother?

## Dot's Brother

Dot's brother wasn't a triangle.
He wasn't under the surface of the page.
He wasn't a cloud.
He wasn't he wasn't he wasn't.
The trouble with Dot's brother Harry was that nobody could see him except Dot.

No, that's not strictly true, because Dot couldn't see him either.

Do you know how the air looks, when there has just been a shower, and the sun has come out again? It looks exactly as if someone has been giving it a good polish, using lots of elbow-grease.

Mr Tremaine used to polish Arthur's bicycle like that, and later on his car, his lovely new custard slice of a car. Well, let Mr Tremaine finish his labour of love and then remove the car, or the bicycle, from the scene, leaving just the polish behind. *That*'s how the air looks, when a shower has come and gone, and the fat beaming sun has gone and come. The air looks as if it's been polished and polished away until there is hardly any of it left. The day is a glittering blank.

Now imagine an ordinary day. How dingy the air is!

16

Splattered by puddles, smudged with soot, covered in dust. But when Harry came along, *his* patch of air was polished up and shiny. It was a glittering blank. Because the space was filled with Harry, there was no air left. Because Harry was invisible, you could see the space he occupied. At least, Dot could. But then, she was looking.

There was another tell-tale sign. When Dot was looking through Harry (which she always had to do since she couldn't look *at* him) the objects on his far side went slightly bendy, as a stick does when you thrust the end of it in water.

I know what you're thinking.

You're thinking: perhaps Dot just *imagined* she had a brother. You're thinking: perhaps she was lonely and wanted somebody to play with. So she made him up. Often children make up a person or an animal of their own to play with.

I can't remember doing so myself. In this respect I seem to be the opposite of Dot. She makes a brother, I unmake one. I had no intention of making him invisible when I put pen to paper. I find myself killing off a character before I've even established him, out of sheer perversity.

Well, the same thought had crossed Dot's mind also. That is to say, she wondered if Harry wasn't just a figment of her imagination. She asked her mother about it.

Her mother said: 'Of course you've got a brother, Dotty dear.'

Unfortunately Dot's mother said these words in a special grown-up way, so that Dot didn't know whether to believe them or not. You've probably had the same experience. Instead of saying them as if they were just true, she said them as if they were REALLY REALLY true. Which strangely enough made them sound like fibs. You think to yourself: hello hello hello, who are *these* words trying to impress?

Mixed in with the really really sound there was a rather sad sound too, as if her mother were trying to cheer Dot up after she'd fallen over.

Her father was even worse. The little giant was sitting in

his chair after a long day at the mine. He had carpet-slippers on his feet and was toasting them on the fender. The fire was leaping about in its grate in the jolliest fashion. You could see the reflection of the flames flickering over his face, but his face didn't flicker in reply. It just looked tiredly and steadily back. When Dot asked her question the words seemed to take a long time to sink in. Then his face turned from the fire to look at her. Naturally the little flames in his eyes went out. But he smiled.

'You make me laugh, my dear,' he said. He pulled her nose with his hard heavy hand.

So she went to ask her Uncle Taylor instead.

# Chapter 2

## The Question of Harry
## (Not to mention the dratted Uncles!)

Before we do anything else, let's evict Uncle Taylor.

*I* never asked him to live with us in the first place. Nor Arthur for that matter, though it was always Uncle Taylor I resented.

So let's grasp him by the shirt collar, studs a–popping, and drag him down the gravel driveway and along the lane.

The lane at the end of our driveway is charming on a nice day. Cow-parsley bubbles from the ditches in June. Or do I mean May? I never was one for clocking vegetables. Today is nondescript in any case: overcast, possibly threatening rain. A tall hedge runs down the far side, allowing only occasional glimpses of fields, sea, our tin–mine. In one direction the lane winds towards town. In the other it wanders, as though by sheer chance, into the village of Trevine. It is in this direction that we drag Uncle Taylor.

One of the first buildings you come to in Trevine High Street is the village pub, which is called the Mare and Foal. It has a creaking sign outside depicting a big horse and a little horse. There is an old bench on one side of the door and Jack Hotchkiss is sitting on it as usual. He watches as the first raindrops land in his mug of beer. He doesn't like being inside the pub because it's too 'poky', so he sits on that bench in all sorts of weather. As Uncle Taylor stumbles past, whimpering and flailing, Jack looks up from his beer to observe him, with mild eyes like a cow's.

Since the rain has only just begun, the large village ladies, wives of tin-miners and farm labourers, haven't yet been wetted enough to retreat. They are still clustered in doorways and on the pavement, and now they turn round in mid-gossip to witness the spectacle. In his tiny chemist's shop the Squeaking Man peers out from between glass window-shelves that are stocked with wonderful stoppered bottles containing liquefied sapphires, rubies, emeralds. Uncle Taylor puts his incompetent hands together by way of beseechment, but there is another ruthless tug on his collar, a despairing moan, and he is off on his travels once more. The village begins to fade away. Fields replace cottage gardens. We yank Uncle Taylor up a muddy driveway and deposit him in a tatty eighteenth-century farmhouse which happens to be vacant.

Uncle Taylor manages to revolve his eyes about his surroundings while he is propelled across the weed-tufted cobbles of the courtyard.

'Quite testful,' he gasps, as he flies through the front door and lands with a thud on the moulting tiles of the hall floor.

It is indeed a nice farmhouse of the homely English sort, though it has fallen into sad neglect. I remember it in happier times, when it was a bustling place, and one of my classmates from school lived there. He went off to the Great War and when he came back there was nobody left but his mother and the dog. All the rest were dead. I think people forget that almost everybody died in that war.

My family left the area shortly afterwards, so what happened next was simply repeated to me, probably by my friend Anne, with whom I exchanged letters for a few years. The farm-boy's name was Robert. His mother died also, after a year or two, and left him high and dry. He shot himself.

He was a chunky boy with very red cheeks, the sort of slow-talking son of the soil who looked exactly as if he wouldn't kill himself, but did. The story was in fact that after he had done the deed he changed his mind.

How dreadful, to be determined before that blast, and to hesitate afterwards!

An even more horrible explanation occurred to me at the time, but of course I'm a children's writer, so I tend to look for horrible explanations.

Robert killed the dog first, apparently, and I did wonder if that might not have proved to be a turning-point. Your faithful companion – who is going to look after him when you're gone? I think people who commit suicide have a strong sense of life going on in another plane after they're dead. Bang bang and before you know it you will be walking your land again exactly as before, except perhaps that the fields won't be as muddy, and mother will be installed once more in the kitchen baking scones. What I'm suggesting, I suppose, is that people may approach suicide in an optimistic frame of mind.

Anyway, bang! So much for the dog.

And at *that* moment Robert changes his mind.

Up until this point he's been thinking of death from the inside, as it were. Now, looking at his dog, he remembers how it appears to the onlooker. He's seen it before so often, all those men lying in the ditches of Flanders like dead dogs.

The Great War did one of two things to the men who survived. It made them want to live, or want to die.

In Robert's case, possibly both in succession. He wanted to die; now, suddenly, he wanted to live. But he's already killed the dog. He's a decent boy, with a sense of duty. He's honour bound to carry the arrangement through, it amounts to an understanding, even if the dog can hardly be said to have understood.

So he shoots himself to oblige his dog.

Then he drags his poor body, riddled with pellets, out of the barn into the farmyard where he's found by one of the labourers, who comes by to discover Robert squirming on the cobbles, putting incompetent hands together by way of beseechment. He's allowed to want to live now that he's proved his good faith. He keeps saying please, like a well brought-up child.

Robert's death leaves the farm conveniently vacant for Uncle Taylor. It became vacant, I suppose, in about 1922, and I've been thinking about Dot as living in 1908 or so, simply because I've been thinking about myself at that time. But not to worry. Children's stories happen outside the realm of history – at least my sort do.

So Uncle Taylor has suddenly become a tenant.

After a few moments squirming on the hall floor he gets to his feet, dusts himself off, replaces his collar-studs, and recovers his dignity. Soon the farmhouse has been restored and renovated to his high, not to say finicky, standards.

What does Uncle Taylor grow? Hardly silver bells and cockle shells and pretty maids all in a row. In real life he cultivated figures. He was the tin-mine's accountant. That's why, I suppose, he was able to do so much of his work at home. He sat up in that bedroom of his, cooking the books – when he and my mother weren't playing their games together.

Uncle Taylor was a mathematician, the best for miles around. He had a delightful numbers farm down a muddy lane, just beyond the far end of the village. Dot went to visit him often. Uncle Taylor was always immaculately dressed, and he never got his hands or even his little patent leather boots dirty, so that he didn't look like a farmer at all. He was the most indoorish outdoors person you ever saw.

Dot asked him her question.

'Come with me, Dot,' Uncle Taylor said, after a moment's thought.

Some 4s were clucking lazily in the farmyard. An angry 5 rushed out of a doorway and hissed at Dot. He ran right up to her, hoping to peck her bottom with his long beak, but she shooed him away. There was a little pond just beyond the yard, on which a couple of 2s were gently bobbing. A field of 11111111s rippled dreamily in the breeze, and beyond it there was a spindly copse, above which a small flock of 3s whirled and flapped about, squawking noisily at each other. Every now and then Uncle Taylor used to invite some of his gentleman-farmer acquaintances to go shooting with him in that copse in order to 'keep the numbers down' as he put it to Dot, who didn't like the idea at all.

At the moment, however, Uncle Taylor was more interested in a field at the very edge of his holding.

'Look,' he said, pointing. 'Can you see what I've got over there?'

Dot scrinched her eyes almost shut so that she could see better.

The field was peppered with small, white, rather puffy-looking objects. For a moment she almost thought they were clouds!

'Are they sheep?' she asked.

22

'No, they're not sheep,' Uncle Taylor replied. 'Though I can see why you might think so. They certainly look white and round, as sheep do in the distance. They are the most useful and versatile of all my stock. They're called naughts. As you know, manure is excellent for fertilizing the soil. Well, if I put the droppings of these naughts into my field of ones, the amount of harvest increases tenfold.'

'My!' exclaimed Dot.

'Or I can float a few naughts on the pond. Naughts float very nicely on water, rather like soap bubbles. The next thing I know, my pond is absolutely teeming with twos.'

'Gracious,' said Dot.

'It's as nothing,' Uncle Taylor replied. 'Tell me, little Dot, have you ever heard the expression "the cuckoo in the nest"?'

'Yes,' Dot replied, remembering nature study at school. 'I know about cuckoos in the nest.'

'Well,' said Uncle Taylor, 'I can be as crafty as a cuckoo. I go to my copse, over there, where the threes roost, and I climb up to their nests. I discard the diminutive clutches of eggs I find within, and replace them with some delightfully large, round, white, naughts. The foolish birds never realize what's happened. They sit upon the naughts perfectly happily and care for them when they hatch.'

'What is it that *does* hatch?' asked Dot.

'The plumpest fowls you ever saw. They are so fat they can't fly. In the end they have to jump out of the trees in order to get to the ground. You can hear them thudding down like coconuts. Luckily they have so much fat on them that they rarely hurt themselves. Then they waddle around my farm like so many penguins.'

'All this is very interesting,' Dot said, 'but I really want to know if I have a brother or not.'

'Well, that is precisely what I'm trying to tell you. But first of all I want to clear away any misunderstandings, and the best way to do that is by introducing the subject of my herd of naughts. Do you know that we can knit clothes out of their wool?'

'Can you really?'

'It is so fine and soft that it appears more like a light haze than ordinary knitwear. We supply it to the Emperor. He appreciates good quality. Unfortunately, most grown-ups do not. You know how it is when you've used a knife so much that it has become blunt?'

Dot was rather pleased with this question because she was not allowed to play with knives. 'Of course,' she replied.

'Well, many adults have used their eyes so much that *they*'ve become blunt too. Naturally, children don't have that problem. They have sharp eyes. On one occasion, this led to a rather embarrassing predicament. The Emperor was in a procession, veiled in a lovely golden haze, pale and rich as if it had been knitted out of sunbeams.

'As usual the blunt-eyed grown-ups had great difficulty making out what the Emperor was wearing. Then a little boy who, as it happens, had visited my farm (as you are doing now, my dear), a sharp-eyed little boy by the name of Mortimer, called out: "The Emperor's wearing no clothes!" He'd realized, you see, that the Emperor's clothes were made of wool from my naughts. But the grown-ups standing nearby misunderstood him completely. They thought he meant that the Emperor wasn't wearing ANY clothes. Pandemonium broke out. The Emperor was mortified. He cancelled his order. The only reason I shear my naughts these days is to keep them cool in hot weather,' Uncle Taylor concluded sadly.

'But –' said Dot.

'Don't you understand?' Uncle Taylor asked. 'What I'm trying to tell you is that just because grown-ups don't see things, it doesn't mean that they aren't there.'

And with that explanation, Dot had to be content. She wondered if she should point out that she wasn't interested in what, if anything, the grown-ups *did*n't see, but rather in what, if anything, she, Dot, did. But she gave it up. There were too many naughts in it. They seemed to be getting everywhere.

Anyway, that was the family.

A cloud-like mother
A small tired giant
An ordinary little triangle called Dot
An invisible brother.

And what, may I ask, about the dratted uncles? I launched in on them right at the beginning, before I'd even had time to draw breath, and now I'm making a proper list I haven't managed to put them on it.

They don't belong, that's the whole point. I resented them. Their presence knocked my real family off-balance in some way.

Of course it has to be said that families in those days weren't as neat and tidy as they are now. They had extras: maiden aunts, orphaned cousins, grandparents (not so often uncles, though). And lots of children. Perhaps it was because there were only the two of us children that I resented my uncles so much. In that respect, I was ahead of my time.

## Arthur

In Dot's garden was a pond, with goldfish. She used to love going down to it on those grey damp days, when the trees look as if they can't be bothered, and the plants are sagging, and slugs and worms are on the march. On days like that, when she felt she needed cheering up, Dot would go and look into her pond. The water would be dim and brown, even more depressing than the world outside; but then, with a flick of its tail, one of her goldfish would appear from underneath a lily pad, looking for all the world like a peeled and graceful carrot. It always cheered her up no end. On the other hand she knew that if you observed a goldfish close to, it didn't look charming at all. It had a grumpy mouth, with thick golden lips, and small beady eyes.

Arthur reminded her of a goldfish. He was her mother's brother, and he lived in their house with them, helping to run the family tin-mine. He was quite graceful and energetic, and all the ladies in the area loved him. He cheered them up. He didn't swim around a pond, of course, but he did ride a bicycle, a lovely shiny yellow one with a big bell on it. Ring! ring! he went, as he careered about the streets and lanes of their part of Cornwall. He was the sort of person who laughed a lot and went to parties. He was sleek and handsome, but when you looked at him closely you noticed that his lips were a little thick, and his eyes were on the beady side. He didn't have much of a nose (but then I always think noses are funny things to have anyway, stuck there in the middle of your face, with two little holes in them, side by side). He was reputed to be a good dancer. Yes, you can see why he reminded Dot of a goldfish. He was attractive but when you looked at him from a certain point of view, not *quite* so attractive.

Arthur's job was to keep the miners happy. He was very good at that. For one thing he adored telling jokes. They weren't always very good jokes, but as he used to say, the secret is in the way you tell them. When he told a joke, his beady eyes would shine, his rather thick lips would curl upwards with glee, and something about the eager little nose would make you go all bubbly inside, waiting for the excuse to laugh.

Why did the...? he would ask.

What's the difference between a something–or–other and a something else?

I am unable to remember a joke for five minutes, let alone the best part of seventy years. I don't think I have a sense of humour. But Arthur did, for what it's worth.

An Irishman went into a public house, he would say.

Ho ho ho, ho-ho-ho-ed the miners.

Arthur didn't simply make the miners *laugh*, of course. He did useful things for them. He hired a barber to give them all a weekly haircut and shave. He organized evening classes for them, though like the little giant they were often tired after a hard day's work and would sometimes snooze during the lessons. But Arthur knew how tiring the men's work was, and he was always thinking of ways to make it easier. He arranged for Uncle Taylor's numbers to be let loose on the mine's money, and with the proceeds he bought pumps and winders, crushers and diggers, pushers and pulleys, all to give them less work to do. He even bought a Man Engine, but I'll tell you about that later on.

When he wasn't at the mine, he was bicycling with the local bicycle club (he was terribly proud of his yellow bicycle), taking photographs with his camera (which had a tripod to rest on, and a cloth for the photographer to hide in, so you wouldn't know you were having your photograph taken: he was very proud of all that too), visiting his many friends, and going to parties.

Thus, Arthur, a sort of bicycling goldfish with a merry quip for all and sundry.

## Uncle Taylor

Well, despite what I was saying, he has of course made his entrance, not to mention his exit. One point that needs to be cleared up, however, is to do with clothing. I loathe it when characters in a book merge together, so that they take their separate courses through the plot but share the same exquisite sensibility, poking-out ears, or Sunday-best suit. My uncles were in fact very different from each other despite being brothers. However they did share one characteristic: they were both ridiculously clothes-conscious.

But of course they were conscious of different clothes.

Uncle Taylor liked fine tweed jackets, the sort that have a little skirt to rest over the wearer's minimal rump, a neat waistcoat, plus-fours; a linen jacket and boater in the summer; patent-leather shoes which fitted like skin over his tiny feet; and, for domestic wear, what the French call *le smoking*. He even wore a monocle, which gave him a magnified eye, and he had a silver-topped cane to prod the ground with.

Chubby Arthur, by contrast, was businesslike in his dress. He wore black or grey suits, sometimes a morning-coat (always neat and well-fitting), often a bowler. I suppose it was his somewhat florid complexion that lightened the effect and brought goldfish to mind (also perhaps his yellow bicycle). In bad weather he had a cape for cycling and a large enclosing topcoat that buttoned up to the neck for when he was travelling on foot or in our dogcart. I can remember an incident concerning his coat when I was eight or nine that well illustrates the difference between his attitude to clothes and Uncle Taylor's.

It was the year in which Uncle Taylor had begun to act strangely. It had been a wonderful summer, perhaps the first weather I can recall as an entity in itself. Uncle Taylor went off, monocled and be-boatered, to walk by the sea for hours

27

at a time. (I watched him once, spied on him rather, and saw him do something very odd indeed, but that's another story. He seemed very depressed at that time.) Summer gave way to autumn, but the beautiful weather continued. There aren't many trees on the narrow peninsula of Cornwall except in the villa-ed enclaves about the towns, but these did themselves proud, erupting into a slow gold conflagration beyond the furthest reaches, so I've been told, of suburban memory. The sunlight was white in that September, cream in the October, copper in November. Even on the barest uplands the westerlies merely breathed. The sea beside which Uncle Taylor walked went from pale blue to sapphire as the seasons wore on, but in other respects remained unnaturally still.

But at last the lovely autumn gave way to a stormy winter. It rained without stopping for day after day. Puddles developed on our lawns and slowly merged to form pools. There was coastal flooding, and children were drowned as far east as Brighton, according to Uncle Taylor, who recounted disaster from the depths of his mysterious taciturnity with a kind of glum satisfaction: they had been plucked from piers and promenades by huge waves. Harry and I were confined to the house for what seemed an eternity. The mine had been shut down because of the danger of seepage, but Father still spent all his time there, checking the shafts, presumably, and doing paperwork. Uncle Taylor had given up his walks, and spent hours looking out of the window into the garden. The rain had taken the last leaves from our trees and pounded them to a brown sludge on the lawns. If you followed his gaze, which I did, having grown curious about his behaviour since my experience of the summer, he appeared to be staring straight at our drenched and leaf-speckled Venus de Milo which stood on the lower terrace. My mother must have followed his gaze too.

'Uncle Taylor,' she said, 'I do believe you are beginning to take an interest in young ladies at last!'

As luck would have it, a few moments later Arthur appeared. He was wearing his big topcoat and a bowler. His coat had been pressed tight against his body with the drenching, and glistened blackly, like sealskin.

'Arthur!' my mother exclaimed. 'You've shrunk!'

28

Certainly he looked smaller than usual but his habitual cheerfulness and animation struggled out through the wet.

'Do you know,' he replied, 'soaked as I am on the outside, I'm dry as a bone within. This coat,' he added, 'is a coat to conjure with. I've never known a coat like it for keeping the water out. We, I, had no trouble from the rain at all.'

'What can have possessed you?' my mother asked. 'To go off on one of your, your! Why couldn't you have just sat in the warm here, and looked at the Venus de Milo with Uncle Taylor?' Suddenly she was shaking with laughter.

'I say, Sis!' exclaimed Uncle Taylor in rebuke.

I looked from Arthur's topcoat to the statue in the garden, and felt I'd made a discovery.

'You look like a police constable,' Uncle Taylor told Arthur bitterly.

And that's exactly how he did look: like a police constable. Arthur wore his clothes as a uniform. Uncle Taylor wore his for ornament. Arthur was of a piece all through, from topcoat to soul. Uncle Taylor dressed in order to beautify, possibly even to camouflage, his tiny personality. *That* was how they differed.

'Heavens, Arthur!' my mother exclaimed. 'You're soaking the hall carpet!'

She had become unusually focused. Wet clothing was a subject near to her heart. Something of the mangle had crept into her normally generous and good-humoured countenance.

'That's because my coat won't let the water through,' Arthur replied with innocent enthusiasm. 'Normally there's a capillary action with wool. The water moves *side*ways, despite the pull of gravity. But this coat has been sealed chemically. So there is nothing to distract the water from going downwards.'

You see, I surely could never have taken in, and remembered, the word 'capillary' from those times. In a sense I must be making this all up. And yet I can see it, and hear it, in my mind's eye and ear. How else can you test the authenticity of the past?

There was a thoughtful silence.

'I think you mean,' my mother said, cheerful once more, 'that your *coat* is raining.'

'You look as though someone has had the sense to fling a bucket of water over you,' said Uncle Taylor with great satisfaction. 'And that is precisely what a tomcat deserves.'

It must have been shortly after that incident that Arthur bought his famous umbrella.

# Chapter 3

## We explore the House and Garden:
## then have Dinner

Dot lived with her family in a big house near the sea. Most of the houses in that part of the world are grey, because they are built of stone, but Dot's was red. It looked like the face of an old sunbaked colonel with green moustaches. The moustaches were ivy, which grew all around the porch that enclosed the front door. The colonel had grey slate hair and staring eyes which closed when the curtains were drawn.

Bother the inside of the house. You don't want to read all about wallpaper and armchairs, do you? I'll tell you what I'll do. If you need a bit of the house for any reason, I'll write it for you. For example, if we're in Dot's bedroom, watching her on her bed as she waits for sleep to approach, and we notice a bit of a chill in the air, why then I'll write a little bedroom fireplace for us all, a black cast-iron one with bunches of juicy black grapes moulded on the sides of it. Then I'll write a pile of glowing coals in the hearth, with some dear little flames playing on their surface, holding hands and dancing in a circle like a group of yellow fairies playing Ring a Ring a Roses. There! The room will warm up in no time. My hands feel less chilled already. But there's no point in having that fireplace cluttering up the page if it's a warm summer evening, and Dot is lying in bed with just a sheet over her. And what about when she's playing out in the garden, or has gone to visit her Uncle Taylor on his numbers farm? A fire would be quite useless then: it would be a waste of coal. So I'll only write in the mod cons, as they're called nowadays, as and when they are needed. As a result, there will be lots of unexpected

31

spaces inside Dot's house, but that's quite appropriate as it happens, since large Victorian houses were full of nooks and crannies.

The garden was full of nooks and crannies too. Or if not nooks and crannies, then places, at least. It was a garden full of different places.

First there was the terrace. This was a paved walkway right up by the house. Sometimes in the morning it smelled of cigars, if Dot's father, and Arthur, and Uncle Taylor (from the farm) had chosen to walk along it after their dinner the evening before. Dot and Harry would find cigar-ends lying on the flags. Once they decided to smoke one.

Have you ever done anything truly naughty? Yes, of course you have. Well, that makes two of us. Three if you include Harry.

Harry went to the kitchen and stole a lucifer when Cook's back was turned. He and Dot crouched in a little alcove that had been built at one end of the terrace to shelter people from the wind. Harry lit the cigar, puffed, coughed, and passed it to Dot. As it approached her, she got a lovely zizzy feeling in the pit of her stomach, made up of exactly equal parts of fear and glee, a delightful concoction.

That feeling is one of the most memorable experiences you ever have in your life. It makes you feel that there's a door inside yourself that is about to swing open; and when it does, goodness knows *what* you'll experience. Of course it stays firmly shut. It's probably locked, when all's said and done.

The only experience Dot was to be given was the feeling that she'd swallowed a bonfire.

There was moss between the paving stones of that upper terrace. You could dig your finger in and winkle strips of it out. They were always slightly longer than you had any right to expect, green on one side and brown on the other.

What else? Two huge pots, that looked like wine-glasses for giants. They were cast-iron, painted white, and with bunches of grapes moulded on the sides just as on Dot's bed-room fireplace: cast-iron grapes were one of the principal crops in that part of the country.

In the summer-time the pots weren't particularly interesting – flowers foamed over their tops. But in the winter Mr Tremaine

32

emptied them of soil and, as the months wore on, they slowly filled up with rainwater. Harry and Dot would peer down and watch the water as it rested against the rusty sides. You could imagine wonderfully nasty things below the surface, like toads.

Round the corner of the house the terrace became more private. It was cobbled, not paved, and it widened out into a little courtyard with stables and outhouses on the far side of it, and a washing-line stretched across. To one side of the stables you could glimpse the upper lawn, though you'll get a better view of it if you walk back to the terrace. Come on then, let's retrace our steps – it's not far, only four sentences.

Here we are again, by the toad bowls.

Beyond the top terrace, there is a step down, leading to the narrower bottom terrace, on which stands a woman with no clothes on, the Venus de Milo. I remember having the notion that the statue had been bought prematurely, before it had been decently clothed. No doubt some demure and comprehensive Edwardian covering was waiting for her on the racks of a stone dressmaker somewhere. Come to think of it, our Venus had arms, so she was actually *over*dressed in a manner of speaking.

Below the bottom terrace was a lawn. It had an herbaceous border down one side, with a goldfish pond beyond it. Dot once fell into the goldfish pond. I suppose if you have one in your garden you're bound to fall into it sooner or later.


When I surfaced I made out Uncle Taylor scuttling towards me across the lawn. He was waving his thin arms and his thin stick. In fact, even though he was running he seemed able to wave his thin legs also. The pond of course was only a couple of feet deep so I was in no danger of drowning. I was simply suffering from the shock of the water and a fear that the goldfish might brush against me. And the pond's squidgy bottom made it very difficult to scramble out, so from Uncle Taylor's point of view it must have looked as if I was floundering.

It is important to note that Uncle Taylor could not swim.

'Oh dear!' he cried, looking despairingly at the troubled waters, 'oh dear oh dear! If only one could walk on it!'

In the middle of the wall that ran down one side of the garden was a green door. If you opened it you found yourself in the vegetable garden. There were row upon row of lettuces, cabbages, carrots, tomatoes, everything you could think of. This garden was completely walled in, so that it looked like a room which had lost its ceiling. The vegetables were like green patterns on a brown carpet. It was always warm in here, so much so that even if the weather was overcast in the rest of the garden, the sun was invariably beaming down when you had passed through the door. If only the zizzy door in the pit of one's stomach could be like that door to the vegetable garden, and swing open (squeakily) in such a satisfactory way. The cat always slept here, on a patch of earth.

Beyond the vegetable garden was a large greenhouse. Dot and Harry weren't supposed to go into it, but they did sometimes. It smelled as though someone had put some soil in the oven to cook. Dot couldn't decide whether she liked the smell or not. The greenhouse was full of flowerpots, seed trays, and potting-out compost. The windows were smeared with a thin coating of whitewash, which gave the outside world a snowy look.

Just beyond the greenhouse was the chicken run. The chickens ran, and scratched, and burbled to each other. They always seemed most annoyed. Dot imagined that they had not intended to be chickens at all, and couldn't account for the mistake. Perhaps they'd planned to be something on a grand scale, like hippopotami. They complained in clucks to each other: 'Before I knew where I was, I was a chicken. It was the shock of my life, I can tell you. Look at me, look at us. When I first saw myself in a puddle, I could have wept.' They were scruffy brown blobs of indignation, on yellow legs. They smelled strong, like boxes that have just been opened after years in the attic.

At the bottom of the garden was a long row of elms. Some squirrels lived there.

There were other people's gardens (equally big) to each side. And fields beyond. Then, in the distance, the grey bulgy outlines of the uplands.

You couldn't see the sea from Dot's house, but it was near, only a few hundred yards away.

34

I'll put the sea on one side for the time being. You can get weary of too much description. It becomes a kind of duty in the end, the cod-liver oil of reading. I blew those chickens up to enormous size just to keep Dot's setting on the go. Heaven knows what I'd do if I tackled the sea at present. There'd be a sinking ship at the very least, with little arms wagging helplessly in the waves.

What we need now is more of the *human* background.

Dot lived with her family in their nice house in Cornwall, not far from the sea. They did this, they did that, lah de dah. There was weather. Seasons. Daily round. Let us watch them as they sit round the table on a typical day.

Sometimes the evening meal was just for grown-ups, and Dot and Harry would have tea in the nursery. That would be when the uncles were both dining. On those occasions, after their dinner Dot's father and Arthur and Uncle Taylor would walk up and down the terrace, smoking cigars.

But blessedly there were other days, when Uncle Taylor remained in his room at meal-times, husbanding his numbers: and of course Arthur always seemed –

But on other days, when Uncle Taylor was at his numbers farm and Arthur was out at a party, perhaps, Dot and Harry would have their evening meal with their mother and father.

I was going to show you what they had to eat, but I've always been very messy indeed when serving food, and it would be horrid to have this nice book spattered with gravy and bits of meat and vegetable, wouldn't it? So I'll give you some plates and you can serve the meals yourselves.

Here is Dot's father's plate:

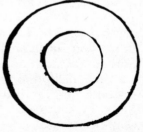

(Remember he's a giant, even if on the small side.)

Now her mother's: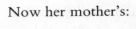

(She had a poor appetite but she made up for it in other ways: Chin chin!)

Dot's plate:

(Healthy growing girl!)
But here's the surprise. Harry's plate is huge! And square! If I made it to scale with the others it would be even bigger than this whole page. So I'll just draw this to be going on with:

Now, please to serve out evening dinner.

A nice big slice of roast meat for Dot's father, or possibly some fowl. Give him plenty of potatoes and vegetables. He needs building up. He was such a *little* giant.

I'm afraid you must only serve teeny-weeny morsels to Dot's mother, or the food will go to waste. She ate barely enough to keep a cloud in the sky.

Never mind, you can heap up Dot's plate. Do it quickly, while Cook's back is turned. Every now and then Cook would decide that Dot ought to be a vegetarian, or only eat white things (like cauliflower and boiled fish). Little girls have delicate tummies, she would announce, shaking her head as if it was the most distressing thing she'd ever heard of. Don't you touch that meat, little missy, she'd warn, or you'll *dream*. Yes, Dot used to think, and what I'll dream of will be slice after slice of roast beef!

There's no need to serve Harry. Being invisible, he ate even less than a cloud. In fact Cook didn't provide him with any food at all. So as you may guess from the picture, Dot used to feed him titbits under the table, rather as you might feed your dog. His plate was the floor!

What did they talk about, while they ate their meal?

Dot's father talked about his mine.

'I don't know,' he said. He was always not knowing things. 'I just do not know. We do the work but we don't seem to achieve the results. Sometimes I don't know how we get by. The corned beef is beginning to dwindle.' (It was a tin-mine, remember?) 'And that new seam of cat-food, which we had such high hopes for: with added pilchard, it turned out to be.' He said pilchard as if it were a rude word, with a little 'pop' on the p. Then he said it again, just as poppingly. 'Pilchard! Cats these days won't touch it. There was a time when human beings would thank their lucky stars to be offered a pilchard. But cats simply turn their noses up at it. They want rabbit. Or Canadian salmon. Pilchard's not refined enough for modern cats. So we have to open every wretched tin, mix the contents with corn and bran, and turn it into chicken food. It's hardly worth the trouble of digging the tins out of the ground. Not to mention eating fish-flavoured chicken. I remember a time when a chicken was a chicken, and a pilchard was a pilchard.'

He looked thoughtfully across the table, as if he were surveying a remote lost world in which chickens and pilchards were kept beautifully separate, and cats ate what was put in front of them. 'And the less said about the tinned peas the better,' he concluded sadly. The tin-mine had been doing badly for as long as Dot could remember.


Certainly I can't remember a time when my father *wasn't* complaining about the mine. And yet I had a prosperous childhood.

37

This, I discovered later, was thanks to Uncle Taylor, and the crops he grew on his numbers farm. Above all, to his expert cultivation of *naughts*.

Dot's mother began on the subject of washing.

'It was such a lovely morning. I stood hanging out the washing. I felt I was standing on the top part of a ship, what's it called? That bit where the captain walks up and down with his hands behind his back. Is it the poop or is that something else?

'Captains don't hang out washing,' Dot said.

'The washing reminded me of sails. On a sailing ship, you know. What *do* captains think about when they walk up and down like that? On their poops. Sit nicely in your chair, Dottie. I suppose they're wondering whether they're going in the right direction.'

'It's called the bridge,' Dot's father said.

'And after that I had a nice lie-down. I do love a lie-down. Whether alone or in company.'

Delete this before I ever *do* anything with this manuscript. *If* I do anything with it. Doing *per se* is perhaps not the point.

As a matter of fact my dear mother once made that remark as we were sitting round the family fire one evening. (She had a bottle of sherry to hand.) There was a pause. My father was thinking of something else. Arthur wasn't there – he was perhaps having a nice lie-down in company of his own. Uncle Taylor went pink.

'My dear Sis,' he expostulated (it was still possible to expostulate in those days), 'do you mind? I'm trying to *suck a humbug*.'

His reaction gave me a pang of fear, just as my mother's remark had done.

'And then I don't know what I did. Time just seemed to fly by. But I did enjoy hanging out the washing. That was something accomplished, wasn't it? Dot, don't drop your food on the floor, there's a good girl.'

Dot meanwhile said very little at table. For the first part of the meal Harry had hold of her ankles and was trying to pull her off her chair. She had to press against the edge of the table to stay put. What made it much harder work was that she had to keep silent so that her parents didn't notice. If they did, she would explain that it was Harry's fault, and her mother would say 'Of course it is, dear,' in that sincere way of hers, and then add, 'But please be a good girl, Dottie.' The strain of trying to stay on her chair was so great that Dot felt as if her eyes were about to pop from their sockets. At one point she couldn't stop herself from whimpering, but to change the subject she immediately said something about captains of ships not hanging out washing.

At last Harry let go, and to keep him occupied she passed him down some food. He was feeling greedy, and nearly bit her fingers, but as always he was easily filled.

'I'm not Anne's friend any more,' Dot said when the conversation at table died away.

'Oh really, dear?' her mother asked.

'She played with Mattie and Edith all play-time, and wouldn't let me join in. I had no one to play with.'

'Oh dear, darling.'

'I just stood in the playground all by myself.'

'Why didn't you play with...?' There was a pause as Dot's mother collected her thoughts. She had a little sip of

'Harry,' she finally concluded.

'Harry's no use. He's a boy.'

'Oh yes. I suppose he is.'

'He has to play on the boys' playground.'

'Oh dear yes. Poor Dot.'

'Harry hardly ever wants to play with me even when we're at home. He's no fun. When we do play he always goes to the lavatory.'

Meanwhile Harry (under the table) said nothing at all. Not even thank you when Dot passed him his food.

I'm not sure what they had for afters. Perhaps it was treacle pudding, with thick custard pocked by the cook's tears.

Anyway, life went on, tum ti tum, until one day...

# Chapter 4

## Dot and Harry at Play

Until my Aunt Fanny!

There's no *until* about it.

Life for most of us is mainly anecdotal, and none the worse for that. Domestic existence is a collection of linked short stories, as many fine children's books, from *Alice in Wonderland* to *Winnie the Pooh*, have established. Perhaps, in the end, a theme may evolve, or a question, at least, may pop up; but there should be a status quo for the theme to evolve from, or the question to pop *against*. Children, vulgar brats, may be eager for disaster, but the author will never make more dignified use of her talents than by constructing a house, setting out a lawn, planting a vegetable garden, cooking a meal. Still to come, the whole routine of Dot's early life: play, school, Christmas, and so on and so forth. Against such manifestations of the status quo, this question of Harry can pop with distinctness, like a banger in a milk bottle.

Oh dear.

AUTHOR DONATES 20% OF ROYALTIES TO CHILDREN'S HOSPITAL.

It makes me cringe to write it. I received what I was going to receive anyhow, and then a quite separate sum, equivalent to twenty per cent of it, was sent on to a children's hospital. My editor – young, creamy-faced, glib – pointed out that despite any reservations I might have, the hospital was going to benefit from a sum of money it wouldn't otherwise have been offered. The book in question, meanwhile, gained free publicity, much more than could have been bought with that self-same amount. My career was in decline; this jiggery-pokery provided a final bump in an otherwise depressing graph.

I have a newspaper photograph somewhere of me in that hospital. I am clumpy in a thick suit (I wore it to look straight-forward and businesslike: in fact I looked well-fed and compla-cent instead) alongside some child in pyjamas in his hospital bed. I had podgy ankles and pearls. I was supposed to be spreading sweetness and light amongst sick and broken infants.

Nonsense.

I was harvesting, like Uncle Taylor on his numbers farm. Increasing sales; cropping pain, sickness, incident, for later use.

And what happened to you, little boy?

One little boy had blown himself up with a firework. He'd put a banger inside a milk-bottle. The last thing he was ever to see was an explosion. When you look into a fire and then away, the fire remains in your eyes until it is slowly extin-guished by whatever it is you are looking at next. But imagine having no new images to cool your retina, so the terrible reaching tentacles of that bang twist and turn within your mind for always.

Nevertheless one can see the attraction, oh yes, one can understand why the little boy did it. What a prospect: making a milk-bottle *bloom*!


Anyway, back to Harry and Dot. Explosions, as far as they are concerned, are some years in the future. Let's watch them at play.

In the days when I was known as a writer, people would sometimes ask me about my career, and I would look back and realize I couldn't remember anything about it. What I mean is, writing is a form of doing, and when you're fully engaged in doing something there is no you to spare, there is only the something. When you review it subsequently, the whole experience seems dream-like. It's almost as if somebody else had been sitting at our desks doing it on our behalf. Which, I suppose, is why writers talk of inspiration. Writers are a hapless lot. On the whole they get precious little credit for what they do, and likely as not what they do receive they pass on to the Muse.

And one's childhood play is the same sort of thing. If one looks back at what one *did* as a child it seems minimal. And

41

yet children are busy people. Sometimes when I realize I can hardly remember doing anything with Harry I wonder if it's because he's dead. But that can't be it. Almost everybody's dead.

Let me see.

Harry liked to stand on his hands. He would sometimes manage to take a few paces, his legs bent forward like a scorpion's tail, his head becoming a red bulb.

What else?

We built a hole in an out-of-sight patch of garden, beyond the chicken-run and concealed by the walls of the vegetable plot. Built is not too strong a word. Children are burrowing animals, and I can remember still the delicious holeyness of that hole. How snug and secure it seemed! Harry had managed to find an empty beer-bottle somewhere, and we drank lukewarm water from it. Until you dig your hole, it doesn't exist, so it is truly your place. For the time being anyway. We got turfed out in due course by Mr Tremaine, who told us that if we wanted to dig, he could find ways of making us useful.

Another time we trudged to school through fog. Harry had his tongue out the while, trying to lick it. Then, when we arrived in class, he told Miss Bowker that his throat felt funny. I was shocked until I realized he was quite sincere. He hadn't made a connection between offering his tongue to the weather and developing a frog in his throat. Poor little chap (he was two years older than me), he did worry about his health. How unnecessary, in a boy born in the late 1890s! (Think of all those futile meals the boys of that generation devoured! It reminds me of a children's game. We went to a party and ate apples, buns, caramels, doughnuts, eggs, fudge, etc etc etc.)

Miss Bowker naturally sent Harry home. She sent me home also, to look after him on the way. As we walked I pointed out to him, with sisterly tact, that he'd brought his symptoms on himself. Needless to say that made him feel even worse, particularly as he misheard what I said, and thought he had *fog* in his throat.

There was no one at home when we arrived.

In these days of mod. cons and working women I suppose that's quite usual, but think how many people had to be absent from our household for it to be empty. All right, the menfolk were at the mine, but even that couldn't be taken for granted, since Uncle Taylor did much of his accounting in his bedroom. And my mother was out. My mother! She who feared the weather. She of the aching head. My mother did not go to drink tea with her friends. Tea is not my tipple, she'd (hiccuping) giggle. Worthy Cornish ladies were not to her taste either. My mother was one of those very feminine women who like only to be with men – which may help to explain why she lived with her husband and two brothers. My mother was female to the tips of her toes and fingers. Hark at plain Jane talking!

Anyway, what matters about her at this moment is that she was *out*. Harry and I found that frightening. A house is grim and empty without a mother in it, like a body when the soul has departed. I remember worrying about whether she might be getting herself into a scrape. I'd noticed the disapproving looks she received from time to time. She was the sort of person who needed looking after. I don't think people always appreciate how maternal or paternal children feel towards their parents. One thinks of James James Morrison Morrison Weatherby George Dupree saying to his mother, Mother he said, said he, you must never go down to the end of the town if you don't go down with me.

Unfortunately our mother must have done just that. So apparently had the cook. I probably imagined Cook draped over a gravestone somewhere, fog swirling round her weeping form. More likely, she was doing the shopping.

And where was the general?

And Mr Tremaine?

The house drifted across its grounds like a brick-and-mortar *Marie Celeste*, watched in fear and trembling by Harry and myself.

Then Harry said: 'Let's go and see the chickens.'

What a wonderful idea! Just what we needed. I took his hand, and down the lawns we went, past the brick walls of the vegetable garden, and round the corner, beyond the greenhouse, to the chicken-run.

The run was a wire contraption fixed directly to the back wall of the vegetable garden, with a little wooden house at one end for the hens to roost in.

For a second I couldn't catch any movement, and my heart plummetted. Surely, surely, the chickens couldn't have deserted us too!

No, there they were, going about their business as usual. Thank heavens.

Harry and I stood side by side, watching them. Chickens are comforting creatures. They scurry about pecking grain for all the world as though they are just completing the task of making their surroundings *im*peccable, with the swift accuracy of your mother removing a speck from your clothing. These chickens differed from our particular mother in two important respects: they were dowdy and they were busy; but those qualities enhanced their value as substitutes. So there we stood, two children weighing perhaps three or four stone apiece, hanging on as if for dear life to a posse of fowl none of whom topped, in all probability, three pounds, feathers included. But the chickens had enough *savoir-faire* to be bad-tempered, and that gave us confidence.

The fog was dispersed by this time, and the day had grown lighter. Shortly though it darkened again, and then began to snow.

Each time a flake landed on a chicken it would shake itself vigorously, and then trot over to a neighbour. Then they would stand together, elbows akimbo, wing-tips on hips, exchanging squawks about the disgraceful weather: first fog, now snow. What was the world coming to? Having concluded the discussion they'd take their separate ways again, scratching at the whitening ground while they still could. Some of the weaker sisterhood took refuge in the hen-house.

I began, very quietly, to panic.

We could perish with cold while we waited for someone to return. And anyhow, what assurance did we have that anyone ever would? Moreover, Harry wasn't well. Now the snow had begun to fall I'd decided that he must be ill after all. A teacher had said so – who was I to disagree? There is nothing like snow for making one lose confidence.

I remember reading an entry from Dr Johnson's journal: *Mens turbata*; it snowed all afternoon.

That's the whole trouble with journals – they encourage you to make entries of that sort. What alternative is there?

Got up. Had boiled egg and soldiers. Thought I wouldn't go shopping as the weather was so dreadful. One can see why it sounds so much better in Latin. The problem is that one does nothing in particular for much of the day (if I'm anything to go by) which means that one's journal has to be filled either with trivialities or with brooding meditations on nothingness: the mind being blotted out, flake by flake.

*My Mother:* Do you know that every time you have a drink a brain cell is lost? I read it in the parish magazine.

*Uncle Taylor:* My dear sister, after a quick calculation, I reckon your head is likely to implode at any moment.

*Mother:* I think of brain cells as little rooms, in which thoughts sit like so many monks. Or prisoners. In one cell there is the thought of a cat. In another, the thought of Cook. And so on.

*Uncle Taylor:* What happens, I wonder, when the demon drink washes their cells away? Perhaps tiny cooks and cats are scattered about the house even now, the size of germs.

*Mother:* How terrifying! I'd better take something to calm my nerves. Give sister a ittle dwink, Uncle Taylor. [She knots her lips into what can only be described as a small pink bow.]

Heavens. Sitting at my desk a life-time later I still find myself looking daggers at Uncle Taylor. All I'm really doing is staring into the middle distance, or rather the near distance, since I'm staring at the wall. The figure of Uncle Taylor I see is merely a germ inside my head, to use my mother's idea. Actually, he *was* germ-like: small, malign, and intricate.

Back to the chickens! (What a rallying-cry! Then *and* now.)

I can see Harry also. He is not a germ. He is wearing one of those bulgy caps boys had in Edwardian England. Big flakes are blotching the scene. He is hopefully watching our scurrying poultry. The picture makes me want to weep. My memory is clouded by his death, eight years or so later, which casts a

45

retrospective shadow over even the smallest events of his life, and makes them ominous.

After all, I was watching the chickens too, and I don't feel sorry for *me*.

At last the adults began to arrive.

First Cook, stern and watchful, eyes dry as a bone. I have an idea there was a dead chicken with its long lolling neck in her shopping basket, but that seems too much like an afterthought.

Then Mother.

She'd been to the doctor's, she claimed. Perhaps she had. She was always complaining of headaches. Then again perhaps she had not. One of the things that made my mother so delightful was that she could be naughty, just like a child, and tell fibs. Anyhow she laughed heartily when she heard our story.

Adult laughter can be a benison sometimes. Chickens become chickens again, and children become childish. Everything shrinks to its proper size. Soon Harry was sliding happily down the banisters. I was reprieved from returning to Miss Bowker as well.

'Since Harry's having the day off school even though there's not a thing wrong with him, you'd better do the same,' Mother said. She had a way of making remarks like that sound completely logical.


Dot and Harry would play together for hours at a time. Harry could do some things Dot couldn't do, of course. He could stand on his hands, for example. Dot tried and tried but she just couldn't manage it. It was the most maddening problem. If you didn't kick hard enough when you were getting off the ground, your legs would become heavier and heavier as they went up into the air. Long before they had reached the proper place, they would feel like logs. And naturally, when logs find themselves in mid-air, they drop directly to the ground. On the other hand (I nearly said foot), if you give a really *good* kick, why then you whizz straight past the allotted spot, and immediately start to fall down the other side. Have you ever been to an orchestra and watched the percussionist playing

46

his triangle? He hits it with his little stick and instead of giving forth a note, it makes a delightful tingling sound. It is as though the stick were really a magic wand and when it strikes it turns the triangle into a cloud of silver fairies, and what you can hear is the sudden flapping of hundreds of filigree wings. Well, even though Dot was more or less a triangle, she didn't sound the least bit like that. When she didn't kick hard enough, and her legs fell out of the sky like logs, she would go aaagh! When she kicked too hard and fell over the other side, she would go THUMP, oooh! She wasn't very musical, I'm afraid.

But Harry could stand on his hands without any trouble at all. He could find the right place in the air immediately: he inhabited a place in the air himself, so he knew all about them. In point of fact, his main difficulty lay in getting his arms to reach the ground. He had a tendency to drift upwards, like a balloon.

I can guess what you're going to ask.

How did Dot *know* he was standing on his hands, when he was invisible?

Well, the answer to that is that when you stand on your hands, the blood rushes to your head. Let me tell you something about this problem.

When I was a little girl, ladies often used to faint. It was quite usual. I think the reason for this was the odd nature of the fashions at the time. You see, ladies were expected to be a bit plumper in those days than they are now. Beautiful ladies, I mean. Ordinary ladies can be plump at any time. (Especially old ones like me.) If you look at photographs of famous music-hall beauties you will notice that they all have slight double chins. I've seen some of your pop-stars nowadays, and they are thin as rakes. But the real problem with these ladies of the olden days was that not only were they expected to be plump, but they were expected to be as thin as rakes as well! At least about the waist. Don't you think that's strange? The poor things were required to be fat and thin at the same time. Large-hipped and wasp-waisted. Indeed they were expected to look very like wasps. If you look at a wasp closely, you will see that its top half is joined on to its bottom half by something that looks very like a thin black thread. And then the lower half swells out in a most juicy fashion. It looks, in short, as if it is in imminent danger of falling into two parts, though funnily enough that rarely seems to happen to wasps. Instead, they have a tendency to get squashed flat. Come to think of it, their lower half is terribly Edwardian in colouring, except that I would suggest that the stripes should be vertical rather than across.

Anyway, these poor ladies who had to be fat and thin at the same time used to wear very tight bodices, in order to hold their fatness in. Unfortunately, though, these prevented them from breathing. If you've ever tried holding your breath you will know that after a while you begin to feel rather faint. Well, exactly the same happened with the ladies. Every so often they would have what was called a 'turn'. They would come over 'rather queer'. And when one of them did, the cry would go up from all quarters: Get her head down between her legs! That'll bring her round! Because, you see, when your head is down, the blood rushes to it, and that makes you feel much better. (If there were no men about, someone could loosen the lady's stays, and let her breathe again. That was even more effective.)


My mother didn't subscribe to any of that nonsense. She was a little on the plump side and softly feminine. Lovely as a cloud. She did have a slight habit of passing out, however, or at least falling asleep very suddenly.


So, you will understand that when Harry stood on his hands the blood rushed to *his* head. This didn't stop him from being invisible, but it did, if you looked hard enough, give his head the faintest, palest hint of pink. If he began to walk about on his hands what you saw was a gently pink bubble, bobbing along over the lower lawn. He was a lovely sight. Dot would skip after him, with outstretched hands.

Another thing Harry and Dot did together was dig holes. Or rather Dot dug holes. Harry *built* them.

They had a special place for doing this, a scruffy patch of ground that lay behind the vegetable enclosure and beyond the greenhouse and chicken-run. A nowhere place, which Mr

Tremaine kept not getting round to, and which had little tufts of grass growing out of otherwise bare soil, like headfulls of unkempt green hair.

Dot dug, as I've said. She dug the earth *out*. But Harry, being invisible, put the hole *in*. She removed what was there already (that is, ground). He replaced it with nothingness. She worked with a garden spade that was about eight sizes too big. She held its shaft with both her hands, lifted it up, (with difficulty) and drove the blade into the ground with all her might. (It usually went in about an inch!) Then she would climb on to the little steps at the top of the blade, grasp the shaft again (the handle part was nearly as high as her head) and let herself fall backwards. She would poke her bottom out to absorb the impact when she reached the ground. Harry meanwhile was able to manage his part of the task much more easily. All he had to do was use his hands to pat the hole into place.

And when the hole was finished, they took up residence in it. Dot loved peering over the edge and seeing the world from low down. The hens in the next-door run were huge, like gossipy ladies in shabby brown dresses. Beyond them, the greenhouse was like a big white ship. The smells were different in the hole too. Before you got into it you could smell chickens, grass and elm trees. When you were crouched inside you could smell dirt, worms, and damp pebbles. Harry and Dot used to fill an old bottle in the kitchen sink, and take it into the hole with them to act as supplies. The water was always warmed by the sun shining through the brown glass, and it usually had some soil in it, so that after you'd had a swig you found yourself crunching grit, but it tasted delicious to Dot and Harry all the same.

The hole was sometimes a house, sometimes a boat, sometimes a tin-mine. That's the marvellous thing about a hole, it can be anything you want it to be.

Here is a strange fact about Harry: he loved to eat fog. He would take great mouthfuls on a foggy day. When you are invisible yourself, fog of course seems quite solid. Dot could hear him crunching as he chewed it. The sound was as juicy and crisp as that made by a horse when it's eating a carrot. What was really odd was that when the weather had cleared you could still see the fog Harry had consumed swirling about inside him. Only when it was fully digested did Harry become invisible again. In the meantime he looked like a boy-shaped cloud. He was his mother's son all right.

# Chapter 5

## Dot and Harry at school

I didn't see much of Harry when we were at elementary school together. He was in a different class from me and when we were out in the yard the boys were rigidly separated from the girls. There was a white line painted across the flagstones to keep us apart, and above it rose an invisible wall. Needless to say I used to feel fascinated by what it must be like on the other side of the wall, where the boys played. Their section of the yard was a mirror image of ours, except for a chestnut-tree which grew in their far corner, but I had the feeling that it would be subtly but pervasively different in some way. You can be in northern France, for example, on a rainy day, with an overcast sky and sodden fields, and yet you know with every breath you breathe that you are not in England. Their rain is not our rain. Of course I'd not been to France in those days. I had come across the problem of boundaries elsewhere, though: in church. I wasn't allowed to go up to the altar-rail to take communion because I hadn't yet been confirmed. I disliked going to church anyway, but what I resented most of all was the smugly serious look on the faces of the communicants as they returned to their seats. They looked as if they'd been let into a fascinating secret and specifically instructed not to share it with you. I think it was that expression, more than anything else, which has led me, all of my life, to associate Christianity with mean-spiritedness.

I don't mean of course that the boys' playground was anything like the altar-rail. If anything, I mean the altar-rail was rather like the boys' playground. The boys often used to gather right by the white line in order to shout insults at us girls, and when they did that they were perfectly ordinary. Sometimes

51

in fact they made little hair-pulling forays into the girls' section. There was nothing untoward about these: they were just what boys *did*. But none of us girls would ever step into the boys' area. Somehow that, by contrast, would seem indecent. I think of the whole business as a kind of graduated freemasonry. When the boys were up by the line, or over our side of it, they were their usual selves. As they receded further and further into their own half, however, they became more and more alien.

And then one day I walked straight over the line and into the furthest reaches of their kingdom.

It wasn't a conscious act – I was simply thinking of something else at the time, heaven knows what. And because there was after all no wall in place, and because their part of the playground was in reality exactly like ours (except possibly for a faint smell of wee gusting on the breeze, from some of the smellier boys) I didn't notice where I was, until suddenly I was surrounded by a gang of leering lads. I don't know whether it's ever been remarked upon that the ragamuffiny sort of boys, the ones whose clothes are a little holey, the ones who think it's clever to shout 'Ya boo!', the ones whose exercise-books are covered in blots, almost all tend to have virtually cubic heads. You can make out edges on them, and corners.

Of course I was frightened. I looked about me in panic. Heads like ruffled boxes stared back. I felt that these boys had the right to do anything to me since I had trespassed on their domain. I was subject to their laws, not those of the girls, nor those of the school in general. For the time being they confined themselves to staring, heavy sarcasm, some jostling, but this wasn't out of generosity, it was simply because they couldn't quite think what would be the most enjoyable thing to do next.

Since looking from side to side hadn't provided me with any escape from those hard eyes, in matching pairs, I looked upwards. I wanted suddenly to remind myself that there was somewhere above or beyond the narrowing circle, I wanted to get what was happening into proportion.

And there, stretching above us, was the chestnut-tree!

It was spring, and the chestnut-candles were out. They were the white kind; I like the other sort even more because they are a colour that doesn't exist elsewhere in nature, so far as

I know, and for which there is no name except the mockery of pink, but the white ones are lovely too. They glowed in the dull south-west air. Each one seemed to have an aura of quietness around it, as real candles are intended to have in church, but these were pure beyond all religion, as only new things can be. There was a backcloth of freshly opened chestnut-leaves, pale green and sausage-shaped. The stately tree was solemn and joyful all at once. Lord knows how I worded the experience to myself at the time – perhaps not at all. I may just have looked at the chestnut-tree blankly, the way objects of nature were intended to be looked at. The candles pointed skywards, rank upon rank. They were brighter than the sky, as though they did indeed shed light.

When I looked down again, Robert had arrived. He was a country lad from one of the farms, red cheeked, stocky, slow talking. I may have mentioned him already.

'Leave her be,' he said. His pronunciation made it 'lave her bay'.

'Myer yer yer,' one of the gang countered, mimicking without words. Then 'ooof' he added, as Robert brought a clenched fist down on the anvil of his head. The blow was so massive and inevitable, the two participants were somehow so mineral in their hardiness, that one expected the recipient to end up essentially the same as before, only smaller and more compressed. Instead, he buckled at the knees and began to cry. And then Robert disappeared in a swirl of enemies. I ran. Crossing the dividing line felt exactly like jumping up on something in off-the-ground tig, only more important.

In afternoon play I saw Robert, not far from the line. He looked battered but in a fitting, almost reassuring way, as an old piece of furniture might. He glanced over at me shyly, uncertain what our relationship now was. It had been, as I understood it, non-existent before. I was equally uncertain. It never even occurred to me that you can say thank you for something intangible, if that word can be used of a fight.

The only thing that sprang to mind, as an appropriate way of responding to Robert, was to prance about and show off with my friends, pretending to ignore him. So I did.

School.

Yard.

Dividing-line.

Dot had wondered and wondered what lay on the other side, and one day she determined to find out. She waited until all the boys were busy doing all the things boys do, like playing, fighting, and talking, and then very very cautiously she stepped across the dividing line and began to explore their playground. Her little feet twinkled over the tarmacadam. Her destination was a huge tree that grew near the railings in the far corner. She had always thought of it as a magic tree, since it had candles stuck on its branches, like a Christmas-tree gone wild.

This playground was very different from the girls'! Have you ever tried learning French? Perhaps you will one day, if you haven't already. One of the strange things about the French language is that even objects that aren't alive are masculine or feminine (that means boys or girls). A door is a girl, for example. And a hammer is a boy. Well, going into the boys' playground seemed to Dot to be a bit like going into a French place. Everything here was apparently a boy, even if it was just the railing fence, or the brick steps leading up to the WAY IN. Of course you'd expect their toilets to be a boy. It had begun to rain a little, and even their rain felt different, more boyish somehow.

Tip toe tip toe she approached the tree. Its leafy branches were like a green staircase up into the sky. Each nook and cranny was illuminated by a candle. She wondered what she would find if she climbed right up to the top. Perhaps an ogre would be up there, eating a pork pie the size of a furniture-van! And in his purse he might have pieces of money so huge that you would have to carry them on your head, as a baker balances his tray. It was worth a try. At the very least she might have an adventure. Her father was too small a giant to bring much excitement along in *his* wake.

She neared the tree. Its leaves pattered gently in the light rain. The staircase stretched up towards the sky, in grand spirals.

And then, suddenly, from behind the trunk, whooping, gibbering, waving their arms about, came

Tad
Bowman
Terror
&
Pig.

The four most horrible boys in the whole school! They were
wicked. The teachers despaired of them. They were ugly. Tad
had a huge nose. Bowman had sticking-out ears. Terror had
starey eyes. And Pig was fat, and grunted. They danced
around Dot like Indians on the warpath, shrieking and howl-
ing in triumph.

'We got you now!' they chorused. They weren't very gram-
matical.

Dot was frozen where she stood. She felt that her last
moment had come.

Finally, in a teeny weeny voice, she managed to say: 'Please!'

'Please!' they all shouted back. 'PLEASE! Oh yes, we're
very pleased.'

That was their idea of a joke. It wasn't much of one but it was
enough for them. They held their sides and roared with laughter. Then they stamped their feet and clumped round her once
more. They all wore great big boots – not, as it happened, to
enable them to stamp and kick more effectively, but because
their parents were rather poor and couldn't afford to buy them
more elegant footwear. Their plonking feet moved closer and
closer to her, their waving fists began to brush her face and
clothes, their rough voices were bellowing in her ears.

And at that moment, when she had just about abandoned
all hope, she had a glimpse of something in the tree.

At first she thought it was simply a stray beam of light,
striking one of the wet leaves. Or perhaps one of the candles,
guttering in the breeze. But almost immediately she realized
what it was.

Harry was climbing down the green stairs!

Carefully, slowly, watchfully, his invisible form descended.
He'd obviously been high up in the boughs all along, observing everything. When he saw Dot looking up at him, he put
his fingers to his lips, to warn her not to say a word.

Now the gang stopped dancing and stood in a row in front
of Dot. It was the time of reckoning.

55

Tad's nose was like a fat animal. Its nostrils stared at her like fathomless eyes. It sniffed. A shudder of pleasure ran through its whole body.

Tad said: 'I smell the blood of an English girl.'

Bowman's ears were pink and wrinkled, resembling the wings of a bat. They craned forward in expectation.

Bowman said: 'I hear a sudden cry of pain.'

Terror's eyes were like... Have you ever read the story of the Tinderbox? There's a dog in it with eyes as big as saucers. I used to dream about those eyes, during my childhood long ago. Terror's eyes were great discs of white, with a tiny speck of iris in the centre of each. They were as big as saucers.

Terror said: 'I spy with my little eye.'

And what did Pig do?

Pig was fat, and grunted.

Then Tad took a step forward, so he was right up close to Dot.

'Now,' he said, in a croaky voice, 'I'm going to jump up and down on your –'

At that very moment, down from the tree leapt Harry, and began to jump up and down on Tad's –!

Then Bowman took a step forward, so he was right up close to Dot.

'Now,' he said, in a screeching voice, 'I'm going to punch you on your –'

At that very moment, Harry leapt off Tad, span around, and punched Bowman right in the middle of his –!

Then Terror took a step forward, so he was right up close to Dot.

'Now,' he said, in a menacing whisper, 'I'm going to grab hold of you and pull your –'

At that very moment, Harry stepped back from Bowman, grabbed hold of Terror, and pulled his –!

Finally Pig took a step forward so he was right up close to Dot.

'Now,' he grunted, 'I'm going to kick you on your –'

At that very moment, Harry let go of Terror, took a little run, and kicked Pig upon his –!

Once again Tad, Bowman, Terror and Pig did a little dance. This time, however, they held their sore places as they did so, and sobbed,

Boo hoo!
Boo hoo!
Boo hoo!
Grunt!

And Harry took Dot's hand, and led her back to the safety of the girls' playground.

'Thank you for rescuing me,' Dot said.

She loved her brother Harry.

Later, a poem was written about the whole incident. Perhaps you've come across it?

> Dotty had a little bro
> His skin was pale as air
> And since he was invisible
> He walked about quite bare.
>
> He went with her to school each day
> And helped her with her sums
> And when the big lads frightened her
> He kicked them on their bums.

I won't get away with that, I don't suppose. Children's editors are *so* puritanical. I imagine it's on account of their youth.

# Chapter 6
## Over the Cliff...

One of the games I liked playing when I was a little girl was called Hot and Cold. One person would have to hide something while the other shut her eyes. It didn't matter *what* was hidden: anything small and convenient would do. I remember using a Brussels sprout of all things. Then the Hider would call Ready! and the Looker would open her eyes again. Everything would *seem* exactly the same. The cat would be pretending to be a dead cat, just as before, lying on the grate of that fire with the cast iron grapes, with its legs stretched rigidly in front of it. (Every now and then, when it thought nobody was looking, it would open its eyes a little and take a quick peep round, to make sure it wasn't missing anything.) *There* would be your bed, and your chest of drawers, and the washbasin and jug *on* your chest of drawers, and your wardrobe, and the ornaments on the mantelpiece, all in place just like the cat, all pretending to be dead. But somewhere amongst them lurked that sprout. If you thought about it in a certain way it could make you feel quite frightened, as though the sprout were a green unblinking eye, watching from a dark corner. Or as if it might go BANG! at an unexpected moment. Anything, no matter how humble, becomes threatening if it's been hidden from you.

While the Looker looked, the Hider would call out: 'You're getting warmer' or 'You're getting colder', according to whether you were approaching or moving away from the concealed sprout. If you were very near, she would just shout 'Hot!' If you were very far away she would just shout 'Cold!'

Now the strange thing was that if you concentrated on the game you would begin to feel warm or cold before you were even told. It was exactly as though the sprout really gave out heat, which of course enhanced the feeling that it might go bang at any moment; and so made the game more frightening than ever.

One day Dot was hunting for her brother, as she did so often. He wasn't in the house. The house was cold. Then she went into the back garden, but that was cold too, though it was a warm summer's day. She went round to the front of the house. Sure enough, the driveway was warm.

She walked down it, her feet crunching on the gravel.

At the bottom of the driveway was a big twirly gate. Dot believed it had been knitted out of iron by a giantess. I had better explain that Dot had come to the conclusion that although her family owned their house and garden from a human point of view, a couple of giants owned it from a giant point of view. In the same way a robin can own part of your garden as far as *he* is concerned, even though you still own it as far as *you* are concerned. And there were a number of signs in Dot's garden of giant occupation. There were the toad bowls, from which they must drink. There was the knitted gate, which I've just mentioned. There were giant billiard-balls on the gateposts at each side of the knitted gate.

I know what you're going to say: if giants truly lived alongside Dot, why did she never see them? The answer of course is that they were too big. They weren't little giants, like Dot's father, they were full-sized ones. It's possible they may even have been *giant* ones. Giants can have giants of their own, just as little fleas can have smaller fleas, upon their backs to bite 'em.

Now, considering how small one's head is (and Dot's head was perhaps a little smaller than most, which is the fate of triangles), it's amazing what can be fitted into it: houses, elephants, pianos, and ocean-liners, for example. But there are some things which do take a certain amount of squeezing. I've always found True Love a bit of a strain, and also World War I. They require a brain version of a shoe-horn. And sometimes things are SO big they cannot be fitted in at all, so we know nothing about them. An ant knows nothing of us, because we're too big to be fitted into *its* head.

Anyway, one thing was quite obvious – the giants did not

59

normally stir outside the front gate. The road the gate led on to was a little muddy Cornish lane, more the domain of gnomes than giants, which wound higgledy-piggledy over the countryside, skirting obstacles as a stream does. On the other side of the lane was a tall, surprised, Cornish hedge. If you followed the hedge a little way, you came to a stile. The thread of warm air led Dot on to the stile.

When you stood on the stile you saw a field sloping upwards, and the sky beyond. But what you heard was the sea. It grumbled or it thundered or it boomed or it lapped, according to its mood, but it always did something. And as soon as you heard it doing its something, you had to run up the footpath to the top of the field, where you could see it.

The sea in the part of Cornwall where Dot lived is a magic sea. Everywhere else it might be grey or brown or green according to the weather; this sea was always blue, except when it had streaks of silver in it. Although Dot knew exactly what to expect when she had run to the crest of the field, the sea always took her by surprise.

There were big jagged cliffs at the end of the field, and about two hundred yards to Dot's right, perched on the sharpest jag of the biggest cliff, was her family's tin-mine. Those of you who do not know Cornwall will probably be surprised by that. You expect ugly industries like mines and factories to keep together in groups, as gangs of hoodlums do. But not in Cornwall. Cornish mines are loners. They like nothing better than to dig their lair on a cliff-top, and peer out of it at the sea. And that is precisely what Dot's tin-mine was doing now.

A mine is like a great black upside-down tree. There is a main shaft, which is like a trunk. From it, other shafts branch out, crisscrossing and interlinking like, well, like branches. Above ground there is a tangle of buildings, like roots that have been exposed to the air. Dot had never been allowed to climb down the mine, though she often felt curious about what it was like.


I used to long to go down our mine at home. It occupied so much of the waking time of the men in my family I inevitably assumed it had a commensurate attraction. I suppose I was born into too privileged a sector of society to think of work as a painful necessity. The male relative most resistant to its charm was of course Uncle Taylor, who claimed that he was able to do the best part of his work at home since his responsibility was figures, and they could be attended to anywhere. One could almost suspect that his calculations were independent of the actual business. Though I suppose that's hindsight. Oddly enough, the first visit to the mine I can recall making was under the leadership of Uncle Taylor. Even more oddly, it was suggested by my mother.

> *My Mother:* It's about time I had a look at it. It's my mine too. Just think of that. My mine!
> *Uncle Taylor* [dryly]: How emphatic.

And so off we went, Uncle Taylor, my mother, Harry and I. I had hopes of going down the shaft but no such luck. Uncle Taylor explained that it was over nine hundred feet deep: the same distance down as the Eiffel Tower in Paris was up. Since I hadn't seen the latter the comparison didn't make much impression on me, but a phrase of my mother's did.

'Think of it,' she said in awe. 'An *eternity* of ladder.'

Instead of exploring, then, we simply went to Uncle Taylor's office. My mother didn't seem to mind: in fact, within a few minutes she and Uncle Taylor were indulging in their usual verbal by-play while Harry and I shuffled about in boredom. And then something strange and rather horrid happened.

Uncle Taylor left the room for a few moments and when he came back his face was completely darkened with soil. Only the whites of his eyes remained clean, and they looked uncannily bright, like those of a Negro or, more pertinently, those of an entertainer in black face.

> *My Mother:* Heavens, Uncle Taylor! Whatever's happened to your face? You have dirt all over it!
> *Uncle Taylor:* [he walks with even more finicky movements than usual, poking at objects the while with his cane. Then, in a deep, most untypical,

big-bad-wolfish voice]: I'm a miner, I am.
I've just climbed up the shaft. I'm very dirty
because of my hard manual labours.

*My Mother:* Stuff and nonsense, Uncle Taylor! Your
hands are soft as a girl's!

*Uncle Taylor* [he prods mother with his stick and says,
with miniature aggression]: And now, by
way of respite, I'm on the *qui vive* for wine,
women and song!

To my relief, Mother turned on her heels and left the office
at that moment. The three of us remained exactly where we
were, not knowing what we should do next. It was all very
well for Mother to leave the office if Uncle Taylor had somehow or other gone too far, but could we, as children, do the
same? Uncle Taylor prodded a few more things somewhat
half-heartedly with his stick, and then gave the two of us a
haughty look. 'What the miner-about-town is wearing,' he
said, as though this explained the whole situation.

At that moment, Mother re-entered the office. I was appalled and incredulous to realize that she had dirtied *her* face too.
Uncle Taylor sighed, with pleasure or relief. 'Not to mention
the mineress,' he added, and then, turning to her: 'May I have
this dance?'

'Whoy sartinly yr lardship,' my mother replied, and round
and round the office they danced. Harry and I huddled against
the office wall, our eyes popping out of our heads. And pop
they well might, since the measures they were watching con-
flicted at the very least with the laws of nature, and, I thought,
with certain other laws as well. Uncle Taylor was too complex
and delicately balanced as a mechanism to undertake anything
so exuberant as a dance; Mother was too lazy. To see them
do so, then, was to see them do something they oughtn't, and
filled Harry and me with corresponding nausea. I suppose that
old fashion for masked balls was to enable people to surprise
not so much each other as themselves, and in that room Uncle
Taylor and my mother were wearing masks of dirt. My
mother's generous skirts swished by us; her ample bosom
swayed just slightly in the wake of whatever inaudible music
she heard. Uncle Taylor's jacket skirts rose from his busy

rump, and his dapper legs were an intricate blur; periodically, as it caught the sunny window, his monocle flashed.

'Heaven preserve us!' Arthur exclaimed.

None of us had seen him come through the door. As he gawped, the dance slowly evaporated. Uncle Taylor's grime seemed to darken with embarrassment, but Mother was unabashed.

'Hello, Arthur dear,' she said.

'Have you seen your...?' Arthur asked ineffectually. He was still wearing his bowler-hat. Now he took it off. I've always suffered from a kind of optical illusion with bowler-hats – I think because they are rounded and usually fit so snugly. I tend to see them as part of the wearer's head, as though only the rim is actually being worn. Thus, when the hat is removed it makes me wince, as when the top is taken off a boiled egg. I winced now, as Arthur's hair, gleaming, well-brushed, rather thin for a youngish man (Uncle Taylor's was rather thin, too, but that was only to be expected), came into view.

'We thought we'd be miners,' Mother said. 'Don't we look sweet?'

'Miners?'

'Dancing miners.'

'I've heard of playing *doctors*.'

I caught my breath. Harry turned and began to look out of the window, as though he'd decided the world at large was more interesting. There was a long pause.

'Well, *we*'re playing miners,' my mother said. She sounded almost sullen.

'You don't *play* at being miners. The miners are a thousand feet beneath this floor, breaking their backs.'

'Well, to be perfectly frank, I don't believe all that skipping about has done *my* back any good,' Uncle Taylor said, and went over to retrieve his cane. He had gone through his embarrassment, and re-emerged. Despite the grime on his face he looked at Arthur haughtily, especially with his monocled eye. Now it was my mother's turn. She wasn't quite looking at the ground, but she wasn't looking level, either. She was looking at forty-five degrees. She took Uncle Taylor's proffered arm. 'Come along, children,' she said.

'You can't go home looking like that,' Arthur said. 'For heaven's sake, wash your faces first.'

'We're not ashamed of honest dirt,' Uncle Taylor said, and he and Mother went through the door, with Harry and me tagging along behind.

Suddenly Arthur roared at our backs: 'It's dishonest dirt I'm talking of!'

'He's not talking, he's shouting,' Uncle Taylor muttered testily, and we continued on our way. As it happened nobody passed us on the way home, not even one of our tin-carts.

Dot turned to one side and looked at the family tin-mine. The winders were winding, the grinders were grinding, and the pulleys were pulling, but she couldn't detect any warmth, at least at this distance. She turned to face forward again. The cool sea breeze washed over her. Unfortunately there was a streak of warmth in it.

I have a mixer tap (so-called) in my kitchen. When I put my head under it to wash my hair, a solid rod of icy water hits the back of my neck. In the middle of the rod, like the name in the middle of a stick of seaside rock, is a narrow seam of boiling water. The effect is so horrid I would scream, except that I don't know whether to scream at the cold or scream at the heat, so I wash my hair instead.

The sea breeze which Dot was experiencing was a little like the water from my mixer tap, except that its coolness wasn't so cold, nor its warmth so hot. The warmth of course was the track left by Harry, who was too invisible to leave footprints. Unfortunately the track led right over the edge of the cliff!

A footpath went down the face of the cliff to a little beach far below. The footpath was obviously the son or daughter of the Cornish lane that went past the front of Dot's house, because it had a very higgledy-piggledy nature. It travelled one way for a while; then it changed its mind and went the other. Sometimes it lost concentration and went briefly upwards. Worse still, every now and then it forgot it was a footpath altogether and became part of the cliff face for several feet, until it pulled itself together again. When you came to these bits, you had to turn your feet sideways and hope they would grip the wall, as those of an insect do.

Dot had never climbed down this footpath by herself. She had sometimes gone down it with Harry, when they wanted to play on the little beach at the bottom. Harry had no trouble with the difficult bits, of course, as he didn't weigh anything, and he would help Dot get over them by holding her hand. But now he'd gone on ahead, and she had to follow. Shall we go with her? I think we'd better, or we won't know what happens next. She won't realize we're there, of course, because since we're only readers (and writers) we are even more invisible, from her point of view, than her brother Harry.

First of all we'll go to the edge of the cliff, which happens to be at the top of the next page.

Off we go!

Down

up

down

down

'Help!'

down

whoops

down

along

down

down

Dot

went

until

she reached a flat part very near

the beach

Dot sat with her legs over the edge of the flat part. She was just about to push herself off, and scramble down the last few feet to the beach, when she stopped. She had realized that the air below the shelf was cold. It was almost as though she'd dangled her legs in the sea. She pulled them back on to the shelf. They warmed up once more.

Harry had not gone down to the beach. That meant only one thing.

Dot rose to her feet. She turned round so that her back was to the wind and water.

She came face to face with the Hole.

The Hole looked like a cave but it wasn't a cave because it was man-made. Tin-miners of the old days had dug it, years and years before Dot's family had come along and sunk a shaft from the top of the cliffs. In fact it joined on to the shaft somehow, and often when they were bored with climbing up the eternity of ladder that led from the deeps of the mine – as far down as the Eiffel Tower is up – some of the younger miners would leave the main shaft and crawl along the network that culminated in the Hole. Then they would hare up the footpath down which we have just come, and arrive at the top before many of the older miners, climbing up the direct way, had managed to reach it.

Dot had never been in the Hole. It was forbidden. You would get lost in the maze of tunnels. You might come across the main shaft in the dark and fall to your death.

But Harry had gone in there. Dot could feel a thread of warmth in the clammy air that lingered, despite the sea breeze, near the entrance, as his last breath lingers near the mouth of a corpse. Dot had followed her brother down the face of the cliff. Now she had to continue after him into darkness.

She turned to take one last look at the day. The summits of the waves were silvered, and a boat with white sails bobbed its way across them, like an angel in a vast web of light. How Dot wished she could be out there in the open, rocking in sea and wind!

Instead, she turned back to the Hole, and went in.

# Chapter 7

## ...And into the Hole

Just inside the entrance to the Hole, hanging from a rusty nail that had been driven into solid rock, were some bunches of candles. They dated from the time when this was the main entrance to the mine. The miners wore a bunch round their necks when they went on shift, so they could light one candle at a time, as needed, and stick it on to a spike in the middle of their tin helmets. There was a tinderbox hanging from another rusty nail nearby. You lit your first candle with that, and thereafter used each candle in turn to light the next.

Dot took the tinderbox down and struck the flint. Soon a little flame was curling about the scraps of tinder in the tray at the bottom of the box. Quickly she thrust the wick of a candle in, and lit it. Then she blew the tinder out, shut the box, and replaced it on its rusty nail. She would only take one candle, she decided. She didn't want to stay in the Hole for any longer than she had to, and when her candle got low she would have a good excuse for coming out, even if she hadn't found Harry by then.

Candle in hand, she set off down the tunnel.

As the daylight dwindled the candle-flame seemed to grow. Then, as the darkness grew, the candle-flame seemed to dwindle. Dot trotted down the long black corridors of the mine in a bubble of light.

The thread of warmth usually kept to the middle of the tunnel, but sometimes it would swing to one side or the other where Harry had avoided an obstacle: a lump of hard rock like a sleeping dinosaur, plump in the way, or a heap of bent and broken tins which had not been up to standard, piled up like the debris in an enormous bird's nest, an auk's perhaps,

68

whatever an auk is. Sometimes Dot would lose the warmth altogether, and have to track back a few paces, when she would find another tunnel branching out from her own, and the thread would be resumed again.

She walked for what seemed like hours, though as you will know if you've ever been unable to sleep, time, like little girls, tends to lose its way in the darkness. The darkness around Dot's bubble of light grew even darker, and as it grew darker it became heavier, and as it became heavier, it pressed on the bubble, so that the bubble became smaller still. Soon all that was left was the tiny flame of the candle itself, shedding no light at all. Dot cupped her hand around it but there wasn't any wind. You cannot protect a flame from darkness. The flame became tinier and tinier, folding in upon itself.

And then, finally, it was gone.

Dot stood, in the depths of the mine, alone. It was so black that she could no longer tell whether her eyes were open or shut. It felt like being in the world before the world began.

Have you ever heard the story of Theseus and the Minotaur? Dot had. At least she'd he d some of it. Miss Bowker was reading it out in class. Theseus, a hero of the olden days, had to go into a Labyrinth in order to fight a monster. A Labyrinth is a very confusing place, where it is easy to get lost, much like a tin-mine. But a lady called Ariadne had helped him. She'd given Theseus a big ball of thread and told him to pay it out as he went along. Then when he wanted to return, all he had to do was pick up the thread and follow it back to the light. A much better idea, Dot had thought, than dropping breadcrumbs, as Hansel and Gretel had done, since those were asking to be eaten by birds, particularly in a wood of all places. Not that there would be any birds in this Hole.

But there might be bats.

Dot shivered at the very thought. Bats could be roosting all round her, black as the blackness in which they lived, hanging on to the roof of the tunnel with their feet. She looked up fearfully to where they might be; or rather she didn't look because you can't look where there isn't any light. Blind people don't *look*. What she did was move her head fearfully.

Doing so shook up her brain a little, and brought a hopeful thought to the surface. Theseus had paid out a thread when he went into the Labyrinth, so that he could follow it back when he wanted to leave. She, Dot, had followed Harry's thread when she entered the Hole. Surely she could follow it back now *she* wanted to leave.

There was no point in trying to go any further without a candle. It would have been different for Harry. He was invisible himself, so he could no doubt cope with lack of visibility. But Dot knew, as children always do, that Now Now Now was time for her to go back to her mother.

She turned round.

It's quite difficult to do that in the dark. What she did was to leave one foot where it was and turn the other round one hundred and eighty degrees. When you do that you look as if you're walking into yourself. One more step and you'll disappear, as that candle-flame did.

But then Dot moved her stay-at-home foot round to match the other one. This meant that she should have turned completely round. She reached out for Harry's thread.

It wasn't there.

All Dot could feel was the chill of the Hole. There was no trace of warmth in the darkness.

She took a step or two forward, groping and grasping and reaching the while, just in case, but the darkness slipped through her fingers. The thread of warmth had gone; just like Hansel and Gretel's breadcrumbs. What she hadn't realized, I'm afraid, is that the other side of warmth is coldness. She was following, or trying to follow, Harry's thread in the opposite direction from before – what could she expect?

The darkness no longer seemed thick and heavy. She only wished it did. She could have grabbed hold of it with her hands and feet and dragged herself along. Instead, it felt thin and slidey, like black mud.

She began to walk again. She had to put each foot down carefully, not knowing where the ground would be. It's very exhausting, walking like that, and gives you a pain in the tummy. On and on she went, step by step. The darkness lay like slime on the uneven surface of the tunnel floor. Twice she slipped, her hands clutching at nothing as she went down. It's hard standing up again when you can't see a thing. You forget which is the right way up.

70

Dot staggered for hours, or so it seemed. Mostly she pointed her head slightly upwards, as blind people do, but sometimes she wagged it from side to side, unable to believe that there was not a chink of light anywhere. Every so often she would stop and ask herself if the darkness did not, after all, seem to have a trace of grey in it. The answer was always NO! Even worse, she would sometimes wonder if the darkness wasn't getting darker. That was impossible, because you can't get darker than black. But it was possible that she was going deeper into the tunnel and if so she might, at any moment, stumble down the main shaft, and fall endlessly, as you do in dreams. Be sensible, she told herself, there'd be lights there, and you would be able to hear men's voices, above or below. But it's difficult to be sensible when there's a cliff on top of you and a tin-mine beneath.

And then, behind her, she heard something.

A little scraping sound, a faint knocking.

She stopped and listened. For a while her heart pounded in her ears, drowning anything else. Then the sound came again. Knock Knock.

Perhaps it was miners? No, the knocks didn't sound human. They were too random, too deep, too menacing.

Dot's father, the little giant, had told her about knocks like these one evening while he was sitting by the fire. (He couldn't have been as tired as he was usually.)

'Do you know,' he asked, looking at the flames, 'that there is something which lives in mines?'

At first Dot didn't realize that he was talking to her. He didn't as a rule. It seemed as a matter of fact to be more likely that he was talking to the fire.

'Dot,' he added.

'Yes, Father,' she replied, surprised.

He continued to stare at the flames, so she did too. Possibly it was another way of looking at each other.

'They call it the Knocker,' he went on. 'You never see it, but you hear it knocking in the shafts.'

'What does it do?'

'Do? It knocks.'

'I mean, to the miners. Does it eat them?' she asked fearfully.

'Sometimes a big hearty miner goes down the shaft, and

71

doesn't come up again. And when we go down to look, all we find is a small heap of nibbled bones.

'Oh Father!'

'My dear, I'm only joking. When there's an accident in the mine, though, the men put the blame on the Knocker. Mining's a dangerous business, you must understand.'

Then Dot's father told her what his men used to do in order to keep on the right side of the Knocker (that is, the *out*side). As most of you probably know, Cornish working-men usually eat pasties for their lunch. For those of you who don't, a pasty is a kind of bag made out of pastry, into which are stuffed onions, potatoes, carrots, turnips, and, if you can afford it, some minced meat. The tin-miners used to take quite large ones to work, because they would be underground for a long time, and because they used up a lot of energy. But they weren't greedy, so they didn't eat their pasty all at once. They would have a bit of it for elevenses, some more for lunch, and a last helping for tea. But to make sure that arguments didn't develop over which half-munched pasty belonged to whom, their wives would cut their initial out in pastry, and stick it at one end of the pasty. Obviously the miners would eat from the other end, so that whatever remained still had their initial on it.

But at tea-time they stopped short of eating that last corner. Instead, they threw it into the darkness, for the Knocker. Perhaps they believed that if the Knocker ate their initial, it wouldn't need to eat *them*. Perhaps they just hoped that consuming all those corners would make the Knocker full.

Just as she thought this, Dot remembered something about the Minotaur. Its favourite food was *girls*. Perhaps its cousin, the Knocker, shared the same taste!

Dot ran.

The knocking followed.

As she ran Dot wondered whether she was running at all. She had no sense of going anywhere, only of the Knocker coming.

Have you ever run for a bus? I used to, in the days when I could still run. You run and run, and the more you run the more panicky you feel about missing it. Part of your mind tries to be sensible. It says: it's only a bus; another will come along in due course; what's the rush?

But you take no notice. It *isn't* an ordinary bus. It's a special

72

bus because it's the bus you are going to miss.

And then, suddenly, before the bus you want so much has even begun to move, you do something very strange. You stop running. You give up.

You still want to catch it just as much as before, but you can't bear running any more, you can't bear the uncertainty. Let it go.

Dot of course wasn't running for a bus, she was running *from* the Knocker. But now she had the same feeling. If I'm going to be eaten, *let* me be eaten. She began to slow down. Let's get it over with. Munch away.

But at that very moment, just as she had given up, Dot saw a light at the end of the tunnel. She began to run with all her might once more.

The light grew bigger as she ran, so she *was* going somewhere after all.

The light was firstly a speck, then a dot, then a circle, then a square, then a boy. It was Harry!

Of course. There was no room for darkness where Harry was, because he took up the space where darkness should be, so there was light.

Dot ran towards her brother's arms.

Though when she arrived she stopped short of them and said, as sisters will, 'Harry! Where've you been? I've been searching for you everywhere! Why did you want to come down this mouldy old Hole? You went off without saying a word!' And more of the same.


Tin-miners call their first glimpse of the light of day, 'greening'. When I went down the Hole, though, and re-emerged, what I saw was the sea, a shock of blue. It was during the very hot summer when I was eight or nine years old. I'd been mooning about for an hour or two, not sure how to occupy myself, and I ended up playing about on the cliff, a lowish one, near our house. There was a very enjoyable footpath on it, down which you had to scramble and jump and twist. At the bottom was a little beach which, unusually for this part of the coast, was covered mainly in pebbles. Harry and I used to regard it as our personal property since we never saw anybody else there.

73

Harry wasn't with me that afternoon, however (he rarely was). He was probably playing with the neighbourhood ruffians.

I became bored after a while and began to probe the aforementioned Hole, as one picks at a scab, with a mixture of enquiry and repulsion, the enquiry in the end just tipping the balance.

This was, of course, the other kind of Hole. Not the product of childish labour, but *un trou trouvé*, as you might say (if you were a snob). A dug hole is a hole that belongs delightfully to you; a hole in a cliffside belongs by contrast to who-knows-who. Harry and I had made the occasional foray into this Hole, but we'd always scuttled out promptly enough. At a certain point – ten, fifteen yards – you sensed that the light had admitted defeat, and you were in the Kingdom of Darkness. At that point, back we always went.

But now I was alone, I found myself going in further. It was a process of acclimatization.

This is an oddity: one is less cowardly by oneself than in company. Wouldn't you have thought it would be the other way round? By contrast, one can be a *snob* by oneself, even though that seems a competitive sport. Look at me, a couple of paragraphs ago, writing of *un trou trouvé*. There I was (and am) sitting alone at my desk, not a tooth in my head, and when I wrote *trou trouvé* I got a lovely golden glow, even though I knew those words would be edited out and no one else would ever read them. Moreover, I then went on cunningly to disclaim them, thus establishing myself as too snobbish even to *be* a snob. All in the solitude of my dwelling!

But if snobbery is personal and ineradicable (I'm sure people even *die* snobbishly – I expect *I* will), cowardliness is all bound up with your relation to other people. Either you catch *their* cowardliness, or you're intimidated by their bravery. You feel that you'd rather establish yourself as a coward at an early stage than let yourself down later. But when you're alone it's a different story. You can't be doing with cowardice, it's too much of a nuisance. I even catch spiders in cups and shake them out on the lawn.

And when I was just a little triangle, I went into that Hole.

Not all at once, of course: it was a process of acclimatization, as I said, like putting your foot into a hot bath, taking it out with slightly less alacrity, and so on, until at last your foot can cope, and the rest of you learns from its example. I went in and out of the Hole a few times and then thought, blow this for a lark, and stayed in. There was nobody outside for me to demonstrate my nervousness to, there were no cowardly gods to propitiate. Nevertheless, even within the privacy of the Hole, my exploration was a gradual matter. I would take a few steps forward, and then ask myself whether I was still all right. On discovering that I was, I would take a few more steps, and stop again. And so on.

Silence.

The silence was so pure you could almost hear it. That sounds a tired paradox but I mean it literally; as though the darkness had a rhythmic beat; as though the black air were breathing.

And then:

Pitter patter pitter patter forward I went, as flouncily and fussily as possible, trying to fill the ominous spaces around me with my noise and movement, so that there was no room for anything else; as abandoned children must speak with raised voices in the depths of a wood.

When I stopped, my pitter patter would slowly fade away and the breathy silence would be resumed. Each time I looked over my shoulder the entrance to the tunnel was smaller than previously. Finally a shelf of rock must have obtruded, or perhaps the tunnel had imperceptibly taken a corner, because the circle of daylight wasn't there at all.

I took another step. Coldness rose from below, as though I were up to my middle in water. I became aware that in the distance there was a drip. Blop blop blop it went, as though someone somewhere, some dark and remote being, had not turned off a tap properly. I listened, transfixed, my ears focused on the sound as sharply as eyes might be on a sight. I began to wonder if I could make out other sounds too, dreadful threatening sounds that lay somehow just out of sight of one's hearing: skitterings, crunchings, knockings.

I turned to run, but couldn't.

I was stuck in the black as if my feet were in pitch. This was nothing to do with cowardliness, this was to do with terror. Somewhere in the far past our ancestral lines cross with those of hedgehogs, rabbits and other animals who freeze when threatened. I felt as though I were turning into a statue.

75

I often used to feel sorry for our Venus de Milo, stuck forever on the lower terrace, ennui in marble. Perhaps indeed it was boredom that finally broke the spell for me. There is nothing more boring than sustained panic.

At last I ran.

I stumbled, groped, thudded into a shelf of rock, but suddenly, after (to be frank) just a few paces, the entrance to the Hole was visible again, and after a few paces more, the sea and sky radiantly filled the aperture. I had safely blued.

Once outside, with that sense of melodrama which renewed daylight gives, I flung myself full-length on the ledge that overlooked the beach, perhaps nine or ten feet below. As I did so I glimpsed someone walking on the shingle, and started to call out. I took it for granted it must be Harry – this was our beach, after all. But it wasn't – it was Uncle Taylor!

I broke off. Uncle Taylor didn't look up. Perhaps he thought my noise was the squawk of a seagull. (I've often noticed that the calls of animals and birds resemble incomplete words.)

Uncle Taylor on our beach! How dare he! The man who, every day, inveigled his way into my house, our meal-times, his sister's intimacy, was strolling along the beach which Nature had reserved for the private use of Harry and myself.

For one thing, how on earth had he managed to scramble on to it? How *could* he have minced and twiddled his way down our tortuous, crumbling footpath? I simply couldn't picture him. That pernicketty cane, those fluttering gestures! He must have *flown* down, like some be-boatered Edwardian butterfly.

Anyway, there he was, taking his constitutional upon some-one else's pebbles. My eyes bulged with indignation. I stared down at him with all the hostility of a Knocker seeing an intruder in its tin-mine.

I had no intention of making my presence known to Uncle Taylor, which meant I couldn't scramble down to the beach nor even retreat up to the cliff-top. Nor did I want to return to the Hole. So I had no alternative but to lie where I was, and watch. And then I came to notice, eight-year-old that I was, that there was something very strange about him.

I hesitate to put it on paper, it seems so trivial. But I knew it was significant at the time, and I'm still convinced it was.

76

Uncle Taylor was limping.

He'd put down his cane – it was leaning against an outcrop of rock. That was logical enough, as you will realize if you've ever tried to use a cane on a pebble beach. Perhaps one could invoke a law of contrarieties (or contrariness). A man who habitually uses a cane when there is nothing wrong with his legs might apparently have something wrong with his legs when he is *not* using his cane. In other words, he uses a limp *as* a sort of cane.

But that explanation is too pat, there's more to it. Obviously, relinquishing his cane must have given Uncle Taylor the idea, but I'm absolutely confident that there was an underlying motive. In my mind's eye I can see him still, hobbling beside the blue sea on that glorious summer's day so long ago. He would walk for a few yards along the shore, just above the wave line, then turn and walk back, but swivelling his head so that it was pointing at the water no matter which way he went, as an animal does when it paces up and down its cage, and stares out between its bars the while. Instead of a regular crunch crunch crunch, the sound his little patent shoes made was a double rhythm like the systole and diastole of the heart: crunch-crunch crunch-crunch crunch-crunch.

I don't know how I formulated to myself what was going on, but I'm sure that deep down somewhere I understood the essential truth of the matter, which is this:

If you limp, you inhabit a limping world.

Which is to say, from your point of view, it is the *world* which is out of kilter.

And funnily enough, this applies even more poignantly if you are making the limp up as you go along.

Uncle Taylor continued up and down in this way for hours, or at least so it seemed to me. Finally, he went over to pick up his cane. I retreated a little way into the Hole. Talk about the devil and the deep blue sea! The Knocker behind, and Uncle Taylor approaching my footpath in front. He went past, and up, and after a few minutes I followed. He was in the garden when I arrived home, armed with his cane, not limping. He had no idea, of course, that I knew of his secret.

## Chapter 8
## *Blow Chapter Eight for now!*

*Mens turbata!*

And on this occasion, the Latin is no exaggeration. Disaster has struck.

I'm too upset to write about Dot, that little triangle. A big triangle is my theme, one moreover stuffed full of naughts, which wobble and bobble and try to go their separate ways. Me. In my mid-seventies. Living in my house in Shrewsbury. Hardly epic subject matter but when you live on your own you have to talk to yourself from time to time. It helps to get things in proportion. And I have more confidence in myself with a pen in my hand. It's my stethoscope, or baton. My magic wand. Some hopes. The last thing my pen is capable of is exorcizing monsters. On the contrary, it's stuffed full of them, drinking them down with its ink. Which is well and good when you're writing for children, since monsters are their diet. But when you're as old as me, monsters are superfluous to requirements.

Of course, the word monster may be something of an exaggeration. But it's a useful term for a being you can't picture, and I certainly can't picture Uncle Taylor's grandson, any more than I could picture Uncle Taylor's daughter, or Uncle Taylor's wife. It's a useful term, too, for a being who is likely to threaten one's very existence.

Anyhow, that's what I can use my pen for, to see how much of an exaggeration monster is.

First: the status quo ante. (What a lovely word ante is, and how remote, even when it's this morning. Once upon a time is nothing but a wistful invocation of ante.)

And then we can let the question of the Grandson *pop*.

Bed of course is one of my stronger points.

I am the most horribly untidy person I know, and I've undoubtedly become worse as I've got older, which is why the last thing I need at this time of my life is for Uncle Taylor's descendant to rear his ugly head. But I *am* frightfully good at making my bed and get great satisfaction from doing so. I tuck my sheets and blankets in so tightly that to enter I have to sit on my pillow and slide myself in completely flat, as you slide a letter into an envelope.

But needless to say, my one tidy habit has irritatingly untidy consequences. As I go down, my nightdress rucks up. I make an attempt to tug it down once I'm in, but with varying success. With the bedclothes well tucked in it's difficult to lift your body off the mattress in order to slide your nightdress under your bottom. And even worse, your arms will only move a tiny way up and down, like those of a toy soldier. Sometimes I'm lucky, and with one economical movement I unwrinkle. More often than not, however, I lie in secret discomfort, like the princess on her pea.

So there I was this morning, my head neatly amputated upon its pillow, my bed sheer and orderly on the outside, tangled within.

First light.

I woke. I knew it was first light because I could just catch the ups and downs of my clothes flopped on my bedroom chair like a melted statue.

I thought of Dot. Yesterday while pursuing her brother she had been pursued in her turn in the depths of the tin-mine by a Knocker, and at the crucial moment had seized up, standing in the dark like a statue until somehow she got going again.

I had a notion of where I was going to send my Dot today. Somewhere more domestic than a cold dark mine-shaft. I was (am) going to send her *under the table*. I myself had an experience under a table once upon a time, and I think I can put it to good use.

So I lay on the bumps of my nightdress, and thought about such things, until interrupted by the distant sound of bottles. They rang faintly from somewhere along the quiet streets, like glass bells.

I like to be up before the milkman arrives, for a particularly disreputable reason which I suppose will become apparent shortly. Still, at least it proves I have a routine. Except that I didn't get up when I heard the milk bottles ring this morning, so that casts a cloud over my good behaviour. I lay in bed and thought for a bit longer. When faced with the prospect of getting up, one can clutch at certain wispy thoughts as a drowning man clutches at straws.

The thought I clutched at this time was that in my childhood there were two knockers. The first was the one that lived in our tin-mine, and that yesterday pursued poor Dot. The second was a man who used to go round the houses of the village near us first thing in the morning, knocking on the doors to wake people up. I suppose he would be more correctly termed a knocker-upper. It was obviously an arrangement which predated the general distribution of alarm clocks. He didn't knock on *our* door, of course, we were too important. In any case, we employed him. He was an Arthur notion, needless to say, like the mine barber. With each knock, a whole family got up. Grown-ups, girls, boys, dogs, cats. Shaking themselves, crawling out of bed, moaning, stretching. House after house, one knock at each.

Anyway, I didn't take my cue from the thought of the knocker-upper, any more than I had from the sound of the milk bells. Instead, I went into a doze, that delicious state which is too low level even for dreams. It's not a state, therefore, which can be described. But my ears must have been working even though my brain wasn't, so I heard something without knowing what it was. As I came out of my doze I wondered for a moment if I'd made the noise myself: if it had been that most shy and elusive of animals, one's own snore. Then I thought somebody might have called out, perhaps the milkman.

No, it hadn't been a voice.

Now I was awake, it came into focus, a shiny sound, folded in upon itself like a knot.

The milkman had dropped a bottle.

What drama!

In an emergency like this, of course, I bitterly regretted that my bed was so tight. If it was hard to get in, it was just as hard to get out again. I had to slide out a bit of me at a time, and pile each one on the pillow while waiting for the next to arrive. And there is a *lot of me* these days to pile up. As a result, therefore, and despite all my hurry, I found myself thinking my fat thought.

Sometimes I think, and sometimes I have thoughts. The first involves exploring pastures new; the second consists of going along some mental footpaths that I've taken hundreds, thousands, of times before: indeed, I've worn the path into existence by following the same route so often. Since I was in a hurry this morning I rushed along my fat thought, taking no notice of the sights en route. I *knocked* my way along it, like Arthur's knocker-upper:

Knock: Plain as a child.
Knock: Brown and freckled.
Knock: Skinny as I grew up.
Knock: Fuller figure all the rage.
Knock [discreetly]: Even prayed for a bosom. Dear God, let it pop forth.
Knock: Blush to think of it. I can feel the tips of my ears turn red.
Knock:
Knock: And then, forth it popped!
Knock: Aged fifty some-odd.
Knock: And now!

Finally I was free of the coverings. I was piled up like jumble upon my pillow. I felt, as so often, like some poor woman in a Picasso painting. I located my legs and swung them out and down to the floor. My nightdress seems flimsy on them these days but at the same time reminds me of something. Yes. Stormy weather. The washing-line broken. My mother frantic. Uncle Taylor dancing attendance, as though upon strings. A sheet, at the bottom of our garden, tangled in trees.

My right foot found its slipper straightaway. But would my left? Of course not. It fussed about, practically at random. I developed that sensation of pins and needles in the brain you get when you are fed up with the extremities of your body. You want to curl your toes and twist your fingers so violently that they drop off.

81

There was a sudden jingle of bottles. Much nearer. My left foot gave up on its slipper and I hurried out as I was, one shoe off and one shoe on, diddle diddle dumpling my son John.

Or rather: slap-slap slap-slap slap-slap, like my Uncle Taylor on his long-ago beach.

Down the stairs.

Across the hall.

Into the sitting-room.

Over to the window.

There was a frame of white round the curtains where they've shrunk. It seems rather unfair, since I've hardly ever washed them. I've not inherited one iota of my mother's joy in scrubbing and mangling.

Item for the Prosecution: the curtains, like much else in my dwelling, have been Let Go.

The float was coming down the road. It was whining like a low-power banshee. The great advantage of gaps is that they let you peer out of the window without opening the curtains. I peered.

It was still very early. Everything was grey. My long unkempt grass was grey. My sagging fence was grey. (The first things the Grandson will see!) My road was grey. It's one of those concrete roads which are normally white, with black seams at intervals which look like liquorice. There was a mist round the trees in the public park opposite, which made them look wobbly. Even their leaves were grey. Everything was grey except, for some reason, the milk float, which was pale blue, and its white bottles.

The milkman was hurrying up the garden path of the horrible man next door. Bottles dangled from his hands like great white fingers. He didn't look towards me. Then he scurried back and turned into my pathway without needing to refill his fingers.

This was the test.

I turned my gaze down, as one turns down the gas.

I wonder if other people can do this? If I look at someone with a certain intensity in my gaze they feel my eye-beams and turn to look back along them. It's rather like my Dot, yesterday, following Harry's thread of warmth out of the house, across the road, over the field, down the cliff, and into the mine. If I turn my gaze down a little, however, the beams fade in proportion, and nobody notices. Perhaps I'm a witch.

Up my path trotted the milkman, head bowed, thinking whatever thoughts a milkman might think. Possibly mourning his dropped bottle. Dropping bottles wasn't characteristic of the man as I saw him. He seemed busy and efficient. Moreover, he was well into his forties, with iron-grey hair, obviously neither gawky nor impetuous. Anyway, no matter what he was thinking of he didn't look up towards me. I had a sudden sense of what he would have seen if he had: a grinning toothless face with cunning eyes, hanging like a balloon against the dimness of the room behind.

Suddenly, at the crucial moment, I found myself shuddering with laughter, and my heart pounded with shock and fright as I struggled to hold it in.

No harm done. He deposited my bottle, picked up the empty, turned and hurried back to his float. Victory once more!

Wouldn't it have been terrible if he had seen me! He would have thought I was spying on him. He would probably have assumed I was senile.

Ha Ha! Serves him right. I *was* spying on him! Who does he think he is, making judgements on people, deciding who is senile and who isn't? He should devote more energy to not dropping his bottles.

And more of the same, I'm ashamed to admit. I told you my motive in getting up before the milkman's arrival was disreputable. I commence each morning by spying in this sneaky way and then gloating over my success. It puts me in a good mood, for a moment or two at least. You would become a very boring person if you were always as good as gold.

Now the milkman had gone I opened the curtains, an annoying chore. Your pull has to go up the curtain and then round a corner in order to get into those little wheel things and make them travel along the rail. I always have the feeling while I tug that my arms are too short (possibly because, in answer to my prayers, my bosom once upon a time popped forth!). The effort made my eyes throb.

Then back upstairs to my bedroom. Needless to say my left

slipper was sitting in full view on the rug beside my bed as if butter wouldn't melt in its mouth. Anyway, having given it a glare I went over to my clothes and inspected them. Not too closely. They were good for another day.

I will draw a discreet veil over the process of getting dressed. After all, that's precisely what getting dressed *is*, so I'm doing no more than a good writer should, adapting form to content. Similarly with the bathroom. Even though I'm alone in the house I always lock the bathroom door. Sometimes I tell myself it's because I don't want burglars to catch me in a position of disadvantage, but of course it's not really that. One locks the door in the end to prevent *oneself* from intruding. It's a way of saying that this aspect of me doesn't have to be taken into account.

So there I was, downstairs once more, marching into my kitchen. It has to be admitted that my kitchen isn't tidy. The best that can be said for it is that it provides a record of my movements. You can reassemble my boiled eggs, and account for my cups of tea. If you had the correct kind of cinema projector you could place my kitchen table into it and play back all my meals of the last week.

On my kitchen table, amongst other debris, was a slice of pork luncheon meat, like a pink letterbox. How can you forget a slice of spam? I couldn't even remember *when* I'd forgotten it. At least I had the sense to pick it up and drop it into my bin, so that's one piece of evidence the Grandson won't be able to lay his hands on. As a matter of fact I didn't *drop* it into my bin. Nothing gets dropped into my bin, because my bin, like the magic porridge pot in the story, is always full. I placed it on the surface of my bin and tiptoed away.

The thought did cross my mind of building on the example of the spam and trying to sort out my kitchen table as a whole. How satisfactory! I could have forgotten that excellent intention so easily if I had not been sitting here for the last few hours, methodically establishing my status quo ante. Actually, tidying up one's kitchen is no hardship, once one begins. The best bet is to grab oneself by the scruff of the neck, as if one were a recalcitrant little boy, and get on with the job with no more ado. In fact, it rapidly becomes a positive pleasure, a voyage of discovery. Ah, my bottle of sauce. Ah, my bread-bin. And then there's the delight of the next time you come into the kitchen. If you simply pick your bottle of sauce up off a horrible table, when required, then it does no more than what is necessary. On the other hand, if you take your sauce out of its cupboard, particularly if its neck and shoulders have been wiped clean, then the very taste seems to have been wiped clean also. All those extraordinary ingredients on the label, those mangoes, tamarinds, goodness-knows-what, come through clearly on to the palate. It's like having sauce for the first time, an appropriate reward for good behaviour.

However, the good behaviour didn't materialize. The intention came and, as intentions will, it went. I think my extenuating circumstance was the sun. The early morning greyness had departed, and sunshine was coming in through my kitchen window, convincing me that today was just the sort of day to be a slut. I decided I would leave my nasty kitchen exactly as it was. Perhaps I would even make it a little bit worse.

I lit my gas and put the kettle on. Then I cast around for a cup. Every single cup I owned was dirty. They were sprawled over my table and working surfaces as if there had been a party. Perhaps there had. Life itself is a party. In my case, all the guests are me. Certainly I was in a party mood. I would wash *one cup*, not a jot or tittle more. To make up, I washed that one very well. There was a brown line round the bottom where the dregs had been, so I inserted a finger and rubbed it. As with so many of my achievements, that one seems double-edged. It provides evidence for both the defence and the prosecution.

Next: the milk. My milk wasn't in the refrigerator, needless to say, it was on the table. I sniffed it. It didn't smell off exactly, but it smelled more milky than it should. Of course there was a fresh pint waiting on the doorstep but I couldn't be bothered to go and fetch it. This would do. My *cup* was fresh, anyway, so I poured some in.

The kettle began to steam. I remember thinking that the steam smelled slightly overripe too. That way madness lies. In any case, it was time to begin my hunt for the teapot.

Teapot.

?

Teapots don't march off.

Where would a teapot go? In the name of goodness?

It was sitting on the table along with everything else, perfectly visible. I'd actually looked *at* it while I was looking *for* it. I must have thought: that's just my *teapot*. What I'm after is my teapot. Perhaps I should concede the Grandson's case: I *am* beginning to live in a world of my own.

No. Nonsense. I've never been able to find a teapot in my life.

Now to find the *tea*.

You have to work for a living in my household. You can't just say, 'I'd like a cup of tea' and have one, like they do in books. You have to earn it. You have to look and look until you're tired out and couldn't care less whether you ever have another cup of tea in the rest of your life. You feel you would like to pour your cup of tea, if you ever manage to make it, over somebody's head. And since there's no one else available, over your own head.

'I am a complete, stupid, horrible, idiot,' I said out loud. I said it slowly, with true hatred in every word. 'I can't even keep tabs on my tea-caddy.'

As though I'd said the magic words, I found it straightaway, behind half a pound of butter.

As in the case of the teapot, it was perfectly visible, but I'd deliberately refrained from looking in that direction. If Uncle Taylor's Grandson ever discovered why, my life would be over. That I know. But at the same time there's no point in conducting this exercise if I don't keep my tally of pros and cons. Butter, I'm afraid, is most definitely a con.

I like butter. I can't bear margarine. I like to think when I open a lovely yellow oblong of butter, of the cow that was behind it. I haven't seen a cow for years, and they seem to me to be old-fashioned to the point of being unlikely, creatures that belong in children's books. Possibly that's why I insist on liking butter.

But I worry about it. I worry about it going rancid. Indeed, I'm beginning to realize I worry about everything going rancid. This morning I was suspicious of the milk. I even had a fleeting thought about the water. Water, for heaven's sake. But butter is the main thing.

On my table, to one side (in front of the tea-caddy), I was aware of an opened half-pound of uncertain age. I deliberately avoided focusing on it, though I could see it clearly in my mind's eye. It resembled some horrid bog flower, with the opened wrapper like sticky silver petals, and the yellow insides, grooved, scraped, contorted, like pistils or stamens or whatever you might call them, those parts that are liable to reach out and grab you. I'm not sure it would do any good to keep my butter on a dish. The lovely clean edges would soon blur, and as for washing the dish out afterwards, the less said the better. The worst thing you can ever touch in your life, no matter *what* you choose to put your hands into, the very worst thing of all, is stale butter in warm water.

Me being me, what happens is this.

I buy a half-pound of butter, and use some. Since I live on my own, and am not a big eater, despite the evidence to the contrary, a half-pound of butter lasts me quite a time. After a while, however, I become frightened that it's going rancid, and I stop using it. But I know in my heart of hearts that it isn't, so I can't bring myself to throw it away. Instead I wait, averting my gaze, until at last enough time has gone by to ensure it really *is* off, and I can throw it away with a clear conscience.

'Why not put it in the refrigerator?' the Grandson would no doubt ask.

No, he wouldn't, since I will make absolutely sure the topic of butter NEVER NEVER NEVER arises between us.

The answer would be in two parts. 1) Putting it in the refrigerator will slow down the whole sorry saga, and make it even more difficult for me to work out what point I've reached. 2) I always forget to put things in the refrigerator.

This butter needless to say was in the in-between stage so I'd been trying to avoid catching its eye. And *that's* how I'd come to overlook my tea-caddy.

By this time the room was filling with steam. I rushed over to the kettle and turned it out. Then I came back to the table, and spooned tea from the caddy into the pot. I didn't warm the pot first, I never do. As a matter of fact I hate people who warm their pots. They are grown-up versions of those children who keep their toys, unscratched, pristine, in the original boxes. Toys were made to be used, and slightly broken. Then I carried the pot over to the stove and poured the water in.

Of course the kettle was now well off the boil, so it would be a rotten cup of tea. Only *I* could get the water too hot and then pour it out too cold. I was so irritated that I found myself pouring the tea straight into the cup without giving it time to brew.

I had a sip. It tasted quite nice. I looked around my kitchen contentedly. Who cared about chaos? The sun was still shining in through the window. I settled back on my kitchen chair and drank my tea.

I was glad when it was finished. It hadn't been very nice really. I'd just pretended it was nice because I was tired of being bad-tempered about everything.

Now it was time to get myself some breakfast. I was famished. The question was, what? I've never been one for cereal. How about a boiled egg? Nice to look at and nice to eat. There's nothing nicer than a lovely egg-shaped boiled egg, in its little cup, with a slice of bread and butter.

Except of course a fried egg.

No, I didn't want all that fuss. Dirtying a pan (or knowing me, making a dirty pan dirtier). Likely as not sticking my thumb in the yolk when I broke the egg, so that you don't know whether to throw it away or make do. Washing my plate afterwards. With a boiled egg, if you're careful, it's just a matter of brushing off the bread crumbs, and the plate's as good as new.

The trouble with thinking about fried eggs is that it makes you lose your appetite for boiled eggs. A frying egg sizzles so deliciously. Boiled eggs are boring, boiled and boring.

Get thee behind me, fried egg.

I would love a boiled egg for my breakfast!

Refreshed by my horrible cup of tea, I got the egg boiling merrily. And there was the bread, in its bag, lying on the table amongst small debris like a beached whale. I do admire sliced bread. I love its sequence. Similarly with sliced bacon, the way each rasher is similar to the one before, but slightly different, as though you're watching an object travel through time. I once had a loaf bag split open on me, and all the slices dropped to the floor, like spilled playing cards. Strangely they stayed in order, so they still resembled a loaf, only they lacked the necessity of bagged bread. They were loosely organized, like a *dead* loaf. Not that I've ever seen a dead body. Just think of that. I belong to a generation where everybody died, and I've never seen a dead body. Sometimes I feel quite left out.

Anyway, it was time to confront the butter. Enough shilly-shallying. I picked it up.

Now, poke your nose out from its burrow, for a little sniff. Sniff.

It smelled as butter always smelled (to me).

On the left, a rich buttery smell.

On the right, a dry odour, somewhat like cardboard or wood.

Possibly this smell version of double-entendre emanates from my nose rather than from the butter itself. Perhaps I have one butter nostril and one cardboard nostril. But together they made up *the* smell, and I couldn't be doing with it. I'm old enough to know what I like, and what I don't like is in-between butter.

I actually spoke out loud. When you realize you're in the grip of some silly foible you feel a need to take it out of its twilit hobgoblin realm into the outside world.

As a matter of fact, all I said was: 'I'll jolly well have my bread...' and then I paused, because I couldn't think of an adjective to describe bread with no butter on it. Finally: 'bald'.

Anyway, a couple of minutes later I was sitting at my table. I had cleared a space in front of me. I had brushed off a plate. I had washed a knife and a spoon. I had even found my egg-cup. The egg was deposited snugly in it. I had my slice of bread to one side. I picked up my knife. I tapped my egg to make a little inroad. Then with a quick, decisive motion: 'Off with his head!'

I suddenly thought of Arthur. I could hear his voice as if it were yesterday. It's normally hard to remember voices. People's faces can come and go in your mind, but voices are normally lost forever, except in your dreams. But I could hear Arthur.

He had a friendship with a farmer's wife, or perhaps widow, at the time. He came home one day, excited and pleased with himself. They'd spent part of the afternoon beheading ducks apparently. He sat by the fire – Christmas was coming: which was why duck was required, I suppose – and told us all about it. I can still see his exuberant piscine features in the flickering firelight.

'It was the most extraordinary thing. Mrs... [*Somebody-or-other*] manned the chopping block. What an amazing creature she is! Not a flinch. I was entrusted with fetching the ducks, one at a time. They led me a dance, as you can imagine. But whenever I got hold of one, it seemed to become resigned to its fate. It would sit quite still in my arms.'

There was a pause.

'A sitting duck,' suggested Uncle Taylor.

'And then,' Arthur continued, 'what was even more remarkable: as we approached the chopping block, each duck in turn would stretch its neck straight out, as if to allow its head to be chopped off more conveniently. It was as though the duck had taken in the whole situation at a glance, and understood that resistance was useless.'

'I would have thought,' my father said, 'that wringing their necks was more usual.'

'I am going upstairs to gag in the privacy of my own room,' Uncle Taylor said, and left.

'Is she a handsome woman?' my mother asked. 'This Mrs... [*Somebody-or-other*]? With her chopper in her hand. Heaped about with headless ducks.'

(The art of conversation still prevailed, in those pre-television days.)

My egg was perfect, exactly as I like them, with the white firm and the yolk soft. I was just about to dip my spoon into it when –

Peeng Pong blip.

My doorbell rang. It always makes that little noise at the end, as though by way of a full stop.

Who on earth could it be at this time in the morning? My heart sank. I wasn't dressed for visitors. I was wearing my slippers, for a start, and of course I didn't have a tooth in my head. Blow them, I thought. If they ring my bell at this time in the morning, they'll have to take me as they find me. I got to my feet and went along the hall to my front door.

Surprise, surprise, it was the horrible man from next door. Who else was it likely to be? He was the only person who ever called, apart from the milkman once a week and the meter reader once a quarter. Only a busybody was likely to press my bell at the crack of dawn.

In my opinion there is a lot of truth in the notion that the body is the temple of the soul. In other words, that your appearance is a good yardstick. I don't mean of course that a beautiful person necessarily has a beautiful interior. In fact beautiful people quite often look rather unpleasant at the same time. Not that there is any ambivalence in the case of the horrible man next door. He has large ugly features clustered in the middle of his face: a grey walrus moustache, a pendulous nose, heavy spectacles. I am always reminded of those spectacles which comedians and clowns wear, the ones with the other attributes attached. If the horrible man should ever take his glasses off, his face would be entirely blank...

His brain was blank also, with that total and abysmal blankness only a compulsive chatterer can possess. He loved to have an excuse to ring my bell. He would pretend to be going shopping, for instance, and come round to see if I wanted anything. Once I almost succumbed. I told him I wanted a piece of chicken. Dear oh dear, the peroration that ensued! I received a history of the chicken, in its capacity as a comestible. I received a ditto, though perhaps more marginal, history of fish. Apparently in the recent past these two histories had coincided, and the one had begun consuming the other. As a result, when you bought yourself what looked to all intents and purposes like a nice piece of chicken, it turned out to be fish-rejects, cunningly metamorphosed into poultry form. Which proved the old axiom: you are what you eat.

The horrible man wasn't trying to wriggle out of buying me my piece of chicken, oh no. He was far too devious for that. What he was suggesting was that instead of going to the local shop, he would go further afield, to a high-class emporium he knew of, where the chickens hadn't been fed on fish-meal. The intention of course was to put me under more obligation to him than I was already. I was perfectly aware of what he was after. His ultimate goal was to be invited into my house! He wanted to poke that false nose of his into my surroundings, and see how messy they were. There is a dog-like prurience about such people, and yet, of course, he'd be clean as a whistle himself. He would be the sort of person who always warmed *his* teapot. The next thing I knew he'd offer to help me tidy up, or decorate. I've met his type before. They simply can't leave people alone.

Anyway, I was having none of it. Quick as a flash, I changed tack.

'I don't think I'll bother with chicken after all.'

'Oh no, it's no trouble.'

'No, really. It strikes me that what I really fancy is a tin of pilchards.'

'Pilchards?' he repeated in astonishment. He said it with a little pop on the p. It sounded exactly like the implosion that occurs when you open a can, as though pilchards were a tinned *word*.

'Cut out the middle-man,' I suggested. 'Or rather, the middle-chicken.'

'But as I said, I can get –'

'No, it's quite all right. I suddenly feel a hankering after pilchards. I have a tin of them in my kitchen cupboard, as a matter of fact.'

'I can buy you a packet of fish-fingers. They're very economical.' His manner suggested that pilchards had been superseded by modern advances – a point of view which consorted oddly with his nostalgia for the chickens of yesteryear. I'm afraid he was improvising hastily in an attempt to retrieve the situation.

'I don't like food with corners,' I said decisively. It was a lie, of course, since as I've already mentioned, I'm very fond of sliced bread, but it put paid to the horrible man for the time being. 'Pilchards will suit me fine,' I went on. Meanly, I let fly one last blow: 'I assume they're not yet being fed on *chickens*?'

But of course people like the horrible man never give up. And here he was again, at this time in the morning, standing at my door and clutching a letter.

'Hello,' he said. 'What a lovely day!'

'Is it really?' I replied. I tried to give the impression that I didn't need to be summoned to my front door to be told *that*.

'The sun is a-shining,' he continued, by way of elaboration. He seemed perilously close to bursting into song. 'I was mowing my lawn yesterday.'

I couldn't help but bridle. He seemed to be implying that I should have done mine. That's so typical of people's attitudes towards writers. I spent yesterday at my desk, helping my Dot negotiate the depths of her tin-mine; the horrible man footled his time away hacking at grass: and then *he* rebukes *me* for time wasting!

'How kind,' I said acidly. 'First of all the weather forecast. Now: Leaves from My Diary.'

The horrible man, unabashed, merely laughed. 'You *are* a character, Miss Watson,' he said. 'I can quite see how you wrote all those books.'

I nearly made some comment to the effect that if only I were left alone I might see my way to completing another one, but I held my tongue. At one time writing books was a routine matter for me, but so many years have passed since I last produced one that I've become rather self-conscious. I feel like a neophyte again, ashamed to admit that I've actually embarked on so grand an enterprise. Virginity *is* recapturable, at least in a literary sense. (In other respects the question hasn't arisen.)

'I didn't write them by mowing my lawn.'

'No, I'm sure you didn't. While I was mowing *my* lawn the thought went across my mind that it might come in handy if I mowed *your* lawn too. It wouldn't be any trouble. I've got one of those petrol mowers.'

I gazed at him in astonishment.

'I thought you'd come to deliver a letter,' I said. 'You might at least try to keep your story consistent.'

Again, he had the front to laugh, or at least to *say* a laugh, as people who are too lacking in intelligence to have a sense of humour often do. 'Ho, ho,' he said, 'that sounds like an author talking!'

'What I'm getting at,' I explained, 'is that you obviously originally intended to come here on the pretext of a letter.'

He looked down at it, all innocence. 'I met the postman at the bottom of your path. I said I'd save his legs.'

'I see,' I replied severely. What a saintly picture of himself the horrible man must have, I thought. Saving the postman's legs. Offering to mow my lawn. He was so adept at erecting a philanthropic edifice around his urge to pry. 'Postmen's legs are not collectors' items,' I pointed out. 'And I prefer my lawn how it is. *Au naturel*. Good morning.'

'If ever –' he began, and realizing I'd seen through him, abruptly gave up. 'Good morning,' he conceded, and began to slink off.

'I'd like my letter,' I said, putting out my hand.

'Oh, of course,' he said, passing it over. 'I hope it's good news,' he added forlornly. I imagined how he must have weighed it in his palm, trying to gauge the contents.

'I'm getting a bit old for good news,' I replied, and shut the door.

Back in my kitchen I sat down in front of my egg and collected myself for a moment. I might be too old for good news but you're never too old for bad. The envelope was handwritten. My mail is normally typed and official these days, and of course it's years since I received a letter from an admiring reader. I'm Out of Print. The letter immediately seemed ominous, I don't know why. Possibly because it was delivered by the horrible man. I have a certain sympathy with the ancient custom of executing the bearers of unwanted news.

I'll copy it out. I like to read with my pen.

> Yes, yes, yes
> Manchester etc
> Recently

Dear Aunt Olive

I hope you don't mind me being so familiar. To be honest, I'm not sure what our relationship is, but I think of you as my Aunt (or should I say Aunty? Aunt sounds a bit formal). I'm the grandson of Edwin Taylor, your mother's brother, so I suppose I'm really a first cousin once removed.

I know the family lost touch with each other years and years ago but to be honest I've no idea why. So I don't know what you know and what you don't know. So forgive me if I'm repeating things you're well acquainted with. My grandfather died in his mid-80s, in 1954 I think it was. I remember him a little from my childhood. A lovely old man, very impeccable in every way. Despite his bad leg he was a great walker, almost to the end,

94

and I can see him now, striding about with his cane.

His wife, my grandmother, was of course much younger than him, but didn't outlive him by much, sad to say, dying also in the 1950s. Their only child, a daughter (my mother, of course!) was named Catherine, after your mother, I think. She married my father in the war (the Second W.W.). I was born in 1945, just after the war ended, so as you can see, I've reached the ripe old age of thirty! Sadly my father was killed in action a few months before, so I never knew him. My dear mother, your cousin, died on the twenty-third of January last, after a long illness. I don't think you ever knew her. She was a gentle and lovely person.

Anyway, after my bereavement it came over me that you and I are the only members of the family still left. Not that I'm exactly alone in the world! I'm proud to say that I have a delightful wife, Margaret, (Maggie to her friends!) who I married two years ago. But it seemed silly for us not to be in touch when we're all that's left. To be honest I have no idea what the problem was that arose all those years ago, but surely we can let bygones be bygones? Apart from anything else, I'm very proud to be related to a famous author! I read your books when I was a child, and thought they were marvellous. Far better than Enid Blyton (oh dear, I hope she's not a friend of yours!)

I'm not literary myself, I'm afraid, as you can probably tell by perusing this letter! As a matter of fact I'm a solicitor. I've not long been out of articles, and am at present working for the council, though I hope one day to be in a position to enter private practice.

Anyway, enough about me. What I'm writing about is that Maggie and I would love to come over and visit you, to talk about old times (and future ones!). We can get to you in a couple of hours by car. We have the day off next Monday (Bank Holiday) so thought we would drive over if you've no objection, arriving towards lunch time. But *don't* rush around getting anything prepared. We'll bring a picnic with us, and we can eat it together. (And perhaps a bottle of bubbly, to commemorate Long

95

Time No See!). By the way, I'm a great D.I.Y. addict (Do-It-Yourself) so please don't hesitate to make a list of any little jobs you'd like done while I'm there. I'm quite an expert at making conversation with my mouth full of nails, while hammering away at something, and I never go anywhere without my tools in the boot of the car. As the boy scouts say, Be Prepared!

There's nothing like inviting yourselves, is there? But don't worry if it's at all inconvenient. Just give us a ring at the number above. (I wasn't sure whether you were on the phone – Directory Enquiries had no record of your number). Or drop us a line. We could always arrange another date.

Well, I hope you don't mind me writing out of the blue. Hoping to see you very soon.

Yours sincerely
Arthur Hodgkinson
Not to mention Maggie!

While I read this letter I could feel my moorings shift, and then break loose. When I had finished, I couldn't speak for some minutes. Not that I needed to, of course. But I couldn't think, either. I simply stared at my irrelevant egg. It stared back at me with an unwinking yellow eye. I have an unwinking eye too, I know how to read a letter. Not to mention that I'm a miner's daughter. I can burrow beneath that I'm-just-a-little-boy-scout-and-I-wouldn't-say-boo-to-a-goose style. It's the epistolary equivalent of those men who don a Gas Board hat in order to rob little old ladies of the life-savings they've hidden in a sock.

I spy with my yellow eye:

Aunty! Tame her from the opening sentences. I've never been an aunt in my life. I've never been a relative of any sort since I was a *daughter*.

'I don't know why the family lost touch with each other'. He says that twice. I.e.: it defies reason. You defy reason. Especially since Uncle Taylor proved to be such a darling old man! Of course he did. He was a darling old man when he was a young man. He'd practised all his life.

Enough said about that preposterous 'bad' leg. Uncle

Taylor had a bad leg in his *head*, as other people have head-aches.

You never saw my father, you never saw my mother, you never saw my grandparents, you never saw my dog Fido, you never saw anyone, yet they were all saints and martyrs, so what was the matter with *you*? Were you blind?

You are a famous author. Ergo you're rich. (Are you listening, you editors?) Just like your friend, Enid Blyton. You can afford to pay a heavy fine after trampling down that lovely and gentle woman (whoever she was) and that impeccable old man who strode so valiantly through his crippledom.

And who is entitled to your loot? I'm your only living relative. I'm the heir apparent. Let's let bygones be bygones: I've got a long *future* ahead of me.

Not to mention the nubile Margaret (Maggie to her friends). She's an Earth Mother, Maggie is. Fecund as a rabbit. The two of us will have the children you never had. We'll spend the money on them you never spent. That *exact* money!

Don't think you can get away with it. I'm a solicitor, dreaded word! Don't try any of this literary hanky-panky on me. And we only live two hours away. We've already reported you to Directory Enquiries. And if you don't let us come on Monday we'll come some other time.

We know what we'll find. You've never heard of the Second World War. You're not able to look after yourself. You can't cook a meal. Your house is falling apart. Yes, this is the crux of the matter. First he aunties me to a jelly then he starts to whack my house with his hammer. And it's true: my curtains have been Let Go. I noticed only this morning. The kitchen looks as if a bomb has hit it. I think anguishedly of my lawn. The horrible man will bear witness. 'I offered to mow it for her, yer Honour, but would she have none of it? No, she wouldn't. She said she wanted it back to nature, or words to that effect. It's difficult to make out what she's saying, toothless like she is. Could be French, half the time.'

They can probably put you in a HOME, once lawn and curtains have been proved. She was sent down, on the grounds of lawn and curtains. And multiple cases of kitchen. Lacked teeth, to be served concurrently. Spying on milkman also taken into account. (Of course the milkman knows I'm there.

97

How one does fool oneself! Just because he doesn't look doesn't mean he doesn't see. You can see with your *ears*, if necessary. It takes a blast of cold air from the real world to bring you to your senses, and make you aware of the games you've been playing.)

I sat for goodness knows how long, staring at the threat the Grandson posed. Then I did a very strange thing. I put my coat on and went off in search of that bottle the milkman had dropped first thing this morning. The cursed letter has shaken my previous way of life to its very foundations, and I think I felt the need to prove it had taken place at all – which is probably the real reason behind this chapter. It's a despairing attempt to give a bit of stiffening to my status quo. I went in my slippers, I'm ashamed to say. No doubt the Grandson could call umpteen neighbours to testify to that, all staring at me from behind their curtains.

I was nonplussed at first because I saw no sign of the dropped bottle on the paths or pavements nearby. And then I noticed a neat pile of glass in the gutter. That's not what I'd been expecting at all. I'd expected to find the bottle where it had fallen, like a flower composed of milk and glass. But instead it had been tidied away. Heavens! The milkman must keep a little broom on his float, for just this eventuality!

I found myself laughing out loud at the very thought. The Grandson would be proud of him. Waste, Death, and Destruction are on the rampage everywhere, and people like the Grandson and the milkman trot about with their hammers and brooms, their mouths full of nails, clearing up little messes and making sure people put the correct labels on World Wars. They pin their faith on Do-It-Yourself!

Of course, it did my case no good at all, laughing out loud in the street like that. It's a hilarity equivalent of smoking a cigarette, not the sort of thing you hope to see an old lady do at all. As it happens, I've never smoked in my life, but I wouldn't mind taking it up now for the express purpose of blowing a puff in that Grandson's face! Trust me to think of ways of making matters worse.

# Chapter 8
## The Land Where Lost Things Go

I remember seeing those astronauts jumping about on the moon like slow-motion children. You don't need all their paraphernalia, of course, you can discover a world anywhere. I discovered one under the dining-room table once, when I was a little girl.

Christmas wasn't far off, the one following that glorious summer. I know because the scene of Uncle Taylor unnecessarily limping along the beach was very much in my thoughts, as events will show. His sinister lopsidedness seemed to undermine his neat little boater and bootees.

I was alone in the dining-room. Harry had been playing with me, but he'd gone to the lavatory and not come back, a habit of his. He'd catch me out in the same way over and over again. I'd play listlessly, waiting for his return, and after a long long while realization would finally dawn. It's one of the oldest deceptions in the children's repertoire, and disproportionately dispiriting in its effect. You feel you've been left behind while the world has gone on its way.

The late autumn downpour must have let up, because it was a bright day. Through the window I could see my mother hanging the washing on the line. A blue wind was blowing, flapping the sheets like sails on a ship. She looked so busy and absorbed in the sun and breeze that my sensation of being left out intensified, as though there were more than the window of the dining-room between us. Perhaps, deep down, I was jealous at seeing my lazy mother working at all. Be that as it may, I found myself wondering how she'd feel if I were dead.

She'd be very brave of course, hanging out the washing just as if her little Olive had never been born. She would stand in

99

that sunny empty breeze pegging and pegging and pegging. But she'd be weeping inside herself, and I would be able to do nothing to comfort her because I wouldn't be able to speak. That's how I imagine death, as a form of claustrophobia: losing the connections between yourself and the outside world. At intervals throughout my life I've had what I call the dwindling dream. Perhaps everybody experiences it, though I've never heard it mentioned, unlike its near relative, the falling dream. In the dwindling dream you seem to get smaller and smaller while your body remains the same size. Possibly Jonah and the Whale is the story of this dream because you finally feel as though you've been swallowed up by some torpid leviathan. You scrabble in desperation at your own walls but fail to get a purchase. You can no longer reach any of your body's knobs and levers. In your panic one hopeful thought crosses your mind: if you cry out, if you scream, you'll break the spell and all will be well again. But you can't scream. You've forgotten how.

The loss of consciousness holds no fears for me. Let me be nothing. Then there will be nothing to fear! But what I do fear is being conscious of my unconsciousness. Surely what happens in the dwindling dream is that your body, on the outside, is asleep while you, on the inside, remain awake. (The falling dream is perhaps an earlier stage in the experience: it involves the sensation of *surrendering to* sleep.) Isn't it terrible to anticipate being so out of control! Not out of control in an exuberant manner like a car rushing down a hill; but out of control like one of those old-fashioned roadsters stalled on a railway crossing in a silent film. Inside, such desperate fumbling! If that is what it's like to die, there is no point at all in composing oneself for death. One faces the inevitability of panic.

No one doesn't.

ONE does no such thing.

There will be no urbane, judicious *one*.

It'll be *me*. I. Sharpened to a wobbling focus, like the dot projected from a burning-glass.

I'm sure eight-year-old Olive worried about such things. There is no moment in life when you are insulated from the fear of death. But after a while she went off and got on with something, as one does.

I stepped away from the window. The room seemed dark and gloomy, after the light outside. The empty chairs sat around the empty table, like knobby old men waiting for a meal. I took a deep breath and plunged below the surface of the furniture as one plunges below the surface of the sea.

Below, it was a different room. It wasn't a room at all. I was in a tiny wood, where all the tree-trunks and branches were straight and smooth. I wasn't on the ground as you are in a real wood, but quite high up amongst the branches, like a squirrel.

There was a row of huge elm-trees at the bottom of our garden. Their branches were always windy and cawing with rooks, and you could often see squirrels leaping from one to another, red squirrels of course in those days. They fascinated me. They were not like animals running about, nor like birds flying. They seemed to inhabit a different dimension from everybody else. They lived in a bendy place with lots of holes in it, like a picture you haven't finished colouring in. Under the dining-table I inhabited a similar place. My eyes did, at least. (My arms and legs were still on the floor, but I didn't take any notice of them!) My eyes hopped from tree to tree.

Every time I moved the whole wood changed, so that soon I felt I'd been travelling for miles. Some sunshine had crept into the window end of the wood, and I headed leapingly towards it.

When I arrived at the sunshine it was like getting into a warm bath. Little white specks circled in the sunbeams like high-up birds. This part of the wood seemed golden and dozy and I shivered pleasantly at having been chilly just now, though I hadn't noticed it at the time. (The general had a particular knack of lighting anaemic little fires that struggled for hours to get going, so our house was often nippy in the winter-time. Perhaps one lights fires in one's own image. Which might explain why now, when I put a match to my oven, my eyebrows tend to fly off.)

When I left the clearing to resume my wanderings, the woods seemed even darker than before.

Once when I was sitting with my father in the evening, he suddenly asked: 'Do you know what happens to your eyes in the dark, Olive?'

101

He asked the question abruptly, out of a long silence, and a chill clutched my heart. Goodness knows what I imagined.

'In the mine we are always in darkness,' he added. 'So we know all about it.'

He made me fetch a mirror and a candle, and showed me.

'The black part of your eyes is little in the light,' he said, 'but it grows when the light is taken away. If you want to see in the dark you have to wait until some of it has got into your eyes.'

Then he slumped in his chair once more, looking at the fire. No doubt his own pupils shrank to full stops.

Away from the sunny place the wood was cold again. It was sinister also. There were so many corners that anything could be lying in wait. Dwarves for instance.

In the darkest part of all, there was a cottage. I climbed into it. The chair seat above me was the roof; the chair legs, with a bar of wood going across, made the window. Outside the trees rose high, high, blotting out the light.

Somewhere in the distance I was aware of a regular thudding. The dwarves were obviously out at work, hitting things with little hammers. I was glad of that. I didn't want to see them winding through the wood with their oversized heads.

It was very quiet. The only birds I'd seen were those high white ones in the sunshine at the other end of the wood, too far away for their singing to carry.

The light at the far end of the table faded and then came back. That must be the Queen, moving across the noon clearing like a cloud across the sky. Now her dark form was lost in the twilight of the woods.

When she finally arrived outside my cottage window it was a shock, even though I knew she was coming. Such apparitions carry shock along with them as part of their stock-in-trade, even when they lack the element of surprise. Her pretend-face was old and wrinkled and ugly, with her beautiful one discernible within it, like a prisoner in a cell. (Wishful thinking of senile author!) One side of her apple was red as meat, the other as green as grass.

'Would she like this apple, m'dear?' Her voice sounded creaky, like a stair.

'No. Thank you.'

'My love, my little one.' Her little eye peered up at me like the eye of an evil bird. She had two eyes, but her gaze was so intense that I was only aware of one. 'Does she not trust me?'

'*I don't want it!*'

'Let me show her.'

The Queen took a bite from the green side of the apple. Her teeth were bright and even in her ill-fitting mouth. The bitten place stared up from the apple like a small white eye.

What could I do?

It was a sort of bargain, one-sided undoubtedly, but binding. Rather like military call-up in times of war. Because the Queen ate, I had to eat too. Of course I knew perfectly well that the poison was in the *red* part of the apple, but it made no difference. A story is a story. You have to follow it through to the end.

The Queen raised the apple to my face, revolving it so that the red side was foremost. I opened my mouth as you might open the mouth of a puppet.

And then there was a roll of thunder.

I stopped on the very edge of my bite.

Thunder?

I looked up at the sky. There were brown swirling clouds in the fixed grain of the table. When I looked down again, the apple had gone. So had the Queen: with the alacrity of someone who hadn't been there in the first place. But the memory of the thunder still rolled in my ears. And as I thought about it, I realized that the hammering of the dwarves had been real too. There had been a distant thudding sound, and then a sort of collapsing rumble. I had effortlessly incorporated the sound-effects into my playing, as one incorporates the ringing of an alarm clock into one's dream.

Suddenly I felt afraid. I pushed my way out from underneath the chair. As objects do when one's in a rush, the chair pushed back, bumping me. Then I was in the dining-room once again.

The window sparkled blue, as before. You could see at once that no thunder had passed by. I looked out. There was the washing, some on the line and some in the basket, but my mother had disappeared. She had stepped out of the scene just as the Queen had stepped out of the wood.

I knew I was being silly. For some reason she must have

come back into the house. And the banging and crashing must have been Harry, up to something in his room. He was the sort of child who frequently gave out loud sounds. I started up to his room to see what he was doing this time.

The bottom of the stairs always smelled of cabbage, whether the cook was preparing cabbage that day or not (though she mostly was). When you climbed out of the cabbage there was the smell of polish above.

I walked towards Harry's room and then turned to one side as if deflected by a magnet. The door to Uncle Taylor's room was a tiny bit open. I suddenly knew that the noises had come from in there.

I went up to the crack in the door.

Uncle Taylor was lying on the floor beneath some chairs. He looked as though he'd been exploring in some strange wood of his own. He had no clothes on except his drawers. He looked slightly fat in that state though he was very thin when dressed. He had a little round tum and his arms and legs were like linked sausages. My mother was on the floor too, though she had her clothes on.

They didn't see me. My mother was laughing, and Uncle Taylor looked embarrassed. Now I know, I thought to myself: now I know why he was limping on the beach. I felt as if I were looking at them through a terrible window, like a dead princess in a glass coffin.

Dot and Harry had been doing *something or other*. I know, they'd been playing at their lovely Uncle Taylor's numbers farm. They always had such fun there!

It was fun, for example, to tie the top part of a six to your finger and drop the round part down, so that it looked like this:

Then you flicked it back up again: 6. Harry and Dot became so skilful they could toss it upwards, when it became a nine. You could do magical things with numbers at Uncle Taylor's farm!

After they had tired of yo-yoing they took hold of a ten and placed the one on top of the naught, sat at each end of it, and played see-saw-margery-daw.

Uncle Taylor had one enormous number which he kept in a big barn. This was the number (approximately):

222,222,222,222,222,222,222,7o1.

It was called a two-two for short. Dot and Harry took it out of the barn (it was quite docile). Dot sat on one of the twos; Harry stood in front of the seven, driving. What fun! Two-two, two-two, two-two!

They had less success with another game they tried. This one was called Naughts and Crosses. I expect some of you have played it. One person has a supply of naughts, the other a supply of crosses, and they take it in turns to put one of them down. The first person to arrange three in a row is the winner. Dot and Harry thought it would be great fun playing this game at Uncle Taylor's farm. Dot gathered together some naughts and Harry borrowed a few multiplication signs from the farm's breeding unit. But it all went badly wrong. The crosses made the naughts *multiply*, so that shortly Dot and Harry were all but buried in them. Luckily Uncle Taylor came along in the nick of time and rescued them. He was very angry. He told them that naughts and multiplication signs don't mix. He said that if he hadn't happened by at that moment, his whole farm might have come to naught. And by that time the process could have been too late to stop. Cornwall could have disappeared; then England; then, heaven help us, THE WORLD.

Uncle Taylor was so upset that Dot and Harry decided it might be wise to leave him to cool off for a while, so they went for a walk over the fields. There was a large wood on the horizon. Harry wanted to explore it.

'It's too far,' Dot told him. She didn't like the look of the wood, which seemed dark and threatening even though it was a sunny day.

Harry took no notice of her, however. He rarely did. He skipped off over the fields.

I expect you've seen the shadow of a cloud race across the countryside on one of those bouncy, breezy days in spring. Well, it was summer-time now, and the sky was perfectly blue, but Harry slipped over that rolling landscape in exactly the same fashion, except that he was a *pale* shadow.

Dot had told a little fib, I'm afraid to say. The wood wasn't too far, it was too near: that was the whole trouble with it. Have you ever fallen, unexpectedly, into a pond? Dot had, remember. One minute she was tootling about her garden, thinking of this and that; the next she was face to face with a goldfish. Dot and Harry arrived in the wood so quickly they felt as though they'd *fallen* into it.

In an ordinary wood the trees are nicely haphazard. There will be the occasional one standing grandly by itself; then you will come across a group of timid saplings clustered all together, looking like thin girls with long hair; and after these, perhaps a bunch of jolly little bushes going roly-poly in the undergrowth. But here the trees were grave and rectangular and evenly spaced. They looked like sentries who had been called to attention hundreds of years ago, and then been forgotten. There were no leaves to be seen, but when you looked upwards you discovered the wood was topped as by a dark lid.

(I think I've had occasion to remark before that trees do not grow profusely in Cornwall, there being, over most of the narrow peninsula, a sea-wind which irons and flattens the terrain, keeping the grass pressed like well-parted hair in a single direction, from west to east, and challenging any vegetation which might wish to grow higher. Such trees as there are tend to be low and tangled since this wind, though consistent enough, acts as a random factor in the development of each, unwinding its symmetry. Perhaps this explains why I seemed so often to have trees on my mind.)

Cornish trees as a rule are few and wind-tangled, but there was no wind in this rectangular forest, and perhaps never had been. Dot had the feeling that though tempests might roar by outside, they would never knock at this door and come in.

The air smelled stale. There was no bird-song. She was frightened.

'I want to go home,' she said. Her voice sounded thin and wiggly amongst those huge and silent trunks.

Harry didn't answer. He was standing at some distance, like a stray patch of misty sunshine.

'Harry, do come on. We've wasted enough time already.'

Even as she spoke, she realized she was saying the wrong thing: or rather, she was saying it in the wrong way. He was her older brother after all; and obstinate; and a *boy*. He flickered a few paces further away, and then turned to face her. He had a certain look on his face as if daring her to speak like that again. If she tried to give another order, he'd be off. What she ought to do was 'get round' him, as they say.

But instead, Dot found herself becoming even more bossy than before. She thought to herself: if he wants to be silly, let him be silly. Why should *I* care?

'All right,' she said, 'you can jolly well stay here if you want to. *I*'m going home.'

Harry immediately hurried deeper into the forest as she knew he would. Blow him, she thought, blast him, bother him. If Harry wants to be a silly ass, let him *be* a silly ass. She turned and began to walk out of the wood.

But when she got near the edge, something made her stop and turn round again. There was Harry, flashing in and out of the trees. But he paused after a moment, as though he'd sensed her watching him. He looked back over his shoulder at her. As she expected, his expression was hard and naughty and determined. But then, without any warning, he began to cry.


I surprise myself sometimes.

No, it was in the *pose*. Looking over one's shoulder.

There is poor Harry, peering over his shoulder at Dot, and weeping; and in Canto XX of Miss Sayers' translation of Dante's *Inferno* we come to the Fourth Bowge of the Eighth Circle of Hell, in which walk the Sorcerers, weeping, with their heads twisted round so that they're looking back at where they've come from while they continue on their way. They

107

twisted the order of nature, so they've now been twisted themselves by order of the Supernatural. But Dante, with his eye for the heart-rending detail, shows pity for them even if the Almighty does not. He sees – and I think this is the most piercing and wonderful piece of information in all poetry – that their tears run down into the cracks in their bottoms. (Also, it's very funny.) And Dante weeps in turn.

Bowge is a splendid word. The Bowges are the trenches of hell.

Suddenly Harry ran.

He rushed off in the wrong direction like a startled pheasant (or a Three!). It was sheer fright that sent him scuttling into the depths of the forest instead of towards safety. And as he ran he continued to look back towards Dot. Even after he had disappeared she felt she could still make out his pale face, misted with tears, in the dim air.

Now it was too late she found her voice.

'Harry!' she cried. 'Harry! Harry!'

Each time she called out his name – and she called it a great many times – it would collide with some nearby tree, then another, then another; and then the next 'Harry!' would join in, skittering off a different series of trees, until it seemed as though the name surrounded her, woven through the wood like a great invisible spiders' web. And then, when at last she stopped calling, it gradually undid itself again, until finally there was only one tiny mournful 'Harry!' far off among the great trees, a small sad voice that didn't sound like hers any more calling back to her from that land where lost things go, the old worn doll that you one day realize you haven't seen for so long, the family puss that couldn't walk properly and was taken to be looked at by the vet, that generation of boys who were on the verge of manhood in 1914. Although there was no weather in the wood it was a cold voice, which seemed to come from a cold land, covered by the snows of yesteryear.

Dot began to run after Harry.

# Chapter 9
## We Meet the Witch

Dot ran and ran until her eyes were bulging and her breath came in tiny packages. (The same symptoms, incidentally, are experienced by old ladies with short arms when they are trying to tug their curtains open.) Nothing in the wood seemed to change, however. The big trees simply clocked by her, one at a time, one at a time. She felt (quite rightly) that she was running Nowhere. Eventually her ears began to ring.

No, they did not. It was bird-song. You can tell how tired Dot must have been by that time, mistaking birds for ears. We all know that sometimes people's ears can be a little unfortunate. Occasionally they stick out so that they do look somewhat like small round wings. I once knew a little girl who had one sticking-out ear and one flat ear, so that however straight her destination she always described a gentle curve. But as a matter of fact, though Dot was not naturally a tidy person *her* ears were fairly neat.

Then, in the distance, beyond the oncoming march of trees, she made out a patch of sunshine. It was a woodland glade! It resembled a great tree of light, with birds fluttering in its branches like bright leaves.

Dot ran towards it with renewed vigour. She ran all over. Her legs ran. Her heart ran. Her brain, throbbing, ran. When you run like that you actually *feel* your brain, like some big fruit or fungus that has grown within your head and is pressing rhythmically against the sides.

And at last Dot tumbled into sunshine, laughing with relief. She sank on to a grassy knoll and felt herself relax. The glade was golden and dozy, and entering it was like entering a warm bath. Above her the golden tree's great branches swayed gently in some breeze they did not share with the forest all around; and the white birds drifted vaguely in eddies of the air. The ground beneath her resembled one of those delicious old-fashioned horse-hair mattresses, full of smooth slopes and valleys (unlike the modern contrivances with powerful springs designed to fling you back up in the air if you should carelessly leap upon them). In short, it was a blissful place. Its ending was quite distinct, like the rim of a spotlight when you are on stage. At one point Dot put her arm out into the rest of the wood, and it felt instantly cold. The experience was exactly like sitting on an island of noon-time, while a sea of dusk stretches away in every direction. Dot lay back on the mattress of the ground, looked up at the wonderful tree which stretched above her like a great chandelier, and let the peace invade her senses until her mind was blank.

If publishers weren't so horribly mean I'd ask mine (who-ever he might be!) to insert a pale yellow sheet of paper at this point, so you would know what Dot's thoughts looked like while she lay beneath that golden tree. However, I know he'd never allow it. He would write me a letter explaining that the cost of employing somebody to paint all the pages that would be needed for all the copies of the book would be prohibitive. Publishers adore using the word prohibitive! Other words and phrases they like using include the following:

> unfortunately (their favourite of all!)
> changeable market
> hard times
> my reader and I both agree
> enjoyed it anyway
> constructive criticism
> better luck next time.

They also use lots of exclamation marks in their letters to show how perky and brave they're being despite adverse circum-stances! (That's another phrase they like.) And in any case publishers like to stuff as many words on a page as possible, just as omnibus companies like to stuff passengers on double deckers. So you'll just have to imagine how it felt to lie in that warm, yellow, *buttery* light, under the great tree of noon-tide.

110

But Dot didn't wake up comforted. She awoke to a sense of bad news, as you do on Monday mornings. Harry after all was a patch of light himself, though small and pale in comparison with this glade, and he was lost out there among the shadows.

Dot gritted her teeth and resumed the search.

Her teeth were an assortment of milk teeth and second teeth, so they didn't grit all that well.

(Meanwhile for me it's Sunday afternoon, and the Grandson and Maggie are due to arrive tomorrow, so *I* shall wake up to bad news for certain. And I haven't got teeth of any sort to grit.

Isn't it strange how, whatever the weather, late Sunday afternoons are always tinged with mauve, like rain clouds glimpsed through frosted glass?)

Dot was on the far side of the tree of light now. This didn't feel like Nowhere, as the hither side had done, it felt more like a place, though a horrid one. True it *looked* just like the other. The towering rectangular trees

I wish I could think of a better word than rectangular for those trees. What I'm describing of course is a series of gigantic furniture legs: a dining-room suite. Though I haven't made that clear. Insert earlier: The forest was a forest to Dot and Harry, but it was a dining-room for a family of giants who were too big for the children to see. The father-giant was the brother-in-law of the father-giant who lived at Dot's house (not the little giant, but the giant giant, the one who drank from the toad-bowls).

Luckily the forest giants weren't in their dining-room, or I would have had some difficult-to-explain legs to deal with. Oddly enough, I did once write a novel in which a character grew an enormous leg, but I've got enough problems here without that. The giants had heard a noise upstairs, and had gone to investigate...

111

But even without legs I've got enough on my plate. The trees have a square cross-section and a rectangular face, though the rectangles are never completed, since they shade off into the darkness above. And of course the rectangles are in three dimensions. Perhaps that means they should end in -oid, like one of Uncle Taylor's more exotic creatures, the dreaded and mysterious rhomboid.

Rectoid?

Oh dear me.

When my father lived with me in his old age, he suffered from piles. A miner's disease in more ways than one. Though as a matter of fact I have a bit of bother in that direction myself, nowadays. In my case I suppose you might say it's a writer's equivalent of athlete's foot. My father used to use a brand of suppositories that went under the dreadful name of Germoloids, though he always called them his Things. 'I'm just going to use one of my Things,' he'd mutter as he set off for the bathroom. He said Things as though it were the trade-name. Blushing, I recall how, when he was getting on my nerves, I'd pull him up about this. As follows:

> *Hard-faced Daughter:* I beg your pardon, daddy?
> *Father* [mutters]: Going up to. Things.
> *H.f. Daughter:* Do you mean you're going up to use one of your Germoloids?

[Father blindly grunts assent. Even as I write I can feel the same directionless anger that I experienced so often during his last years.]

> *H.f. Daughter* [continues]: Well, why on earth don't you say so? How can I be of any help to you if you won't let me know what's wrong?

How could I have helped him, in any case? Putting in a suppository is a private matter. The more trembly and vague your hand, the more determined you are not to have an audience. I wasn't just callous in such episodes, I was unintelligent to boot. See how, writer that I am and was, I allowed myself to endorse the name Germoloids. Things is much the better word.

In due course my father's list of ailments (piles, poor circulation, ulcers, arthritis, and a sort of all-embracing senile terror) grew so long that he wasn't able to go to the chemist's himself, so I was deputed to get his [mutters] Things for him. And how did the hard-faced Daughter fare?

*H.f. Daughter* [in clear ringing tones]: I would like a packet of Germoloids, please...

...So far, so good. At least she's consistent. But if you follow her spoor you'll soon discover that it leads us round a corner...

        .

     .

  .

    .

        ... *Bitch* [continues confidentially]: ... They're for my father.

I say this now, now I am almost the age my father was then: You spyhunters don't have to chase Kim Philby and the like as far as Moscow, you can find treason and double treason beneath the surface of a random old lady like myself. I wish, father, diminutive careworn giant that you were, how I wish you could see your old old daughter now, blushing with shame.

The towering rectangular trees disappeared into the darkness above, the ground remained flat, there was no undergrowth. The woods no longer felt deserted. Dot had the unpleasant feeling that other things were about, just out of sight. You half expected to come across dwarves, but she couldn't see any. Perhaps they were hidden behind the trees. Hopefully they'd gone off to work as dwarves do. Dot hurried on, through the silent, dim, and sinister woodland, for what seemed like miles.

And then, suddenly, she stumbled upon a cottage.

There it was, right in front of her!

113

She had no idea where it had sprung from. She stopped in her tracks and looked at it.

There was no more light here than elsewhere in the wood, but the cottage was so spick-and-span it positively gleamed. The walls were whitewashed, and there were green shutters on each side of the windows. A small heart had been cut out of the middle of each shutter. The windows themselves were made up of little diamond panes. The glass looked black, as it usually does from the outside, so you couldn't see in.

There was a trellis round the front door, on which roses rambled, the first flowers Dot had seen in the wood. Strangely they were dark blue, though this may have been an effect of the dim light. The roof of the cottage was made of red, thick-sliced tiles, and there was a delightful crooked chimney at one side with smoke wafting up from it.

In front of the cottage was a small garden, with more flowers planted in rows, strange glassy ones this time. They tinkled as they grew. As Dot watched, one of them came into bud. The bud swelled and then opened with a delicate shattering sound, revealing a white flower like a milky diamond. Its beauty hurt Dot's eyes.

A garden path, made of yellow, green and blue stones, led up to the front door. In the middle of the front door was a brass knocker.

The cottage was as pretty as a picture, but Dot couldn't help feeling a little frightened. What could it be doing in the middle of this wood? Nevertheless she had no choice but go up to that front door and knock on the brass knocker. Harry might have passed this way.

She walked up the garden path. Nobody stirred within the cottage at her approach. But as she got nearer her feelings underwent a peculiar change. Her tummy still fluttered, but now with hunger rather than fear. She realized that (probably as a result of all the exercise she'd taken that day) she was absolutely starving. And seeing the cottage from close quarters she wondered what on earth she'd been afraid of.

Its walls were a thick creamy white, like that hard icing you see on wedding cakes, with little points of silver light spangled upon the surface. When she glanced up at the roof Dot realized it was tiled with slices of bread, liberally coated with raspberry

114

jam. Moreover the front door was the thick soft red of uncooked strawberry jelly (everybody, except grown-ups of course, knows that jelly is much better chewy and raw). The knocker was the delicious yellow of Cornish clotted cream toffee.

We used to get Cornish clotted cream toffee from a shop called Pooleys. Hammer toffee, it was called, because it was made in great slabs and broken up to order by a grave middle-aged man in a white apron who wielded the tiniest hammer you ever saw. It was a dwarf hammer, suitable for carrying out repairs on doll's houses. Before the inroad was made the slab of toffee lay like thick sunshine on the counter. Harry didn't like clotted cream toffee, as a matter of fact. He used to say, with a certain amount of glee, that it reminded him of sick. His favourite was treacle toffee, which I in turn couldn't bear. There was something about its sweetness and chewiness which made my teeth want to fall out with shock (which they finally did umpteen years later). When you swallowed it the soft lump burned your throat.

The tasty look of everything was too much for Dot. Her butterflies were ravenous. She opened her mouth tremendously wide and took a huge bite out of the cottage.

At the very moment she did so, a great shadow fell upon her. A thick shadow: she *felt* it fall.

As you probably know, ghosts don't cast a shadow even when they are standing in the noon-tide sun. Witches, however, are the opposite. Their shadows fall on the most overcast of days; indeed, they fall in the night-time. There is no darkness as black as the shadow of a witch.

Dot turned, gagging on a mouthful of crumbled brick, limey whitewash, dry wood shards.

Sure enough, standing on the garden path and looking down at her, was a witch.

The witch was beautiful. She had dark eyes, a straight pure nose, full red lips which were slightly parted to reveal even pearly teeth. Her skin was clear and pale. Her beauty was

115

threatening. Worse still, as you gazed upon her you realized the truth of the saying about beauty being only skin deep. You know how, when you look at an old person's face, you can suddenly become aware of a young person looking back at you from behind all the wrinkles, like an animal peering out from behind the bars of its cage? Well, the witch was like that, only the other way round. When you looked at her teeth, your first thought was that they were bright as stars. Your next thought was that one day they would fall out, and then her mouth would be black as night. When you looked at her nose, your first thought was how aquiline and imperious it was. Your next thought was that within the strictures of its narrow triangle a fat bulbous one was straining to break through. When you looked at her dark eyes, your first thought was how brilliant and striking they were. Your next thought was: what will happen to them in the dark?

The witch had the beauty of her prime, not the loveliness of first youth. Small wrinkles were apparent round her eyes and mouth, like the first cracks in an edifice that would one day collapse on its foundations. Dot looked at the beautiful serene pale witch and discovered an old hag within, drooling, cackling, shaking bony fists at her.

The witch was dressed normally, in a tall pointed black hat with a brim, a long black cloak, elbow length black gloves with the fingers cut out, knee-length lace-up black boots. All in black, in short, which of course set off the paleness of her skin to advantage.

But when I say *black*, I'm guilty of an understatement.

Go down your deepest mines, where dread Knockers live and breed.

Go through farthest space, until the stars go out one by one, as the lights of Europe went out once upon a time.

Gather your blackness from such places, if places they be, by the armful. Bring it home, iron it flat, cut it out, and make your witch's garb. This is clothing that swallows light, and its very shadow darkens darkness.

The witch's face hung palely below her hat, above her cloak, as the moon hangs. You will remember that a golden breeze washed the tree of light, making its leaves flow and sparkle. Well, the witch had a dark wind of her own, so that her long black hair frothed and foamed about her face and shoulders, though to Dot the air of the wood still seemed flat and stagnant.

The witch spoke. Her voice was like starlight. That's a strange thing, incidentally. Everybody knows how a star sounds, yet nobody has ever heard one. One thinks of words like tingling and tinkling, or, for the most prominent and blazing stars, crystalline. For a low star on a warm summer's night: plangent. All these starry words could be applied to the effect of the witch's voice. For its upper register, the twins first mentioned. For its middle range the next on the list. For its lowest, most captivating tones, the last and most beautiful of all.

'Has she mistaken the old saying?' the witch asked, her voice sounding like a frosty xylophone.

'You know how the saying goes,' she plinked, like ice-cubes in a glass: 'I'm hungry enough to eat a horse.'

She looked at Dot for a second, her eyebrows like a pair of question marks. 'What this miss is eating is my *house*.'

Dot tried to say sorry, but the words couldn't get past the unswallowable rubble in her mouth.

'She is not as thin as her brother,' the witch said. Dot jumped, and looked up in hope and in horror. 'But some fattening will not come amiss.' The witch laughed. Each tee and hee sparked silver for a moment as it flashed from her mouth. 'A miss!' she repeated. 'It will not come amiss for a miss!'

So saying, the witch stepped towards her front door. Her hair brushed against Dot as she passed, like a black tentacular sea. She took up a big key that swung from a chain on her belt, and inserted it into the keyhole. The lock screeched. The door groaned. Then the witch stood to one side, and turned to face Dot once again.

'Please to come in,' she softly chimed.

117

*Mens*, even more *turbata*. Yes, I'm back. It's Chapter Eight again, that Bowge. The evening of Bank Holiday Monday.

# Chapter 8
## That Bowge

Sometimes one has a very bleak view of an event in prospect but then, when it actually takes place, it proves to be different from one's expectations. That was true of today. I expected it to be dreadful, but it turned out to be a catastrophe.

The morning began as usual. The glass bells rang. I got up. I couldn't find my slipper.

But at that point I changed my routine. I did not hobble downstairs and slink behind my front-room curtains. I did not spy, with my little eye, the milkman's arrival. No. Today *was* a day for being as good as gold. Today was a day for being above such things as milkmen. I remained in my room.

Needless to say, there is a law of compensation in such matters. The more one tries to rise above earthly constraints, the more they pluck one back.

What I'm getting at is: one puts one's milkman behind one. One stays in one's bedroom for the time being. One resists temptation. And then you can't get the milkman out of your mind. You develop a fear of being incriminated by accident. I imagined going down to pull my curtains in all innocence, placing my tiresomely short arms into position, taking a deep breath preparatory to the tug, and then, just at that moment, the milkman would appear on the doorstep, and today of all days would be the day he'd choose to glance up. I could claim till I was blue in the face that I was simply there to open my curtains, but the Grandson would never believe me.

Because of this dread of irony, of being caught *in situ* – red-*bodied*, you might say – I determined to stay in my bed-

118

room until I was completely satisfied that the milkman had finished with my house and had gone on his way. But then of course the inevitable happened. I stood there for what seemed like hours, hardly daring to breathe for fear I'd miss hearing him deposit the bottle. I couldn't even pluck up the courage to get dressed (mind you I'm never in a hurry to do that) or go to the loo. In my mind's eye, I pictured him creeping up my path and placing my milk in position without a single clonk, as though it were a time bomb. Perhaps it was there already, ticking away. I would still be standing here like a statue when the Grandson and Maggie arrived.

In some respects, despite the difficulties of the craft, writing children's books encourages mental indiscipline, as does living alone for years and years. As a result it wasn't difficult to imagine my milkman as some sort of secret agent or saboteur working on behalf of the invading forces. You can stand cold sober in your bedroom, wearing a hideous nightie, one shoe off and one shoe on, and think such thoughts, even though another part of your brain, if brain isn't too strong a word, knows perfectly well that you're being ridiculous.

But of course the bottle *did* sound at last and I could come to life again. The day had begun with a triumph, albeit a smallish one. Carried along by a sudden surge of optimism, I dressed without even thinking about it. I must simply have given my limbs carte blanche. It was almost as though I had a fairy godmother to do the honours, though any fairy godmother belonging to me would be at least a hundred by now. How revolting to visualize such a person creaking in in tutu and ballet shoes, waving a wand. For the most part one seems to grow old at the proper speed, but every now and then you are able to glimpse how grotesque the process is. In addition to which, Cinderella is my least favourite fairy story. The main purpose of the genre is surely to flesh out bad dreams, not to show how some little prig is given everything she wants. The only good part is when the booty vanishes at midnight.

Anyway, fairy godmother or not, *I* was dressed for the ball. Dress, cardigan, slippers (the second one had hove into view, as it always did once the milkman had gone).

Slippers?

I couldn't let the Grandson see me in slippers. They weren't glass ones, either, but sad nylon objects with pompoms on the top, blissfully comfortable. They would provide clinching evidence, at the end of each leg, that I couldn't cope. The time was when I loved nice shoes. When I put them on I'd understand why Arthur liked to have his bicycle and later his car glossily polished. Shoes gave me a sense that my loose ends had been tidied up. I was fined to a point, two points. But that was all over, long ago. Nowadays I wear slippers and, for shopping, a pair of blue court shoes that have become rather like boats, and are all the more comfortable for that.

I took them out of the wardrobe, and looked at them with a newly critical eye. It's funny how you can borrow other people's eyes. Literature would mean nothing if that wasn't the case. I'd never met him but I was able to see my shoes with the Grandson's eyes – solicitor's eyes. They (my shoes) were scuffed and worn. They were not up to scratch. He no doubt would have Uncle Taylor's handmade patent leather bootees coursing through his blood, and my shoes would fill him with distaste.

It was at this point that I had an idea. It was my first of two this morning, both of them ultimately disastrous. But even now I think my first idea was inevitable. It seemed to arise naturally out of the course of events, and therefore had an authoritative and convincing ring to it. As a result, of course, it brought all my optimism back and filled me with glee.

The events were as follows. Although I'd known all along that I'd never be able to get my house to look presentable by the time the Grandson arrived, on Saturday last it had occurred to me that there *was* something I could do to enhance his first impression. My front door was in a bit of a state. It had been painted red some years before, but the paintwork had long ago begun to blister and crack. It's probably an index of the sort of person I'd become, in those halcyon days before THE LETTER arrived, that the only way in which this state of affairs had registered on me was that I got a certain delight from pressing these pimples from time to time, much as a child gets pleasure from picking at a scab. Last Saturday, though, it struck me that I could go out and buy myself a sheet of sandpaper and a pot of paint. I could rub down the worst of the bumps and slap a new coat of red on. It might at least start things off on the right foot. (Unfortunate phrase.) So I duly went out, bought paint and paper, and that afternoon started work.

I rubbed down in the way I do practically everything except write books: I started out with great perfectionism and attention to detail, and then after an hour or so I thought blow this for a lark, and finished the job any old how. And then I levered off the lid of my tin of paint.

I could hardly believe my eyes. The paint was blue!

I even poked at the surface with my finger, to see if for some inscrutable chemical reason it was red underneath, but no, it was blue all through. I looked at it with horror and indignation. The tin was red, with white lettering. I'd taken it for granted that a red tin would contain red paint. This may be naïve of me but it still seems the obvious way to market a tin of paint: put your blue paint in a blue tin, and your red paint in a red tin. After all, I know about tins. I come from a tin-mining family.

After a close inspection I found a blue dot on the lid. It was about this size: O. That was all you had to indicate the colour of the paint, except for the word Blue tucked away almost out of sight. The red was an irrelevancy. Or worse, the red was a kind of Yah-Boo on the part of the paint manufacturers, a way of saying: *you* might have the execrable taste to want to paint your front door blue but if you had any sense at all you'd paint it red just as we've painted this tin. The irony *is*, of course, that much as I resent the tone of this remark, I happen to agree with it. I wanted nothing more than to paint my front door a rich, smooth red, deep and somehow rubbery, as thick paint is: like raspberry jelly. And here I was saddled with a tin of *blue* paint!

My indignation abruptly gave way to a feeling of relief. I was let off the hook. I could retreat with honour. I'd shown willing. It was obviously written in the stars that I should present a scabby, peeling front door to the Grandson, so why worry?

But now, on the Monday morning, something else entirely seemed to be written in the stars. On the one hand I had a pair of disreputable scruffy blue shoes. On the other, a tin of shiny blue paint. The conclusion was obvious.

Needless to say, the tin of paint wasn't on the other hand at all. Words are so much more co-operative than things. I finally discovered the *thing* on the front doorstep where I must have left it two days previously. Goodness knows what the milk-man thought about it. Needless to say I'd also forgotten to replace the lid, so the paint had developed a thick crust which I finally had to peel away by hand. Then of course I had to begin my search for the brush I'd bought specially (specially to paint the front door with, that is). But at last the paint was on the bedside table, I was sitting on my bed, my shoes were on my lap, the paintbrush was in my hand, and I was ready to begin.

The brush had been bought with my door in mind, not my shoes, so it proved both rapid and cumbersome. I concentrated, though. My tongue was wedged in my right cheek, where it has gone since time immemorial to make room (presumably) for my brain, which expands to cope with a crisis. My eyes, by contrast, shrank with the severity of focus, so that they felt hard as marbles in their sockets. My hand barely shook. In a matter of moments my shoes were slick and gleaming. What an achievement! I felt the cackling satisfaction a hen must experience on laying an egg, *two* eggs. My shoes were rejuvenated. In fact they looked better than they had when I first bought them.

I slipped them on. They even seemed to fit more snugly than they had before. They had been miraculously converted from con to pro, and I felt ready to face the day.

Perhaps not my kitchen, however. I'd avoided it during the hunt for the paintbrush and I hesitated about going into it now. My nerve nearly failed me. There was so much to do. If anything I'd let it become even more shocking during the last day or two, on the basis that a cleaning-up was imminent anyway.

I shut my eyes as I opened the door. I thought of my shoes. I pointed my head downwards at my feet.

One.

Two.

Three.

Open!

In point of fact I only opened one eye, in order to be on the safe side. Yes, it was all right. There were my shoes, freshly painted. I must pin my faith on them. I opened my other eye. Then, slowly, I lifted my eyes up until they faced the kitchen. It looked as though a bomb had hit it. The bomb of course was me.

Once again, I felt a surprising sense of relief. For days I'd been aware of the task ahead. I had to tidy my kitchen up to make it fit to be seen by the Grandson. Now I looked at it from a practical point of view. I was now the sort of person who had nearly painted her front door. I *had* painted my shoes. I'd skirmished with DIY, in short, and was in a position to make an off-the-cuff judgement. The kitchen was out of the question. It would take hours. I'd left it too late. The last thing I needed was to be up to my elbows, in a muck sweat as Mr Tremaine used to say, when the visitors arrived. I needed to be on top of things, not in the middle of them. I required an aura of calm.

Since it was manifestly impossible to transform my kitchen in time, the solution was simple: I would have to ensure that the Grandson and his Maggie stayed out of it. I would keep the door securely shut, and sit them in the living-room.

I spent the next couple of hours tidying up my living-room. This wasn't such a task. There was my bureau with the Dot book on it. Well, papers are sacrosanct. Authors are expected to have tatty and tangled drafts. If the Grandson wanted to be related to a writer, *let* him be related to a writer. Books by other people are a different matter. They believe in making themselves at home. Some were sitting in armchairs, others were lying on the carpet. Miss Sayers' Dante was lolling on the hearth. I put them all back anyhow on my bookshelves. I could arrange them later.

Later is another country, as is the land where lost things go, except that the climate is different. There are no snows of yesteryear. Instead, a mellow putative sun continuously shines. At one end is the sea. The wavemaster is Botticelli, so the waves are green, small and regular. (Turner is in charge at the other place, with a shipwreck in every breaker.) The sea teems with pilchards. At the opposite end of the kingdom, as far from the sea as it is possible to be, is a chicken-run, where chick-chick-chick-chick chickens cluck contentedly and

123

lay their little eggs for tea. In between is a huge library, where all the volumes are shelved in perfect order, like a three-dimensional telephone directory except in this case *I* am represented, indeed there is a vast collection of my works, far more than I have ever written. All round the library are formal gardens with lawns cut in stripes. Somewhat elderly and remarkably serene people stroll about, the sort you sometimes see in the novels of Trollope, Mrs Gaskell, and Henry James. I'm thinking particularly of that man in the opening pages of *The Portrait of a Lady*, who enjoys his cup of tea so much.

Personally, I'd hate to find myself in Later. I'd much prefer the other place. It's more elemental. In any case, it's where I'm actually heading, as we all are.

There are various cups and saucers to clear up. Also, I'm sorry to say, an ancient sandwich. Perhaps owing to the prevailing atmosphere of the room it had become rather bookish, the bread being dry and papery, like thick pages. I didn't investigate the contents. Of course, the fact that my kitchen had, as it were, been formally Let Go simplified this part of the tidying up no end. I merely had to take the errant crocks in there and shut the door on them.

The next task obviously was vacuuming the floor. There was a sprinkling of dust, crumbs and whatnot all over the carpet, like very fine snow. I've got an ageing and redoubtable hoover which I've never quite trusted. I sometimes wonder if, in its roar, it's expressing the accumulated bitterness, anger and distress of all those generations of servants and slaves which it's replacing. Also (like many of its predecessors) it doesn't pick up all that well, and I have to work it backwards and forwards over the same patch of carpet till sometimes I feel like screaming myself. It has its lair in the cupboard under the stairs, and getting it out is enough of a problem to start with, as it clings on to my coat, my wellington boots, and the other odds and ends that are scattered about in there.

Nevertheless I'd approached the cupboard door and girded my loins for the inevitable tussle, when a thought struck me. Though it's been relatively sunny this summer I've found the weather very much on the coolish side, and when I collected my tin of paint from the doorstep first thing, today seemed no exception. It was unlikely that it would be warm enough at lunch-time to go out for this alleged picnic, so we'd be having it in my living-room (since my kitchen, where I have my dining-table also, had been declared out-of-bounds). Therefore it might be a nice idea to have a little fire. When I say nice I mean of course strategic. I mean that it might prove to be evidence that I'm still on top, that I'm perfectly capable of giving the Grandson a run for his, or rather, my, money. Normally I just switch on my two-bar electric fire. I position it by my bureau and direct it straight at my legs. My upper half, protected by the desk lid, remains cool, and able to think about Dot; my lower half grows hotter and hotter. I can recommend this arrangement thoroughly, if you happen to be interested in writing books. But a real fire, dancing in the grate when the Grandson arrives: what could be nicer? There was the added bonus that it would mean postponing the use of the hoover till after I'd got it going.

I cleaned out the grate, screwed up some newspaper and put it in, found some kindling outside and made a lovely little nest of it on top of the paper, and then brought some small pieces of coal in, and laid them like black eggs on the kindling. I read somewhere recently a remark to the effect that one makes a fire in one's own image. Perhaps it was in Dante. If so, my image was in good form for the Grandson, whatever might be said about the state of my reality. I put a match to the newspaper. Flames danced.

And then my doorbell rang.

I looked around appalled at the ash on the hearth, the what-not on the carpet, the coal-bucket on my easy chair. They couldn't have come already! I glanced at the clock on the mantelpiece with the absent-mindedness of panic, since it was many years slow. It came from the old family house in Cornwall, and still recorded their time. But you don't need a clock to tell the time, any more than you require a thermometer to test the temperature of your bathwater.

Ping pong blip.

The bell rang again! Whoever-it-was was not to be kept waiting. Which narrowed it down to two, in my judgement: the horrible man and the Grandson. Well, *I* decided who should be kept waiting and who should not be kept waiting, not that dratted bell. I put my elbow into the time of day

125

and felt it, so to speak. It was later than I'd thought, elevenish. Where on earth had my morning gone?

I'd played statues with my milkman.
I'd had an extensive search for my pot of paint.

ong ip.

I'd painted my shoes.
I'd inspected my kitchen, and given it the thumbs down.
I'd tidied up my sitting room.
I'd lit my fire.

The list seemed substantial until you put it up against a list of the things I'd *not* done.

Washed my face and hands.
Had a cup of tea.
Had something to eat.
Tidied up my kitchen (see above).
Cleared up after lighting my fire.
Hoovered the sitting-room.
And even (shame to tell!) gone to the lavatory.

To be fair to myself, I'm not absolutely sure about the last item. Sometimes my body goes to the lavatory while my mind stays put. Which I suppose is a lot better than the other way round.

At that unexpected thought I did something idiotic. I laughed my head off, just as I had a few days previously when I'd found that dropped bottle on the street. The threat of the Grandson might not have put my house in order but it had certainly shined up my sense of humour.

Bonk bonk.

The Grandson had resorted to knocking, having probably by now used up my bell. The chances were it *was* the Grandson, rather than the horrible man, at this time of day. He'd had ample time to drive here from Manchester.

I looked around at my living-room. It was in a dreadful state. Another half an hour and it would have been like a new pin. Trust the Grandson to arrive during the storm before the calm (which in my experience of weather is the order in which these events happen). Blow him. Who cared? I was tired of worrying. I would have to impose my will upon him in the manner advocated by that late nineteenth century German philosopher whose name I cannot spell. The other word I cannot spell is diarrhoea. (I've just looked the latter up, but I can't look up N— because I own a dictionary, not an encyclopaedia. I've always intended to buy myself an edition of the Britannica, but I suppose I must resign myself to the fact that it will now be forever inaccessible, in that splendid library in the Kingdom of Later, shelved not far from my own Collected Works.) When we die we turn into a word, just as small dead animals which children bury in the garden turn into a sort of chalk. Imagine being a word that nobody can spell, and remaining forever in a cul-de-sac of European letters, with diarrhoea as your sole companion!

Believe it or not all this time I was still laughing. This is partly because most of the last page has been taken up by anachronistic thoughts (i.e. thoughts dating from NOW rather than THEN), but also because I'd deliberately left my laughter on, rather as one simmers a saucepan. In fact, as I stumped towards the door I turned it up. I wanted my laughter to cling on to as I opened the door on the Grandson and Maggie, just as I'd clung on to my freshly painted shoes when I opened the door on my kitchen.

Hee hee ha ha hoo rang out as I put my hand on the latch. Then, very audibly, I stifled the paroxysm. Ooop. My laughter was the equivalent of a sort of pen. You know, the one an editor holds in his hand as you approach his desk, and then very very regretfully surrenders. His eyes are glued to the letter he is drafting. He raises them with great difficulty, as if they've gone stiff and need oiling. Then they look at you for a long moment of studied blankness, of comprehending incomprehension. Then suddenly it's 'How lovely to see you!' 'What a treat!' 'I was only talking about you last year to Hump, you know, our Mr Leg-it, who has to go from shop to shop actually *disposing* of the books that we writers and editors tinker with at a safe distance from the hurly-burly of the retail trade. I said to him, "I do not understand, Mr Hump, why a wonderfully original writer like Olive Watson doesn't sell by the *ton*, while an old, between ourselves, hack like Enid Blyton writes the same book over and over again, and they forever come back for more!" Let's go to lunch, my dear. Tell me all your news.' And so on, ad boredom. None of it matters, what he says. He's lying about Enid Blyton. You do not need to enhance my books by running hers down, there's no necessary link between the two. In any case, if Enid Blyton walked into his office he'd lick her *boots*. But what interests me is that pause before he allows himself to register your presence. That pause when you overlap with his preceding activity. I hoped my stifled laughter could achieve a parallel effect. Create a certain amount of Grandson-resistance. Be testimony of previous, and more engaging, commitments. Not of course that I had any plans to *gush*, when the door finally swung open.

It was a pity I'd thought about that business with editors. When the door did swing open I emphasized my preoccupation with other concerns by staring at its back rather than at my visitors and so by a natural sequence of ideas remembered the flaky paint on its front and my somewhat random rubbings. As a result there was no editorial aggression in my oblique gaze; more a depressingly nun-like modesty. I could hear my visitors breathing in front of me.

I finally managed to unglue my eyes and look up. I immediately fastened on a large, downward curving mouth with thick parted lips. It was a mouth poised to do something, but for a moment I couldn't think what.

Then I realized. It was poised to pass a large round bubble. A goldfish mouth.

My eyes stepped back a little and I took him in more as a whole. He was bigger built and taller than Uncle Taylor – that's why I'd looked him in the mouth rather than the eyes. He was unnervingly familiar.

'Arthur!' I said.

'That's right,' he replied.

'No,' I tried to explain. '*Uncle* Arthur.' I'd never called him uncle when he was alive, and it was strange to do so in retrospect.

'I'm only a nephew, I'm afraid. It's you who's the *Aunty*.'

He smiled, as well he might: it hadn't taken him long to get that aunty out of his armoury.

'The *late* Arthur.'

'Far from it, I hope. Let me introduce my wife.'

A small figure appeared from behind him, as if she'd just climbed off his back. I've always resented those intricate, exquisite-looking women. I have a mental picture of the 1920s positively teeming with them, all with cropped hair, and straight-down dresses, and appealing, inward-pointing legs. They used to smoke cigarettes and talk about men in that coarse fashion in which men are alleged to talk about women. They got on my nerves. There was always an implication that they wished to let bulls loose in their china-shops. I found that hypocritical, somehow: one had a mental picture of bulls bruising and gashing themselves to death on unbreakable crockery. This did not correspond to my notion of feminine charm. Generosity of scale and of heart are what appeal to me, the qualities I associate with my mother. Vulnerability; not a fragile veneer.

She reminded me of someone. Someone in particular, I mean, not simply a whole generation. Dainty as a fairy but hard as nails. Sly. Perhaps worse. Her eyes were pale green. Her nose was tiny. Her lips were delicate, twitching with self-possession or amusement or both. Possibly she was murderous. Then I remembered.

'Tinker Bell!' I exclaimed.

'Maggie, in point of fact,' she replied in a voice that was cool yet soft round the edges, like ice wrapped in muslin. She gave me a sparkling smile, much as one might flash one's tiara, if one possessed such an object, a smile that was ornamental rather than sincere.

I tried to reciprocate, and only then remembered my lack of teeth. I felt my gums despondently with my tongue. My smile leaked away, like a burst tyre.

'Please to come in,' I mumbled.

'Thank you,' they both said, and in they came.

I showed them into the living-room.

'What a lot of books,' the Grandson said. He went over to the shelves and began to inspect not the books but the shelves themselves. Tinker Bell scrutinized the room at large.

'Why don't you sit down?' I asked her. 'Let me take the coal bucket off the chair. I was just lighting the fire.'

As I spoke my mouth felt horribly imprecise, due to the lack of teeth. Also my voice sounded old and croaky. Tinker Bell turned her calm gaze upon me. Stupidly, instead of looking back at her, I dropped my eyes to my feet. And it was then that I had a horrible shock.

My shoes were a smudgy mess. Half the paint had come off altogether, so that the previous surface showed through. Funnily enough, although this was the first time I'd noticed it, my eyes knew exactly where to look next. On the carpet in front of the hearth was a mass of blue smears, where I'd knelt. How *could* I have? I was like one of those Japanese pilots in the last war who deliberately crashed their aeroplanes. I'd painted my shoes and crashed them into my own fireplace. My eyes whizzed despairingly round the rest of the room. Oh heavens, it was everywhere. There was a sort of plimsoll line in blue near the base of my chairs and bureau, smears on the wall, splashes scattered in various locations on the carpet. How I could have missed the latter, when I was inspecting it with a view to bringing out the hoover, don't enquire. It seemed impossible that a couple of square inches of paint could occupy so much space. Loathing and contempt for my incompetent, baggy, blue-stained self (yes, there were blobs of blue on my stockings, as though the paint had managed, by some sort of capillary action, to climb up my legs), an acute dislike *of* me *for* me, precipitated in my breast like acid. I opened my mouth to speak and then remembered it was a horrible toothless old mouth and closed it again. There was Tinker Bell, so accurately formed; here was me, a sloppy approximation. I could feel I was about to burst into tears, and to forestall it I fled from the room.

When you flee, you have to flee *some*where.

When you retreat *from*, you have to go *to*.

I don't mean simply as regards place, but also as regards behaviour. You have to do something next. In a book you can end a chapter with a door slamming and boo-hoos erupting from behind it. And then begin the next one:

The following morning Dot felt much better.

What a pity you can't have chapters in real life. I would have

130

given anything to be getting up the following morning at that point in time. But I wasn't. It was still that point in time and I was stuck in my hall while the Grandson and Tinker Bell were stuck in my living-room. No matter how much you lick your fingers the page just won't turn over.

But I had to do something, and what I did do constituted my second disastrous mistake of the morning. I went upstairs and into the bathroom. I opened the medicine cabinet, took my mother's false teeth out, and popped them into my mouth.

To understand why I did this you have to go back – back as far as my mother, I suppose. She had lovely teeth. An irrelevant phrase comes into my mind: deep and crisp and even. That's how her teeth seemed, as white as snow. But occasionally when she opened her mouth wide, perhaps to laugh, as she did so frequently for most of her life, perhaps to cry out, as she did in her last illness, when she didn't laugh at all, I would catch a glimpse of something else. Something ominous. Something that detracted from the teeth. I never quite identified what it was because I always averted my gaze too quickly. I didn't want to know.

It was only when she was dying that I discovered that her teeth were false. They were made of exquisite porcelain and each one was wired by a tiny gold thread to its plate. The plates themselves were made of some kind of resin (this was long before plastic, of course) which was the colour of that horrible, dead-fish clay that you see heaped up when workmen are digging deep holes in the road. It was these plates from which I'd always glanced away. My mother had hard clay-coloured gums above and below her entrancing smile.

My father kept the teeth. False teeth were a valuable commodity in the old days, because of the gold. I remember years later, during the Depression, pawn-shops were full of the disembodied smiles of the poor. Not of course that this had anything to do with my father's motives in keeping my mother's teeth. He simply wanted a memento of her; he was a great sentimentalist. I suppose I am too, because when he died I kept them in my turn, as a memento of *both* my parents.

So that explains how my mother's teeth came to be in my bathroom cupboard. What it doesn't explain, of course, is why I had no false teeth of my own. There is no sensible

131

explanation. It may have been partly because my own teeth had not been extracted professionally, they had just fallen out on an amateur basis. But the fact that they hadn't been replaced was still an inexcusable oversight, another example of my sloppiness. I have Achilles' heels all over me, the way some people have warts.

I inserted my mother's false teeth in an impulsive and panic-stricken attempt to exorcise at least one of those Achilles' heels, to tidy up one little bit of that higgledy-piggledy chaotic old me which had been exhibited before Tinker Bell's cool gaze.

I slipped the false teeth in. I wiped my eyes with a towel. In a rare moment of forward planning, I went to the lavatory. And then I returned to the fray.

The Grandson and Tinker Bell were standing as though marooned in the middle of my living-room. On their faces was that look of surprise and mild resentment that people have when someone they are talking to abruptly turns into a frog. I noticed that Tinker Bell was wearing a heavy perfume that made the room smell depressing, rather like an Anglo-Catholic church.

'Are you all right?' asked the Grandson.

'Yes,' I intended to say, realizing at exactly that moment that my mother's mouth must have been bigger or smaller than mine, or at any rate arranged differently. When I spoke, her teeth failed to open. I could have been sitting on my own knee, like a ventriloquist's dummy.

'We thought we'd go for a picnic,' the Grandson went on. 'It's a lovely day.'

'Isn't it too cold?' I stumbled out.

'You're never too old for a picnic,' he insisted.

'We've got it all ready,' Tinker Bell put in.

'I've just lit the fire,' I said as best I could. I put my hand in front of my mouth while I did so.

'It's a lovely day outside,' the Grandson repeated.

'It's a lovely day *inside*, now I've lit the fire,' I replied as firmly as possible.

'We could have a picnic here,' Tinker Bell conceded.

'I'll make you a cup of coffee,' I suggested, as though it were a part of the bargain.

'You sit down, *I*'ll make it,' Tinker Bell said.

132

'We didn't come all this way to make you work,' the Grandson added, taking me by the elbow and leading me to a chair. Tinker Bell left the room meanwhile, in pursuit of the kitchen. Oh lord, my kitchen.

'I love getting picnics together,' the Grandson said. 'In fact I like anything to do with cookery. Sheer greed, when it comes down to it.'

Cookery wasn't a subject that rewarded interest, in my day. Ironically, the more hierarchical class-structure of the time had a levelling effect on the cuisine. The poorer people cooked themselves simple working-class fare. But the poorer people were also employed by the richer people to cook for *them*, so the richer people ate simple working-class fare also. When I last stayed in an hotel, which was some years ago now, in the nineteen-fifties, I discovered that there were heavy scones still for tea, and over-cooked vegetables for dinner. Which proves that mediocre traditions are more authentic and more robust than elevated ones.

The great let-out, in our household and no doubt many others, was the wonderful Edwardian institution of the picnic. Cook must have been excused duty when outdoor food came to be prepared because I remember everybody claiming how delicious it was. Uncle Taylor could sometimes come near to tears when confronted by watery cod or dried-up beef as dished out by Cook's podgy and tear-freckled hand. I can see him now, perching that tidy bottom of his on an outcrop of rock somewhere and fanning himself with his boater. My mother would lie relaxed on the grass, in a pale flossy dress. You could bend the social rules at picnics, that was one of the great attractions. Women couldn't lie on their carpets and stretch lazily, like a cat. But they could lie in a field. It was a very intricate indoors society, but much more free-wheeling *en plein air*. Come to think of it, I did come across my mother prone upon the floor sometimes, snoring sweetly, but I'm sure she wasn't typical. At the picnic, Arthur would be prancing about saying, 'Those clouds over there, they're cumulus, I'll stake my life on it. Or nimbus. Which means it's set fair for the day. Good as a barometer, nimbus is. Look at those dandelions. They're smaller than the usual ones, I'll swear

133

to it. Charming flowers. All that nonsense about wetting the bed.' And his busy orange face would stare fondly at the dandelions, looking not unlike a dandelion itself, in so far as a goldfish can. While my father would sit quietly by the picnic cloth, and stab a finger at the grass with his characteristic tired inquisitiveness, as though to determine whether this might be tin-bearing terrain. Harry and I would cavort, as children do. Harry would stand on his hands. I would try to. Perhaps we'd play hide-and-seek.

And as for the picnic itself!

Look it up in *The Wind in the Willows*. Moley and Ratty ate picnics of the same sort. They were Edwardians too. After gorging, Arthur, my father, Harry and I would play catch or cricket, while Uncle Taylor and mother continued to gossip together, Uncle Taylor sipping a red drink, mother gobbling a brown one.

'Come to think of it,' said the Grandson, 'why on earth has Maggie gone to make coffee?'

I know why, I know why, I thought in that dark recess I now occupied, behind my mother's teeth: so that she can write an inventory of disaster, like some air-raid warden.

'Because,' the Grandson went on, 'ta da! Champers!' He raised a bottle. He wasn't as cosmopolitan as Uncle Taylor, who liked to cry *voilà!* or *voici!* as he produced one of his treats for mother; nor as scientific and enthusiastic as Arthur, the *real* Arthur, who would immediately exclaim upon the wonders of the drink and speculate on how they had managed to introduce bubbles into the bottle. But if he lacked these surface qualities, the Grandson had a solidity of his own. He was large. He was robust. He was coarse-grained, hardy, sun-tanned; overcooked, one might say, like Cook's long-ago slices of beef.

'Maggie!' he called in his beefy voice. 'Forget the coffee! Bring a tea-towel instead.' He turned to face me. 'I wrap a tea-towel round the neck of the bottle,' he explained. 'I like to open champagne proper!' He winked to enforce the irony.

I turned my mind to tea-towels. I owned them but I didn't seem to use them a great deal. On the whole, I reflected, that was a bad sign. They would bear the marks of neglect.

Tinker Bell re-entered, as did her scent, almost as though it were a separate entity.

'Perhaps Aunty would like some coffee,' she said. I was *her* aunty too, apparently. 'It was she who suggested it.'

'Who's she, . . . ?' I began, but I had such difficulty getting the words out that I lost my thread. All I could think of was a remark of my mother's: *something the cat's coughed up*. She would say it to Harry or myself when we were dressed even less tidily than usual. I can hear her voice now, laughter curling round its edges: 'Olive, you look like something the cat's coughed up!' She only said it to shock Uncle Taylor, who would clap his hands to his ears or even to his breast, and stagger slightly as though he'd been shot. The remark I was looking for was that staple of nursery sarcasm, for when the third person has been used impertinently: 'Who's she, the cat's mother?' But of course apposite tartness eluded me at the crucial moment, just as other rhetorical elements have always eluded me when I needed them most. I could make a sad catalogue of traitors and deserters, chief among which would be:

flashes of wit
original insults
the punch-line of jokes
clinching arguments.

Needless to say when the battle is over, they creep back, cowards that they are, and return to their posts in my mind as if nothing had happened.

'She means you,' the Grandson exclaimed.

Still over-busy mentally because of my missing remark, I chose this of all moments to become pedantic, forgetting completely the difficulty of negotiating my mother's teeth. 'Does "she" refer to me or her?' I asked.

The trouble was, since the teeth wouldn't open, the words had to be squeezed underneath them. All sorts of peculiar and even contradictory things happen when you squeeze words flat. S becomes sh, for example, so that Does sounds like Dosh. By contrast, sh reverts to s, so that She turns into See. 'Dosh see . . . ?' You've heard it before. It's how drunk people talk. My mother used to talk like that sometimes, and NOT because of her teeth.

135

'I'm sure Aunty will partake of a little champagne. Keeps out the rain. Takes your mind off the pain. See, Aunty, the literary tradition in our family hasn't gone down the plughole yet. I *don't* think. Where's the tea-towel, girl?'

'I couldn't find one,' Tinker Bell said. She shrugged her shoulders and rolled her eyes, very briefly, towards heaven. She only had a tiny face to work with, yet she manoeuvred her features with the instinctive strategy of a Napoleon. The eye-rolling meant that my kitchen was an unmitigated disaster; its brevity suggested that she wanted to conceal the harshness of this verdict from me. But of course the eyes are the most public part of you. Her whites flashed their message with the clarity of a mirror-signal from a hill-top. Everybody has done this with an irritating old person: grumbled about her eccentricities NOT QUITE INAUDIBLY. To be frank I've done it myself in relation to the horrible man, who isn't even old, just horrible beyond his years.

I countered Tinker Bell's instinctive strategy with another example of my talent for defeat. I pretended to be obtuse! It makes me cringe to write it, if someone as large and popped-forth as I now am can be said to cringe. And yet as a writer I pin my faith in the fact that there are certain areas of human behaviour which are common to all, and I'm convinced that deliberate and perverse obtuseness is one of them. Don't ask me why. Perhaps it's simply that you get suddenly bored. You've tried so hard to catch that bus. You've painted your shoes blue. You've put in your mother's false teeth. Now you think: let it go. Blow it. Perhaps I didn't want to go there in the first place, wherever there is.

'I didn't notice it was raining,' I said, as though the Grandson's poem had only just sunk in. The teeth made me say nobis instead of notice. 'It *is* a bit chilly, though. That's why I lit the fire.'

'I think it's terribly terribly hot,' said Tinker Bell.

I was quite prepared to engage on that front. I actually put out my hands to the fire and rubbed them together.

'Anyway,' said the Grandson, 'let's have some champagne, to cool you down. Or, alternatively, to warm you up. I'll open it without a tea-towel for once, even though I feel as naked as a matador without his cape. But I *have* brought glasses.'

136

From his picnic bag he produced three champagne glasses and lined them up on my bureau. He unwired and popped the champagne, and poured it out.

'Aunty first,' he said, bringing me over a glass. Then he passed one to Tinker Bell and picked up one himself. '*To* Aunty, in point of fact. To the family get-together, in every sense of the word.'

I forebore to ask what senses, if any, get-together might have. Instead, I raised my glass.

And it was at *this* moment that my Bank Holiday Monday finally became a nightmare.

N.B. A nightmare can be simply a farce with the sense of humour removed.

I raised the glass to my lips. Bubbles fizzed to the surface. The sharp scent they gave off mingled strangely with the odour of burning coal and Tinker Bell's dreadful perfume, and the resulting concoction, unexpected and unallowable-for as a witch's brew, proved to be precisely what my dratted nostrils couldn't handle. I went through that moment – impossible to say whether it is long or short – when the will is suspended, whatever N— might suggest to the contrary, when what is about to happen is as hard and definite and unavoidable as if it had happened already.

And then I sneezed.

My glass of champagne went, who cares where it went? My mother's teeth shot directly into the fire. They landed, in conformity with that same law which governs buttered toast and grapefruit juice, directly on the reddest coals. The grey plates immediately started to soften and fold, the mouth finally opened, the wires melted and the teeth began to move. It was as though, from across all the years, from the very flames, my mother's mouth was trying to say one last thing to me, but whether it was a reproach or a warning I couldn't tell.

# Chapter 10
## A Gingerbread Life

The witch's cottage was as delightful on the inside as it was
without. It was also extremely tidy, so I will write about it
in a tidy way.

1. Item (that just means something in a list), a bright fire
   in a burnished grate.
2. Item, kettle whistling merrily on hob. For whereabouts
   of hob, see Item 1, above.
3. Item, glittering andirons on each side of Item 1.

> *Arthur* [years and years ago, to our diminutive general
> who was polishing the andirons which stood on
> our sitting-room hearth): Do you know why
> andirons are called andirons?
>
> *General:* No. [The general was not renowned as a con-
> versationalist but since her principal companion
> was Cook, whose sobs were on a hair-trigger, it's
> hardly surprising she tended to be wary.]
>
> *Arthur:* Because they're irons wot you can 'old in your
> 'and.

[His big lips opened and closed as he waited for her response.
Small round expectant bubbles rose to the ceiling. Do you
know, I think there were grapes even on the moulding of
that ceiling. Our house must have been festooned with
them, like some rampant iron and plaster vineyard. The
general's thin face looked up at Arthur gravely from her
kneeling position on the hearth. Then she burst into laughter so suddenly, so violently, so uncharacteristically, that I
thought for a second her head had exploded. Arthur didn't
laugh. His eyes looked down at her in triumph. His mouth

continued to open and close slowly. Blop blop blop. Something caught at my chest as I saw his expression. Perhaps it was the first glimpse I'd had of male victory. Back in the grate our shaking general seemed a *true* Cinderella, one who would *never* be invited to a ball. Any castle pertaining to her would be unequivocally in the air. Her carriages would always metamorphose into pumpkins, her footmen transmogrify to mice. Heavens, perhaps Arthur was what she'd been offered instead of a Fairy Godmother!]

4. Item, quarry tiles on floor, smelling of polish.
5. Item, cheerful rug positioned on Item 4, in close proximity to Item 1.
6. Item, two easy chairs, as soft and flouncy as fat girls at a party.
7. Item, in pride of place, taking up a whole wall, a vast Welsh dresser on which was
8. Item, a huge china dinner service. Dot had never seen plates and cups so thin and hard. When you held them up to the light you could see right through them. After Dot had been in the cottage some time the witch noticed her looking at them. 'She admires my china, does she?' the witch asked. Dot nodded. 'Does she know what sort of china it is?' Dot shook her head. In a low, thrilling, plangent whisper the witch told her: 'Bone.'
9. Item, a dining-table, of oak. Set for two.

The witch pointed at Item 9, with a long red fingernail. 'She must be dreadfully hungry,' she said, 'if she tried to eat my cottage.'

Suddenly the witch laughed. Her laughter was not plangent, nor crystalline, nor tinkling, nor tingling. It was screechy and raucous, like the laughter of a hyena.

Dot tried to explain, but her mouth was still horribly full of masonry. Anyway, there was nothing *to* explain. So she started to cry instead. Luckily, she had a handkerchief. She took it from her pinafore pocket and wiped her eyes. Then she wiped her nose and while her hanky covered the lower part of her face took the opportunity to spit quietly into it. Then, as inconspicuously as possible, she put the silky bag of rubble into her pocket. Luckily the witch was busy talking.

'One knew a witch once,' the witch said reflectively, 'who built herself a cottage out of sugar and gingerbread. When one says built, one means of course she arranged for some dwarves to do it for her. Dwarves are not very intelligent but if one keeps one's eye on them they make excellent little workmen. Certainly her cottage looked a treat when they'd finished. But a person ought to have seen what happened when it rained. Dear oh dear. One has to admit the cottage did look a fright, as a person will know if she's ever dropped her birthday-cake into the bath.'

At the thought of Dot's birthday-cake being dropped into the bath, the witch laughed once more, as she did a few pages ago. I said then that her laughter sounded like a hyena, but to be completely honest with you, I only wrote that because I was tired. I had had a very busy time the day before, what with visitors coming, and I don't think I'd quite recovered. You know how it is, when you're on the spot you say the first thing that comes into your head. As a matter of fact I've not the faintest idea what the laughter of a hyena is like. But I *do* know how the witch's laughter sounded. Sometimes a strong wind blows, and the gusts make a rushing sound as they pass through the trees, and a whine as they scrape by the house. In the distance you can hear the clatter of bouncing tins; the rolling sound of a dustbin lid being hoopla-ed down the road; the crack and flutter of tossing newspapers. If you are out in the wind yourself you will hear the chatter of your own teeth as you shiver with its penetrating cold. All that was how the witch's laughter sounded. It came with a great rush, like a wind, and there were sounds of disturbance within it.

'Oh dear one,' the witch said, when her laughter had blown itself out, 'here one is, laughing oneself. But a person has to have a sense of humour; otherwise life would be so dreary. Sometimes one sees a motor-car accident, or hears of a child dying of some horrid disease, and it is all one can do to raise a laugh.'


When I was stumping around that hospital for sick and broken infants, be-pearled, be-suited and be-smiled, touting my wares, I had a rather eerie experience of which the witch's

140

callousness has reminded me. I had just seen the little boy who'd blown himself up with a banger, and was feeling quite shaken. Anyone would have thought the wells of pity must be flowing freely by then, and indeed I can remember having to brush a tear away, for fear my editor's publicity people would take a photograph of it to use in their advertising campaign. I was walking down a corridor towards the girls' ward when from a closed-off room I heard a little voice cry out 'Maman! Maman! Je souffre tant!'

Hand on my heart, hand on my popped-forth and unsuckled bosom, my first reaction was, how lovely! how exquisite! That perfect, unexpected, enunciation of the French, the pure crystal quality of the little voice: it made me *tingle*. There was a long second before the desolation of what she was saying sank in. It is in that second that the world's atrocities are committed.

I had a try at reading Aristotle's *Poetics* once but it (or they) seemed a scrappy bit of work, to say the least. Nevertheless I've pondered since on the problem of *purging*. I think it's incumbent on writers to put their minds to such things, particularly children's writers, who have to portray violence more frequently and more directly than most adult ones. It all boils down to the fact that people can find enjoyment in disaster. There is nothing the general public likes more than a good plane-crash! What Aristotle proposed, therefore, was that we should put plane-crashes and such-like *on the stage*, so that audiences would have the chance to get them out of their system, and behave in a slightly more civilized fashion when they come across real ones. Possibly Aristotle meant that this would purge one's sadism and I'm-all-right-jackery, and leave pity and fear to get on with their work unsullied. Or perhaps pity and fear have just been mistranslated.

'Never mind,' said the witch, 'one does one's best, in the face of all odds. But to return to the subject of sound building practices. Has she ever come across the three little pigs?'

The witch's dark eyes swooped down on Dot as a teacher's eyes do when you don't know the answer. Surely Dot had come across them on Uncle Taylor's farm? He raised other stock besides pure numbers, though all his animals had num-berish tendencies. There were six geese a-laying, two turtle doves, four calling birds; and, she was positive, three little pigs. (As far as vegetables were concerned, he had quite a large plantation of potatoes: one potato, two potato, three potato, four; five potato, six potato, seven potato, more!)

'Yes,' Dot finally whispered.

'Of course she has,' the witch agreed. 'All children have. One got to know them quite well oneself. The first little pig was a lazy porker. He wanted nothing more than to flop all day in the muck. He built his house of straw. The second little pig was a greedy porker. He wanted nothing more than to slop all day in the trough. He built his house of twigs. The third little pig was a careful little porker. He did exercises. He ate a well-balanced diet. He kept himself in trim. He was quite delicious.'

'But,' said Dot, finding her tongue at last, 'he built his house of brick!'

'Certainly he did,' said the witch. 'His house was entirely wolf-proof. But that didn't save his bacon.' She smiled at Dot. Her teeth were as regular as the teeth of a saw. 'Whatever one's faults, one is not a wolf.'

'I've got to go,' said Dot.

'But one was just about to serve dinner,' said the witch, pointing again at the table.

'I can't stay.'

'There is no such word as can't,' the witch told Dot, sound-ing for the first time like a normal grown-up. This made her seem, if anything, even more frightening. You can, after all, close your book on a witch. Flip. Bonk. There: she's stuck within the pages like an insect, with perhaps just a black-gloved arm waving feebly from the side. But grown-ups are a different kettle of fish. You can't shut your book on them. I had some grown-ups visiting me the other day whom I didn't want to see. I thought to myself, if only you were simply witches and ogres I would know what to do. Since I'm the writer, I'm in an even better position than a reader can be. *I can cross unwanted witches and ogres out!* But of course with grown-ups that's no help at all. So I had to make them cups of coffee, and ask them how they were, and ensure I was well

142

scrubbed, and in general do all the things one has to do with reference to grown-ups to prevent them from doing something terrible to oneself. But they will still do something terrible if they want to.

Dot was perfectly well aware of this. She felt a sharper pang of fear at the witch's grownupishness than she had at her witchery.

'I can't I can't I can't I can't I can't,' Dot replied.

'One knows the sort of children who are petulant and whining. They have runny noses and are often very *thin*.'

'I've got to look for my brother,' Dot said. She hadn't meant to mention him, but the situation was desperate.

'Her brother?' repeated the witch.

'Not my brother,' Dot said, suddenly frightened for Harry.

'*Not* your brother?'

'I mean, he's my *not*-brother.'

'He's somebody else's brother?'

'No, no. He's my pretend-brother.'

'Oh, silly girl! She doesn't have to pretend with me! I'm a creature of pretend already.'

'I've got to look for him,' Dot repeated weakly, feeling she'd been outwitted.

'There is no need,' the witch said, flashing her smile. 'She has found him already. Her brother has been here all along.'

The witch pointed yet again at Item 9, the dining-table of oak, set for two. Dot realized she hadn't properly followed her point before. She had been fascinated by the elbow-length black gloves, with the fingers cut out, and by the long elegant finger that did the pointing, with the long blood-red nail at its tip. It was as though the witch had been pointing at her own point. Now, however, Dot wrenched her eyes off it, and directed them at the oak dining-table, set for two. And at this point she had the biggest shock of any she had received on this shocking day. For there, seated at Item 9, was

10. Item, her brother Harry.

What made it even stranger that she hadn't noticed him before was the fact that he looked like a normal boy, though very thin. He bore no resemblance to a stray patch of sunshine. He

143

didn't at all look like some lambent leaf that had drifted through those marching rectoidal trees from the great tree of light and fluttered into position at the table. No, he looked like an ordinary little boy, a real one, even. Dot thought about what the witch had said a few moments ago: *You don't have to pretend with me. I'm a creature of pretend already.* If Harry was a pretend–brother when you were in the real world, at home with your mother and father and the odd uncle or two, then perhaps when you were in the pretend world – in a wood under the table, in a cottage belonging to a witch – why then, hey presto, in these surroundings, he was an *ordinary* little boy. Though very thin.

'There!' exclaimed the witch in triumph. 'She has reached the object of her quest!' She smiled broadly, once again revealing those beautiful teeth, white as pearls, hard as diamonds, sharp as the teeth of a saw. 'And doesn't she feel,' the witch added, in quite a different tone from any she had used yet, a cajoling or wheedling tone, 'that the plumpness of her brother is reassuring evidence of one's hospitality?'

'No,' Dot replied. 'I don't. I think he's very very thin.'

The witch cocked her ear, to listen to her timid voice. Then she laughed. Trees rushed. Houses whined. Tins bounced. Lids rolled. Newspapers cracked and fluttered. Teeth chattered. She laughed long and loud. Then she spoke. 'He's exceedingly plump compared with how he was when one could see right through him.' Her voice, musical still, sounded plump itself. 'Exceedingly plump indeed.'

Dot recognized the truth of the witch's words, however unpleasantly they were spoken. Uncle Taylor had tried to explain to her from time to time some of the secrets of number husbandry. He'd told her that the difference between one and a million was as nothing compared with the distance between naught and one. Harry had crossed a similar divide: he'd gone from invisible to very thin. Now, as in the case of a one, the witch would no doubt be able to stick as many naughts on him as she liked and plump him up no end.

Which she immediately proceeded to do.

She ushered Dot into the other place that had been set at the table and announced that dinner was ready. But although Dot was hungry, as we have already seen, she didn't want to eat at the witch's table for fear of poison.

144

'Harry and I have our dinner at lunch,' she said. This wasn't strictly true, but she knew a lot of children did.

'Ah yes,' said the witch. She was picking up the pieces of cutlery in turn. She hah-ed on each one, gave it a quick wipe with her cloak, inspected it fiercely and quickly, the way the nit-lady inspects your hair every year at school, and replaced it on the table.

Dot looked around the room for a clock, but there wasn't one, so she glanced out of the cottage window at the steady dimness of the wood.

'I mean,' she asked cautiously, 'it's not lunch-time now, is it?'

'It may be, and it may not,' said the witch. 'But it is dinner-time, because one is just about to serve dinner.'

And with that, the witch went out of the room to her kitchen, and began to bring in the most enormous meal Dot had ever seen, course after course. It seemed to go on for ever.


Children's books are full of food. Hansel and Gretel is about nothing but eating. There is the everlasting tea-party in Lewis Carroll. And think of all the picnics in Enid Blyton. All those sardine sandwiches! All that ginger-pop! Yet in my limited experience I've gained the impression that children aren't particularly interested in food. Certainly they're not ceremonial about it in the way adults can be (though connoisseurs of my kitchen will note this doesn't apply in my case!). Perhaps we authors feed our children in order to make sure that they're alive, as a mother blackbird pushes worms down the craw of its babe. Grown-up characters meanwhile fall in love, which is *their* way of establishing an independent existence. When Enid Blyton children go off on a wizard picnic with not an adult in sight they prove that they're emancipated from domestic ties (notwithstanding that the goodies have been prepared by Mrs Chubby, the farmer's wife, with whom the children are staying because they are recovering from the measles, or because their parents have had to go to India). On the other hand, when you have to eat willy-nilly you are as much in an adult's power as a tiny baby. Witches are always offering children food, which in one respect is odd, since when

145

people ill-treat youngsters they're more likely to starve them. One traditionally associates witches not with bare cupboards, and empty tables, but with steaming cauldrons. I suppose the original sisterhood were tribal ladies who on account of their venerable years had the task of maintaining the sacred fire and stirring the communal stewpot. Cooking after all is a form of magic, because you convert food from one state to another. Into the pot goes your nasty raw meat, your eye of newt and your leg of toad, then you let it hubble-bubble for a while, giving it a good stir from time to time, prick it, pat it, mark it with b, and hey presto, out comes something hot and appetizing, like *bouillabaisse*, or *boeuf à la bourguignonne*. Or in my case: boiled egg and soldiers.

Dot and Harry had dinner at the witch's cottage, and they were served:

apples
huge heaps of beans ('One has a magic beanstalk,' the witch explained.)
cockles and mussels, alive alive-oh
doughnuts
golden goose eggs
a fishy on a little dishy
goose-gogs
one-a-penny, two-a-penny hotcross buns
icecream
jelly on a plate
kettlebroth
lemonade
gingerbread men

Dot was usually happy enough to eat gingerbread men whenever she had the chance (not to mention the wonderful jellybabies you could buy at Pooley's, the nearest sweetshop to her house) but the ones the witch brought in looked up at her so beseechingly that she began to have doubts about the rightness of munching them. Perhaps they had their own, gingerbread lives to lead? But the witch was watching her.

She picked one up and began to eat it, taking little tiny nibbles
so as not to hurt it too much.

nuts in may
oranges (and lemons)
pease pudding in the pot, nine days old
quinces
rabbit pie
duckling

'I can't eat this,' Dot cried, when the duckling was placed
before her.
'Why ever not?' asked the witch.
'It's so ugly,' Dot whispered.
'Ugly?' The witch peered down at the duckling, and as she
did so, Dot noticed something about her that she hadn't
remarked before, something which set a little fledging of hope
fluttering in her chest. 'Ugly,' the witch repeated. 'Ugly.'
And then the witch put her hand into Dot's dish and carefully
felt the duckling. Her fingers had the same spidery carefulness
that a doctor's have when he feels your pulse, as though it's
red hot. 'Oh no,' she said. 'How foolish one has been! After
one has taken the trouble to sit at one's block and behead ducks
with one's little hatchet. This is not duckling after all. It is
swan! Nevertheless,' she went on, wiping her fingers carefully
on a napkin, 'nevertheless, swan is a great luxury. It is eaten
by queens and princesses, and people of that sort.'
Dot summoned up her courage to glance again at the swan.
To her surprise it looked elegant and appetizing, now she
knew it was swan and not ugly duckling. This is quite a common experience with food (and other things). Imagine being
offered a piece of chicken, say, and discovering it to be silvery,
and scaly, and fish-tasting. Ugh! On the other hand, imagine
being offered a pilchard and discovering it to be beige in colour, goosepimply in appearance, and chewy in texture. Oooh!
But reverse the names, and the dishes are perfectly satisfactory.
Which suggests, strange as it may seem, that on occasion
names matter more than things.
As she munched swan, Dot pondered on what she'd noticed
about the witch. It had suddenly struck her that the witch was,

to say the least, short-sighted. Now she *had* realized, she marvelled at how she'd never noticed before. The witch's eyes looked at you penetratingly, with a piercing gaze, not because she had powerful eyesight but because she *hadn't*. Her eyes always had to be turned up to maximum. They looked at you with blind aggression, like the eyes of a cat.

Now she realized this, Dot also noticed something else. The witch's eyes weren't as impeccable as the rest of her. The irises were jetty black, of course, which is why one received such a formidable first impression, but the whites weren't exactly white. They were a little off-colour, as though – unlike all the other burnished and glittering objects in the cottage – they could do with a bit of a polish. There was a delicate line of pink round their rims, as if the lids had only recently been cut out, and hadn't yet healed up.

In her excitement Dot found herself veritably gobbling swan, as though her jaws insisted on keeping pace with the speed of her thoughts. Possibly the witch could only see murkily, as one might see dim objects at the bottom of a pond; perhaps she couldn't see at all, but relied on her other senses as blind people do, on her sense of touch, of hearing, of smell. And of taste. If this was true, perhaps Dot and Harry could somehow evade her in her twilight, as a couple of minnows might flick past a pike.

What had worried Dot most about the predicament in which she and Harry found themselves was the way in which the witch behaved when they had finished one of her courses. She would prod and poke at Harry, squeaking and muttering with pleasure as her finger squidged into his increasing plumpitude. More sinister still, she would make a strange request of him.

'Point his finger at one, boy,' she'd say.

Harry would obey, perfectly happily. Dot was astonished at how at-home he was in the cottage. He seemed to share none of her own fears and anticipations. He always ate heartily, often humming the while, and obviously never troubling himself with any thoughts about what the witch's motives might be. When he poked his finger out Dot wanted to cry No! No! but instead had to restrain herself and watch what happened in frightened silence, like a rabbit.

As we know, Harry was already quite visible when Dot

148

first arrived at the cottage. Nevertheless the witch could still pass her hand through his finger, as one might pass one's hand through a candle-flame. Soon, however, his flesh had congealed so much that it was no longer possible to do so, and she contented herself with giving the finger a doctorish feel with those long-nailed, semi-gloved, careful fingers of hers.

Now, though, Dot decided to try an experiment. Luckily there was a piece of swan bone on the edge of her plate that would do admirably. It was thinner and shorter than Harry's index finger, which made it ideal for the task she had in mind. More importantly still, she made sure that there was not a smidgeon of swan flesh still attached to it.

At last they had finished their helpings. As soon as she heard their knives and forks clink down upon the plates, the witch came in from the kitchen.

'One trusts the swan was satisfactory?' she asked in tones of slightly oily starlight. She always became rather cringing at the end of a course, as if hoping to procure a tip.

'Yes,' said Harry. Just as he was becoming easier to see, so he was becoming more definite as a person. He never said please and thank you, and he ate rather greedily, and on a vastly bigger scale than in those far-off blessed days at home when Dot fed him scraps under the table. In other words, he was becoming more and more like an ordinary brother.

'Yes, *thank you*,' said Dot pointedly.

'Oh, he doesn't need to learn table-manners,' the witch put in. 'Not at this stage. It's too...,' she paused, then added with an evil smile, 'it's too *early*. He is too young and too tender, yes, too tender in *years*, for such considerations. Let him bolt his grub and smack his chubby little lips. It does one's own appetite good to see him. Moreover, a terse yes had the advantage of frankness. When one flings a leftover pie at one's pig, one makes do very well with its responding oink.'

'But *I* said thank you,' Dot protested. 'And I'm younger than him.' Then, with great nobleness and bravery, she added, 'I'm *more* tender.'

'And she's *not* grateful,' replied the witch. 'Therein lies the difference. It means so much to me to find a welcoming home for that swan, in little Harry's accommodating tummy. She was the sweetest singer in all my flock.'

'But swans don't sing.'

'They do before they die. That's the wonderful thing about death. Most creatures sing, with more or less success, when they encounter it. Death is a lyrical occasion, if one has an ear for its harmonies.'

'Anyway, you thought it was a duck.'

'Which made its swansong a still more sweet gratuity. And talking of which, there's a little something which one likes to be offered at the end of a repast. Harry, point his finger.'

At this moment, quick as a flash, Dot made a warning gesture to Harry, and offered the swanbone instead. Harry looked on in amusement, obviously under the impression that his sister was playing some sort of a game. Meanwhile, the witch put out her hand and in her delicate way began to feel the bone. Dot's heart thumped with relief. The witch hadn't noticed. Then her relief turned to despair as she saw a grin light up the witch's features.

'Just as one anticipated,' she intoned, in her sweetly musical voice.

'But he is still so thin!' complained Dot.

'He is hard and solid,' replied the witch, 'which are the requirements in this case. When one is faced with a will-o'-the-wisp, what matters is the extent to which one can give it *bone*. Observe.'

And then the witch did something terrible.

She gripped the bone firmly in her right hand. Then she grasped its tip with her left. Then suddenly, jerk. There was a SNAP that made one's blood run cold. Harry cried out, as though he could feel pain in a swan's bone he wasn't even touching.

'How one does like a finger with a bit of snap,' the witch said in tones of great satisfaction.

'But –' said Dot. She couldn't think what else to say. She was flabbergasted. After a few moments, however, enough of her flabber had returned to enable her to get out a weak reproach, 'that was his finger!'

'Fingers are neither here nor there,' the witch replied. 'They are merely an index as to how things are going. They are simply pointers. Oh! Hark at one! Pointers indeed.'

Harry, fortunately, had lost interest in this conversation.

He was shifting about in his chair, tinkering with his cutlery, and generally doing all the things children do when they have to remain at table after finishing their meal. He was also humming under his breath. The sound gradually grew louder and louder until Dot realized with horror that he was singing in an unexpectedly sweet and harmonious voice.

'Shut *up*, Harry!' Dot whispered fiercely. But she was too late.

'And just listen,' the witch went on, nodding her head in time with Harry's singing, 'at the dear boy's charming melody. Whilst he is contenting himself in this harmless fashion, perhaps we should adjourn to the kitchen, and perform some ladies' business there.'

Ladies, Dot thought, in frightened disgust. Me, a lady. The *witch*, a lady! But then the witch placed a hand like a ring of steel about her arm, and propelled her from the room.

The witch's kitchen was as well-cared for as her sitting-room, with a sparkling porcelain sink, well-scrubbed zinc draining-boards, and a tiled floor which was obviously regularly dusted, though at present a little chopping block was positioned in the centre of it, with small tufts of swansdown lying about nearby. Dominating all was a great wood-burning cooker, made of cast-iron which had been black-leaded, so it glowed dully while the lower part flickered red from the flames. It had a glass window set into its massive door, quite in the modern style, so that you could look through and see how your cooking was getting on. There was a hot-plate on the top, where a huge brass cauldron winked and bubbled.

Near the corner were two wooden tables, which were obviously used for the preparation of food. On one of them was a big jar of sugar, several bottles of spices, all sorts of nice things. On the other, though, the ingredients looked dreadful: heaps of slippery, slimy, slithery objects. The witch explained.

'Though one serves each of one's guests the same delicious meals, what goes into them has to vary a little. She knows the saying: You are what you eat. Since she is a girl, she had to eat those delightfully girlish comestibles on the first table.'

'But, surely,' Dot protested, puzzled, 'that means I am a girl already.' She glanced quickly down at herself, to make sure. Yes, there was her dress, like a triangle. 'And I am,' she added, feeling rather confused.

151

'Ah,' the witch went on, 'if you are what you eat, it is also true that you eat what you are.'

Once more Dot felt a chill of fear at the witch's words.

'And talking of cookery,' the witch continued, 'one would be grateful for some help. Please to open the oven door to feel if it's hot enough yet.'

Her heart sinking, Dot turned to the oven, squatted down in front of it, and opened the door. The heat strode out to meet her.

'It ot!' she cried, unable to draw breath.

'Put her arm in to make sure,' insisted the witch. 'It needs to be very very *very* ot.'

Dot pushed her arm forward where it didn't want to go. Yes indeed, the oven was quite dreadfully hot. She was just about to withdraw her arm when there was a rushing sound from behind her.

Dot twisted her head round to see. The witch was coming towards her, arms outstretched, as blind unstoppable and headlong as a runaway train.

Quick as thought, Dot darted to one side.

With a terrible cry the witch hurtled into the oven.

Most of her did, anyway. Her arms and legs wiggled round the edge of the door for a time, but Dot stuffed them in too, and then began to shut the oven. That required all her strength because although the oven was large, it hadn't been designed to accommodate grown-ups, only children.


I accompanied my then-editor (the one before that luminary who took me hospital visiting) to the great display of children's literature held in Munich just after the Second World War. It was an exhibition designed, so my editor told me on the flight, to 'reconstruct the innocence of Europe'! These editors! That one was barely out of school, or university, or the army. He was barely out of something, that was for certain. Editors, like policemen, grow younger every year. Anyhow, one publishing house put the kibosh on that elevated aspiration by exhibiting a grand new illustrated edition of Hansel and Gretel. It was amusing to watch all those bookish businessmen, those publishers and booksellers (I wasn't at all sure what I was doing there, as a mere author) slapping their foreheads and waving their arms in outrage. A tasteless reference to the gas chambers, and so on, and so forth. How comical that even in this day and age, even in this business, people can still subscribe to the belief that children are more innocent than grown-ups. And yet, as I say, some of these editors were still practically children themselves. Possibly that's the source of the difficulty. The fact of the matter is that children know the same things that adults do, but they know them in a different way. Like all good stories, Hansel and Gretel is about the world in which we live.


The oven had a glass door, and Dot was able to see the witch peering out, her limbs scrabbling. As she grew hotter her mouth opened to scream, and Dot saw that her teeth had begun to melt. They narrowed as they ran together, so that they looked as if they had been changed from human to animal teeth. Strangely, taking all the circumstances into account, she looked exactly as a dumb brute does when you catch it in the act of devouring an ugly meal.

Harry came in.

'Sis!' he cried out. 'Don't tell me you're still hungry!'

'I'm not hungry,' Dot told him. She pointed towards the roasting witch. '*She* was hungry. She was just about to put you in the oven.'

'But I was in the other room.'

'Well, she tried to put *me* in the oven.'

'Make up your mind.'

Now Dot thought of it, what had just taken place *did* seem a little odd. She wondered if she could possibly have made a terrible mistake. The witch was short-sighted, when all was said and done. Could she have just been trying to close the oven door, not realizing Dot was still in the way?

'Perhaps she wanted me for befores,' Dot said desperately. 'You would have been the main course. She's been keeping us prisoners here. She kept feeding us.'

'Her grub was very good, that's for certain. And as for being a prisoner, did you try the door? Why didn't you get off your chair, and just go home, if you wanted to?'

'I'm sure she wouldn't have let us,' Dot said, nearly in tears.
'Oh well,' said Harry. 'Let's go home *now*, in any case.'
'Harry,' Dot whispered. 'You don't think...?'
'Don't worry about the witch,' Harry said consolingly. 'She was only pretend anyway.' Then, after a moment's thought, he added: 'Perhaps that's why we got on so well together.'

# Chapter 11

## Christmas is Coming

After his safe return from the witch's lair, Harry went into a long slow decline. Dot didn't worry about it at first. They had both been eating so much it was time they slimmed down. In fact Harry was so fat to start with that sometimes the other members of the family *almost* seemed to notice him. But shortly he grew thinner, and less solid, until finally he was just how he'd been before their adventure. And then he grew thinner and dimmer and less solid still, until eventually even Dot found it difficult to tell whether he was there or not. When he stood in front of something he hardly changed its shape at all.

Summer gave way to autumn, and then autumn gave way to winter. There were rainstorms. Dot loved to watch them from the window of her house. The rain was like silver hair blowing on the wind. Harry took no interest. As the seasons dwindled he also seemed to go from light to dark, sitting in some corner of the room like an unregarded patch of shadow.

Finally Dot got so worried that she went to ask Uncle Taylor about him.

'I remember,' she said, 'what you told me about your naughts. Please, Uncle, may I have one? I would so like to give it to Harry, and plump him out.'

Uncle Taylor thought about her request for a moment. 'No, my dear,' he said at last. 'I do not think that would be wise. Harry is so nearly a naught himself, that an additional one might have the opposite effect from that desired. It might simply serve to increase his *naught*iness.'

'But what am I to do? Poor Harry is so sad and small. I must help him somehow.'

'Christmas is coming,' Uncle Taylor replied. 'That might have the desired effect. There was once a child called Tiny Tim who suffered from much the same difficulty as your little brother, but Christmas did the trick.'

So Dot and Harry waited for Christmas.

At least Dot did. What Harry was waiting for she didn't know.


When I think of Christmas and childhood I think of my friend Anne. It's fair to say I fell in love with her as Christmas approached one year – that year, the year in which the other unsettling things occurred. How strange. It's become more and more apparent to me as I write this book that the pivotal year of my life was 1908, or perhaps 1909, when I was a little girl of eight or nine myself, rather than 1916, the year in which I'd always thought everything changed for ever.

Anne was a year or so older than me, though we were in the same class at school. Our relationship had been somewhat chequered up until that point, but as Christmas approached it became more and more intense. Christmas makes you freer with your feelings. In wet play, as the stormy weather continued, we'd stand near the big metal fireguard of the classroom fire and talk interminably. Sometimes I'd look into Anne's eyes and feel quite swoony. They were so blue it was like looking right through her head. Her cheeks were delicately pink and she had golden bubbly curls. I felt proudly proprietorial to have her as a friend. Needless to say, *my* eyes and hair were brown. I had a glum sense that everything I looked at for the rest of my days would therefore have a brownish hue. Perhaps I hoped that Anne's pastel shades would rub off on me. Certainly I loved to stand so close to her that we touched. Anne didn't seem to mind. She might not even have noticed. While we stood side by side, holding the hot rail and looking at the fire, our smocks would wash against each other and somewhere, perhaps on my shoulder or arm or hip, there'd be a little hard lump of touch, which was like having a tiny bit of Anne of my own.

The coal in the classroom fire burned strangely, becoming pink as soon as it was lit, and hardly flaming at all. Instead it

156

melted, like butter in a pan. I can remember how fascinating it was to watch a knob of butter disappearing through the floor of a saucepan, leaving an oily puddle behind. The school coal went soft at the edges just like pink butter, and ran in hot fizzing rivers. It smelled sharply sooty, a smell that was both pleasant and horrid at the same time. I discussed it with Anne. Being in her company made me want to be clever, to *earn* her, so to speak.

'It depends on which nose you use,' I said.

We put our hands over our mouths and laughed. I'd meant to say nostril but nose was better.

'I've one nice nose and one nasty nose,' I added.

We laughed even more. When we laughed together the rest of the class disappeared. It was like being by ourselves somewhere white and hot. It was like being under the one sunny tree in a gloomy wood.

When the classroom came back it was big and dim. The double desks stood in rows, on stiff rectangular legs. The grain on their lids was very prominent, like tendons showing through dead flesh. For a moment you could hear all the noise of the other children, as if everybody was screaming at once, until suddenly you forgot to listen, and the room became normal again. The long window that ran along the side of the room was always fogged up, and during wet play the children drew finger pictures on it which began to cry as soon as they were finished.

We talked exhaustively about Christmas. I had a paper spider which Mother had made me. It started off with twenty-four legs and was suspended above my bed on a long thread. Each evening, before I went to bed, I would tear one of its legs off, to record the passing of the days before Christmas arrived. Anne, I imagine, had an Advent calendar like normal children.

'That doesn't seem Christmassy to me,' she said, suddenly deciding to be hoity-toity. A tendency towards hoity-toitiness is inevitable with pretty little girls like Anne, that is to say, with little girls who are pretty in the way she was pretty, with an English rose, or peaches-and-cream complexion, just as choler is inevitable with red-haired people.

'It's a Christmas spider. Mother always makes me one.'

'I don't see what it's got to do with Jesus.'

'Jesus, Jesus, meek and spider,' I offered hopefully, but Anne chose to plunge deeper into her hoity-toitiness and left me blushing.

'I think it's horrid to pull the legs off spiders just because it's Christmas,' she said.

'They're not real.'

'Your dolls aren't real, but you don't tear *their* legs off.'

I couldn't think of an answer to that. But then: 'I've got a doll which the head comes off,' Anne added. 'It's called Edward even though it's a girl doll. I don't want girls to have a loose head.'

I wobbled my head and made it nearly fall off into the fire, but Anne was already thinking about something else.

'What are you going to do at Christmas?' she asked.

'We always have a great big fat huge turkey,' I replied. Uncle Taylor did the honours with it every year, because Cook always went off to stay with the one member of her family who had survived catastrophe, some remote cousin who lived in a place thick with blizzards and roaring winds, so that Cook always returned with influenza and earache. In the meantime Uncle Taylor coped as manfully as he might with the turkey. He would enter the dining-room triumphantly carrying it aloft, as a spindly dapper person might come in bearing LIFE upon a platter, except that in this case the turkey was dead of course.

'I'm going to have a party,' Anne told me. 'With girls. We're going to have presents from the tree.'

'Oh,' I replied, thinking: how boring I am! How brown! Pitting a gobbly old turkey against a proper party with girls and presents from the tree. 'We have parties all the time,' I went on valiantly. There was some truth in it, I suppose. Night after night my mother would say, to me, to Uncle Taylor, (never to father), 'Let's have a party. I feel like a party. I want to get tiddly.' And get tiddly she would. 'And Arthur's always going to them,' I added. 'Nearly every night. Uncle Taylor says he goes to chase women.'

Suddenly one of those extra feelings that Christmas makes you prone to swept over me. I pictured women running round a house, holding their skirts, and Arthur in hot pursuit, puffing and panting. It made me want to laugh and yet at the same time I had a large echoey sensation in the pit of my stomach, one of those magical zizzy feelings that banal stimuli so often seem able to evoke. I looked at Anne. She was looking straight back at me like a soldier at attention. I knew at once that she felt the same as I did. We simultaneously went pink and melted like the school coal.

I had so many emotions that Christmas that they became wearisome. They were all bound up with the old rhyme:

> Christmas is coming
> The geese are getting fat
> Please put a penny
> In the old man's hat.

I would lie in bed, having first torn the leg off my spider, with that verse thumping in my mind. I began to feel I *had* to repeat it, like saying my prayers. If I failed, perhaps somebody would die. I'd have to roll my head from side to side on the pillow to keep this inward recitation on the go. And then at last something would give way, I would become sleepy, and the Christmas sensation embedded in the rhyme would seep through me.

The ingredients of Christmas were as follows:

Fat ladies in red plush dresses, with Arthur galloping hopefully in their rear.

Church. Yes, even I, agnostic and anti-Christian as I was, couldn't exorcize the church at Christmas-time. Instead of just being bored and smelling the horrible damp scenty smell and trying not to listen to the vicar droning at the front, I'd get the lovely, piercing, happysad sensation here too, just as I would when imagining Arthur going to parties. The ladies of the congregation would no longer appear overdressed and holy, and while they stopped short of running about, skirts up, in full squeak, they at least seemed suddenly sweet, even their hats. I'd have the feeling that almost anyone or anything, whatever one most wanted to imagine, might be hiding in the folds of dusky light in the further recesses of the church. The pillars and vaulting became springy, as though on tiptoe, no longer heavy and prison-like as they usually were. Something would tremble on the verge of taking place. Not God, more exciting than God.

And, of course, Christmas carols. It never snowed at Christmas but carols were the next best thing. When you sang Silent Night, Ho-oly Night, the words were like snowflakes themselves, dropping down out of the darkness and turning everything white. Then the second line, dee da dum, da da dee, was like sledging over little bumps and nearly but not quite leaving your tummy behind.

Anne's party at last came round.

There was a huge Christmas-tree, with candles on it. As their flames swayed one had the impression the tree was moving, as though there were breezes in its branches.

We girls stood in a neat queue, and each took a present off the tree in turn. As you came up to it you could smell the green of the branches and the hot scent of candle-wax. The presents were wrapped in red crêpe paper and tied with green twine. They were fastened to the branches with little bows, and you had to be very careful undoing them in case you disturbed the candles.

Anne's father stood beside the tree to make sure none of the children burnt themselves. He had a full head of hair, turning grey, with a sprig of holly in it. His face was very red and his breath smelled of drink, like my mother's. As each girl approached the tree he said something which sounded so rude it frightened me.

'Watch your step or you'll set fire to the 'ole 'arse,' it sounded like. Only when I got to the tree, and the message was directed at me, did I suddenly understand. He didn't come from Cornwall and he pronounced things differently from the locals. Come to think of it, my family didn't come from Cornwall either, but of course you discount yourself. Uncle Taylor said he was common.

When I looked up at Anne's father, I saw a tuft of hair in each nostril. His eyes were bright and red-rimmed. I remember thinking they looked as if they had been cut out, as you might cut out paper decorations. They peered down at me greedily, though I had the impression that they didn't see me at all. They were horrid eyes. His fingers were fat and puffy, and they felt too soft, boneless, when they gripped my arm and took me up to the tree. Luckily he let go when I got within reach of it.

160

The branches were green and slim. Each present pulled its own branch down a little, as if it were being weighed. I saw mine immediately, a narrow, rectangular parcel with OLIVE on a little label hanging from the twine. The redness of the crêpe paper glowed and dimmed in the puffs of candlelight. My Christmas feeling became so strong I thought I would burst.

Then Anne's father's hand began to move toward my present.

'I'll take it off,' I said quickly.

'Careful ven duck,' came the spiritous unChristmassy voice from behind and above.

My hands began to shake as I thought of those fingers waiting to take my present down for me if I didn't get it off the tree quickly. I raised my hand and knocked a branch a little; one of the candles wavered, but the ogre didn't notice. Please hand, I thought, go to the parcel without knocking anything else. My hand fluttered obediently up to the branch above the parcel and began to undo the bow. My other hand waited underneath the parcel. When my first hand pulled the twine the parcel dropped gently into my second hand, as sweetly as a laid egg.

I turned away from the tree and trotted triumphantly round the ogre.

'She darn believe in 'urry,' he said. As though his words contained a hidden burden, I suddenly realized his hand was sweeping towards my bottom. Trot turned to scuttle.

'Now she's give me the lie,' the ogre said. 'Watch her go!'

It was only a few paces to the varnished floorboards on the far side of the carpet, where the ogre wasn't allowed. That was a safe place, like the safe places in tig. I stood on my floorboards and watched as the next little girl approached the tree to get her present and have her bottom patted. Then I inspected my present.

There was another little bow in the twine to open it with, as tiny as if it had been done up by a fairy. I pulled at its loose string; the twine fell off and as if by magic the crêpe paper opened itself, like a flower opening. Inside was a flat box of silver cardboard.

Anne came across and bowed her head over it as if she didn't know what was inside either. I did that when I gave a present to Harry or one of the other members of my family. I'd know what whatever-it-was was and yet, as the person opened it, I *wouldn't* know what it was at the same time. I could see my present from the inside, when it was what I had bought, and then from the outside, when it was a parcel someone else was opening.

'I'll give you a clue,' Anne said.

Her head was very near the box as if she'd gone short-sighted. The gold of her hair dangling over the silver made it look as if the present ought to be hers anyway. I'm so brown, brown, brown, I thought. It made me angry. Why should Anne have everything? If she told me what her present was she'd be taking it away from me, and giving me something ordinary in return, something that might just as well *be* brown.

'I don't want one!'

Anne looked at me, merciless as a child can be. She had heard what I said, and was going to take no notice whatsoever. Suddenly she sucked air in through her little nose, very roughly, so it was more or less a snort. That was obviously the clue.

'If it's perfume,' I said, my voice trembling with rage, 'I'll never speak to you again so long as I live.'

I'd wanted perfume for years and years, since time imme-morial. I *needed* it. Sometimes I'd steal a dab from one of the bottles on my mother's dressing-table, but then I'd have to try all day not to be smelled by her. Not that she would have minded in the least; quite the contrary. In fact, she'd found out once and roared with laughter, in that rich way she had. Her laughter spoiled everything. It turned the perfume from grown-up to babyish.

I'd once tried to summon up courage to ask for perfume as a present, but I knew my mother would laugh again, and then the perfume wouldn't be worth having. Luckily Arthur had given me some scented soap for my birthday, so what I did was wet my fingers, rub them on the soap until it went sludgy, and then smear some of the mixture behind my earlobes. That worked quite well, though after a while the soap dried and made my ears go stiff. And since it wasn't proper perfume I wasn't sure whether the scent carried.

162

If Anne's present was perfume then her clue would have spoiled it, as my mother's laughter had. The thought brought me near to tears. Anne's horrid sniff had made my lovely present go wrong, as a sum can go wrong. I wanted perfume SO MUCH, but if this was perfume it wouldn't be a surprise. On the other hand if it wasn't perfume it would be a surprise but it wouldn't be perfume.

What a dreary surprise: not getting perfume when I expected it.

'It's the wrong sort of box for perfume, silly,' Anne said. 'You don't get perfume big and flat like that.'

Of course! I felt warm with relief. It was all right if the present wasn't perfume to *start* with! Only if it *could* have been perfume, and *wasn't*, would it have been spoiled, because then it would have seemed as if what was in the box had changed into something else. I patted Anne on the neck, so that some of her golden bubbles were squashed under my palm. She bent her head sideways, half because of the tickle, half to press my hand in turn.

'Open it, silly,' she said.

I carefully lifted the lid off the box.

Inside there was tissue paper, and underneath that something white, folded, trimmed with lace.

I stared at it in horror.

Now I understood Anne's sniff. My present, my lovely present, my present that could have been *any*thing, except perfume of course since it was big and flat, turned out to be... a handkerchief. I nearly wept.

Perhaps Anne understood. Perhaps she even regretted her sniff. Certainly she did as much as possible to retract it.

'It's not for blowing your nose in,' she said. 'It's like ladies' ones.'

I lifted the handkerchief out of the box and unfolded it. The edge was like spiders'-webs and the blowing part in the middle was so small and silky you could *see* you were never intended to use it. My feelings swung.

'It's got your letter on it,' said Anne.

So it had, in one corner of the blowing part, a tiny o in pale pink. It looked like the door to a miniature, exquisite world, a pink world.

'Oh Anne,' I said, glad I could be sincere, 'it's the best present I've ever had.'

Anne gave me a pleased look. Then *her* mood changed. A ripple passed over her face as a breeze passes over a field of corn. Then it was gone and she looked the same as before; but underneath she was different.

'I've a better hanky than that,' she said coldly. 'It has a lace bit in the middle as well as round the edge.'

I don't care, I thought. Let her *go* hoity-toity. Let her be jealous of my hanky. If she's jealous of it, that proves it's mine.

Anne realized the trap she'd fallen into at the same moment. 'But yours is *nice*,' she added hastily. 'I chose it with Mother.'

Too late! The hanky was mine for keeps now, whatever she said to get it back.

Anne did a hum, as if she hadn't a care in the world, then danced off to the Christmas tree to join the other children and the ogre.

Then the party took over.

We dipped for apples in the kitchen (so water wouldn't get all over the sitting-room carpet). Then we played O'Grady Says, with the ogre naturally enough taking the role of O'Grady. Next, pass-the-parcel. Then we had tea. One thing after another. You didn't have to think, you were borne along on a chattering stream of excitement.

After tea there was Postman's Knock, and then my favourite, Farmer's In His Den. *And* I was chosen to be the dog, the best part. I only wished I dared to run about on all fours and bark, as Arthur had done once when we played it at home. As a matter of fact Arthur looked more like a fat little pony than a dog, but a dog he was in his own mind, because he became so excited that he bit my mother's foot, and she finally had to hit him on the head and shoulders with Uncle Taylor's stick to stop him jumping up at her.

I tried my best. I woofed once. But I didn't do it loudly enough, and nobody noticed. They were all busy singing and going around in circles. In any case it was such a timid and self-conscious woof, it came out disguised as a cough. I didn't try again, but stood silently with the others in the centre of the ring. Not being a successful dog had made me bad-tempered. I thought wistfully about being like Arthur. He was always jolly because he simply did what he wanted to do and never minded what people thought. Or rather, he had no sense that other people were thinking at all.

Perhaps it was appropriate that I'd become a little glum, because at that very moment, while I was standing with the other selected children in the Farmer's Den, and the remainder wheeled around us, while the game was in its full, final swing, disaster struck.

# Chapter 11

## The Approach of Midnight

'Now children!' cried Anne's mother. She was very large as befitted the wife of an ogre. She was wearing a tapestry dress that made her look upholstered, like a sofa. My mother wasn't wasp-waisted, but she never resembled furniture.

'And what does the big hand say?' Anne's mother enquired. She was pointing a podgy finger at the grandfather clock in the corner.

'Five minutes to,' we groaned in chorus.

'And the little hand?'

'Seven.' The groan was even more marked, as more children understood the significance of the exercise.

'So it's time to get ready to go. Some of your mummies are out in the hall already, waiting for you. Don't forget your presents, dears, and a very merry Christmas to you all.'

The chorus vanished, with the abrupt termination of the party. 'Merry very mass,' came our scattered and disheartened replies.

I said nothing. I was beyond groaning. There was no language for *my* exclamation. I simply stared at the clock in horror. Five to seven. Five to *seven*!

Often when dealing with an uncooperative world, I've glared at it in the hope that sheer eye-power will make it give way. I did so then. I stared at that clock as though each of my eyes were a dial, with five to EIGHT on it. I tried to project my dials across the room.

Anne sidled up to me.

'Is your mummy here yet?' she asked, as though I could know without even leaving the sitting-room. Her tone was warm and sympathetic: there was something about it that

166

suggested my mother prone upon the carpet, back at home. I looked back at Anne as blankly as possible, hoping that the eights were fading from my eyes. 'She ought to have come by now,' she continued, in sweet concern.

'It will be Daddy in the trap,' I said, to get my mother off the hook. 'Or Mr Tremaine, if Daddy's still at the mine.' I had a sudden nostalgic picture of my inaccessible home, on a summer's day for some reason, with rows of jaunty cabbages growing in our walled garden, and Mr Tremaine bending over to keep them in order. He was so thin and spiky that his bottom made two separate pyramids against the seat of his trousers, as little girls' bottoms sometimes do. The cat was snoozing on a patch of warm earth nearby. Home!

The other girls were trooping out towards the squabble of mothers in the hall. I followed, hoping to escape Anne, but she came with me.

'Do you like your hanky?' she whispered confidentially.

'I love it,' I whispered back.

'What bliss,' she replied. 'I knew you would.'

I held the hanky box more tightly. The crêpe paper was scrinched round it in deshabille. I knew Anne wanted to take it back. Not really take it, just act as if she owned it, and had given it to me out of the hoity-toity goodness of her heart. It's strange how diverse things can get heaped up and tangled together. If Anne knew that I'd mistakenly informed my mother that the party was going to end at eight, my handkerchief would be, in a manner of speaking, back in her clutches.

In the hall, mothers in winter coats were pecking and fussing over their offspring. I found my own coat, unhooked it with a jump, and put it on.

Anne's mother noticed me and came over.

'Your mummy hasn't come yet,' she said severely.

'It'll be my father,' I replied, as though that correction cleared up the problem.

The last of the other guests had gone in a rush, as people do when you have nowhere to go yourself. The front door was still open, however, showing an oblong of sheer black in the fussily ornamented house. I looked at it in hopeless fear, as if it were a black pool into which I had to plunge. The last trap clattered confidently off.

167

No it hadn't. I realized I could hear another, waiting just down the road somewhere. There was a faint grinding as a metal-clad wheel moved a little, backwards and forwards, the half-clop of a restless horse, a snort.

'Here he is,' I said, before I'd even planned to say it. 'Goodbye. Thank you for my present. Merry Christmas.' I rapped out the politenesses as though they were a series of orders, determined not to give Anne's mother any chance of checking up. Then I bolted through the door.

Anne said: 'Wait. I'll come down the path with you. Please Mummy, please – !'

The door shut. The handkerchief had escaped her grasp. Nobody would know the vehicle at the gate was any old pony and trap. I was free. For a moment I felt exultation, like another sort of Cinderella. Then the darkness washed over me, and I was the dreary sort of Cinderella after all, despite my distaste for her. I was all alone, on the far side of a door, ill-equipped for night-time. Black rhododendrons prowled the edges of the garden path.


Dot and Harry wait for Christmas. Dot tears the legs off her spider. She has Christmas thoughts: ladies in red dresses. No, keep wicked Arthur at a distance. It's hard not to think of him, though, on his yellow bicycle, ringing his bell, while a pack of jolly ladies in red plush scamper in front. Replace them with Father Christmas, also in plush red. Then church. Then carols, sledging over the ups and downs of Silent Night. Then the Invitation. Perhaps a herald. Blart of trump. Swish of silk. Doff of plumed hat.

'Princess Charming is giving a Ball on Christmas Eve. Everybody invited. Look forward to your company.'

Tweaks moustaches. Flounces off.

Much rejoicing.

Then realizes: Harry *isn't* everybody. He isn't *any*body.

Dot primps and preens herself. All little girls have a touch of the Ugly Sister in them.

'*I*'m going to the Ball. *You* can't come.'

Harry sits in the corner. He snuffles. His discontented whimpers prey on her mind after a time.

Jealousy is well covered in literature, but there's one aspect that's never been done, to my knowledge, at least. The point of view of the person who *causes* the jealousy. Imagine, for example, that all your generation have been killed off in the First World War. That leaves you as the only person still able to go to the party. You live your life surrounded by the silent jealousy of the dead.


Dot doesn't want to be the Ugly Sister after all. She decides to be the Fairy Godmother instead.

You can come. Hide in a corner. There is a wonderful tree. Presents beautifully dot its green cascades, like salmon in a waterfall. An ogre guards the tree. He is hideous, with a glowing face and two bulbous noses. He chases Dot but she is too quick. She takes her presents. There is no present for Harry. Games. As above. Banquet. As Dot munches first course, aware of piping voice from under the table:

> Midnight is coming
> Harry must get plump
> Pom pom pom something
> La la la hump, or bump.

Dot passes down food. Her hand is almost bitten off. Young Harry has his appetite back.

By the time the meal is over, Harry is not so much nothing as almost. At any rate, Dot can catch glimpses of him. He begins to join in the games. In Farmer's In His Den for example he is the dog. He becomes so excited that he bites the Princess's foot, though since she is wearing a glass slipper she doesn't notice. Poor Harry runs around for a while with the popping eyes and the agonized smile which, in my experience, can only be attributed to one of two things:

1. Biting on a glass slipper when you expected to nibble on a naked foot.

2. Eating an ice-cream when you have fillings in your teeth.


Strangely, your fillings can give you gyp even when you have no teeth left, just as amputees allegedly can feel pain in non-

169

existent legs. I went to France a couple of years ago, and made that discovery.

I'd noticed an advertisement in the newspaper for a special-offer coach-trip, and decided to apply. Not that I take a newspaper of course, but it was wrapped round something I'd bought, and luckily happened to be moderately recent. Unluckily, as it turned out. I was tempted because I love France so much, and it was so long since I'd last gone. The coach journey seemed endless, and there was a dismal atmosphere on board, emanating from that battery of grey and bald heads. I can talk! I was as grey and bald as the rest of them, which was what made it so dismal. The coach ride was a public statement that we were too poor or too old to own cars, and that we could only afford to go to France for a single day. The most positive emotion any of us could feel was perkiness in defeat.

It was drizzling when we finally arrived. My clothes felt slept-in even though I hadn't slept. Everyone else went off to the gewgaw shops to keep out of the weather. I, however, sat determinedly on the beach. Not determinedly, that's too dignified a word. Perkily, if one can sit perkily. I told myself that rain in France felt different from rain at home. And, as everyone knows, in northern France you can sit all alone on a rainswept beach, and blink your eyes, and *voilà!* there is an ice-cream vendor beside you. So I bought an ice-cream, and bit into it. Imagine sitting on the sands, alone (the ice-cream vendor having vanished as magically as he'd arrived), rain pattering on grey and balding head, and ice-cream pain flashing through one's jaws from non-existent teeth! I wanted to cry out, though even in extremis sensed it would be a faux pas. Old lady, alone on beach, clutching ice-cream in the rain, not a tooth in her head, screaming.

Anyway, of course, as far as Harry was concerned it wasn't an ice-cream, it was a glass slipper, which as you know is the next best thing. He forgave the Princess instantly, however, for this royal deception. Emperors wear clothing made of naughts; princesses wear slippers of glass. Indeed, glass is simply a hardened version of nothing, when all's said and done.

And truth to tell, Harry was smitten with the Princess. This was hardly surprising, because she was beautiful indeed. When you looked into her eyes you felt quite swoony. They were so blue it was like looking right through her head. Her cheeks were delicately pink and she had golden bubbly curls. Her white dress sparkled with silver; her feet, in their glass slippers, were like tender jewels. In one detailed hand she clutched a tiny handkerchief, white silk with lace about the edge. If you looked very closely (and possibly Harry was the only guest able to do this) you could see a tiny initial picked out in pink in one corner. It was the initial o. It stood for O Princess!

As the evening wore on, the Ball became more grown-up. The children's games gave way to dancing. Naturally, the Princess had many would-be suitors, each of whom wished for the opportunity of taking a turn round the ballroom floor with her. They queued up in an orderly, embittered line, as people do for the bus. But Harry didn't wait; he was at the head of the queue each time. Whoever the Princess chose, he took the floor with her also, flittering round the hall like a sprite. He was a wonderful dancer, of course: just like a piece of music personified, and like a piece of music he was all over the room, even though you couldn't see him. Although as midnight grew nearer, Harry seemed to become more visible. Possibly it was as a result of digesting the food Dot had given him. But his visibility came and went.

All children know how it feels to wake up at night and see a figure in your bedroom. It stands there silent and shadowy, looking down on you. You can imagine a hateful smile upon its lips. Then you blink your eyes and it's gone, just like that. When you are in a car or on a bus, and it's raining, the windscreen wipers go bloop bloop back and forth, and each time the raindrops vanish and the windscreen can start afresh. So Harry would begin to form, a pale bendy figure like raindrops on glass, and then Dot would blink and he'd be gone again; and then he'd begin to form once more. Her eyes were smarting with smoke from the great fire in the ballroom, from the lamps, from the cigars of the men; Dot had to blink quite often. Sometimes she found herself wondering if her brother was actually made of the tears that formed in her eyes. How silly, to think such thoughts just as midnight was approaching,

171

and he was becoming more visible all the time! What a foolish sister she must be, to imagine a brother made of her tears!

Particularly because, for the first time since Dot had released him from the clutches of the witch, Harry was full of pranks and high spirits. You'll never guess the things he got up to. I'll tell you about one of them.

Here is the Lady Tinker Bell, dainty as a fairy, hard as nails. She stalks across the ballroom, her face like a hatchet, her green eyes aglitter, her dress perfection. When she smiles it looks as though she is wearing a tiara in her mouth, to match the one upon her hair. And *look* at her hair, children. Imagine soldiers marching over a great plain, tens, hundreds, thousands, millions, all in step, left right left right, so that after a while they do not seem like men in formation any more, but liquid humanity. Tinker Bell's hair was like that, so in step left right left right that it was liquid hair. Except that it was a hard burnished liquid.

I cannot bear women like Tinker Bell. They become the nastier kind of headmistress, the beastlier sort of Mother Superior, the chilliest variety of cold weather witch.

Harry didn't like the Lady Tinker Bell either. He didn't like the way she looked right through him. Poor little Harry's own hair stood to attention. But then he had an idea.

Now, to understand how Harry happened to get this idea, you'll have to know something about another character we haven't seen yet. There was a butler at the king's palace. He was a gnarled old man with a sepulchral voice and a creaky back. He wore shabby finery and his wig was always skewwhiff. You know how some people have an irritating habit of clearing their throat before they speak? Well, the butler didn't do that, but he did something very similar. He would clear his *mind* before he spoke. When the wordy part of your mind isn't being used, the sounds that are stored in it form a soft and soggy mess, which goes something like this: 'Werroit-dah!' Nice people dispose of this lump of noise in private, out of consideration for others. They do it inside their heads, which is a nice, dark, secret place, with soundproof walls. But not the butler, oh no!

'Wer-roit-dah! want a cup of tea, yr Majesty?'

'Wer-roit-dah! people at the door, yr lardship.'

'Wer–roit–dah! Cook says goose is orff, marm.'

When Dot arrived at the Ball he had announced her thus:

'Wer–roit–dah!, jesty, luhds, lidies, gentlemen: Dot!'

When Harry had arrived at the Ball he had announced *him* as follows:

'Wer–roit–dah!!:    !'

Now the Princess's court was not a wealthy one. Everyone had to *muck in*, as Dot's father might have said. He meant that the mine was a family responsibility. Dot's mother never said anything of that sort: indeed, just the opposite. 'Heavens, I can't be expected to pull my weight. I'm far too heavy.' Then she'd peal with laughter – she had a rich sense of humour, Dot's mother did.

Mucking in and pulling your weight meant that the butler didn't merely buttle, but also had to do odd jobs about the palace, including painting, which he loathed. As the day of the Ball approached he'd been asked to put a lick of paint on the ballroom door in order to give the guests a good impression. Just to be spiteful he'd bought blue paint instead of the red he'd been asked to purchase. As he painted he creaked and muttered to himself, and he prefaced every mutter with a wer–roit–dah! The outcome needless to say was not something that would give the guests a good impression at all, because he made a smeary blobby mess of his work.

But – typical of this grumpy and untidy butler – he left his paintpot and brush lying about after he'd finished the job. And needless to say, Harry's sharp eyes had spotted them.

Have you ever poured ink on your blotting-paper? Perhaps children don't get the chance nowadays, in this age of ballpoint pens. I used to love watching the blue spread over the pink. It seemed to travel at exactly the same speed as mercury rising in a thermometer. There is a true fascination in watching something move when it isn't *being* moved. Another thing that travels in this way, and at the same speed, is the incoming tide.

Now, at the Ball, yet another unmoved movement was taking place, in the region of Lady Tinker Bell's legs!

Lady Tinker Bell's legs, it need hardly be said, were as just-so, as spot-on, as side-by-side, as breathtakingly parallel, as her hair. They were strong, and they narrowed beautifully

173

as they went down. With a mallet you could have driven them into the ground like tent-pegs. There was only one thing that marred their prim and symmetrical perfection: from her dear little, ridiculously expensive, made-in-Italy shoes upwards, at blotting-paper speed, those legs were turning blue!

It was Harry, of course, painting them!

Tinker Bell danced on, oblivious at first. After a while, however, she noticed that some faint oohs and aahs were beginning to spring up around her, as a wind springs up in a tree. Then she heard people say, 'Look at her!' 'What a sight', and 'Well I never', but even then she suspected nothing. Indeed, I'm afraid to say that in her vanity she mistook these remarks for admiration. A woman like me, she thought to herself, has to put up with certain intrusions on her privacy. How I envy these other women, who are not so exquisite, and who can go through life without people taking notice of them. Sometimes I almost wish I bulged a little, or had sticking-out teeth, so that nobody would wish to look at me twice.

The remarks grew louder: 'Talk about blue blood!' 'Perhaps she's got cold feet!' 'I always thought it was blue for a *boy*', and so on and so forth. The giggling blossomed into nasty laughter.

One would almost think, thought Tinker Bell, that these rude people are looking at *me*. No doubt they are all boss-eyed, as common folk often tend to be. They look in one direction and see something in quite another.

She continued dancing, if not with her usual aplomb, at least with more aplomb that you or I would show. Women like Tinker Bell have aplomb running out of their ears. By now the people around her had stopped dancing altogether, so that they could devote all their attention to staring. They began to point. Even Tinker Bell couldn't convince herself that, common though they might be (by her standards) they were actually boss-*armed*.

At last Tinker Bell looked down.

Truth to tell, Harry hadn't painted her legs very well. He was a worse painter even than the butler. Instead of giving Tinker Bell's legs a nice smooth even finish he'd splashed paint all over the place.

Tinker Bell took one look, burst into tears, and fled from

the ballroom, never to be heard of again. Even her tears, scattered over the dance floor, were *hard*, and sparkled in the candlelight in crunchy little heaps. Funnily enough, it's the hardness of those tears that makes me feel sorry for her now, wherever she is.

I'm sure you will agree that Harry had been a very naughty boy indeed. I do hope *you* never do anything like that, children. I certainly won't. Luckily, as midnight approached, Harry stopped his pranks and became much more serious.

The approach of midnight is a wonderful thing. It is the Christmas of night-time. And naturally when the night is Christmas Eve, midnight becomes more midnightish than ever. The candles grew brighter; their flames began to bulge. People's faces also grew brighter; they too began to bulge. The music was sweeter, the dancing more felt. What it is to see plump gleeful men in tight trousers sketching the intricacies of a tune upon a ballroom floor! And all those women in their best dresses, dancing towards girlhood again.

But Harry's attention at this stage was taken up completely by the Princess, and well it might be. In her white and glittering gown, with her blush-pink skin and her spun-gold hair, she was a princess indeed, and as midnight approached she seemed to flower like a snow-rose. Harry became mad with impatience for the minutes to tick by, and his time to arrive. When he looked at the grandfather clock at the far end of the room he stared so hard that his eyes became visible: they were like twin dials, with twelve o'clock on each. Meanwhile the grandfather clock, in its obstinate fashion, insisted on showing twenty-six minutes past eleven, or thirteen minutes to twelve.

But at last there were only a few minutes to go. Harry elbowed his way to the front of the queue that awaited the Princess. He went completely invisible for a moment, as though to gather his strength and then, finger by finger, toe by toe, now a bit of leg, next a portion of arm, now hair, now the tip of his nose, bit after piece, he began to appear.

The Princess watched his arrival with astonishment. In fact, just as the clock began striking twelve she dropped her handkerchief.

Harry watched it slowly fall from her tiny hand, and then he bent down to pick it up for her. He straightened again, and

175

held it at arm's length towards the Princess. She raised her hand to take it from him. At the moment her fingers reached the handkerchief the clock struck twelve.

At last Harry was visible completely, as an object is when you finally get your binoculars focused on it. But then Dot switched her attention back to the Princess and at that point she got a terrible shock.

The *Princess* had disappeared.

All that was left of her was the handkerchief, which was once more falling to the floor, even more slowly than it had before. It did a rock-a-bye-baby in the air, like a blossom falling in the springtime.

Harry, tears welling from his eyes, bent down to pick it up.

## Chapter 8

## Rears Its Ugly Head Again

I can't put it off any longer. It reared its ugly head again right in the middle of my nice Christmas scenes. The church, the Christmas carols, the rest of the jiggery-pokery. I didn't believe in the jiggery-pokery then (when I was little) and I don't believe in it now. But there's always one part of you that takes delight in the paraphenalia of it, the thought of robins perched on spades, of fir-trees covered in glitter, of houses huddled cosily in white valleys. The other side would find it depressing: callers stuffed with bonhomie as a sandbag is stuffed with sand; stockingsful of superfluous hankies and yet more stockings; the endless grey shilly-shallying drizzle that deepens the sludginess of the lawns and guarantees several more months of imprisonment.

But I am a children's author, and I have to put up my Christmas decorations as all good children's authors must. Pin up my bits of holly. Erect a Christmas tree. Arrange a party, complete with traditional games. And just as things are getting into full swing plop through my letter-box drops not a card or a present, but a letter. At least one should be thankful for small mercies: it wasn't delivered by the horrible man, masquerading as some kind of midsummer Santa with a sackful of fishless chickens on his back. Moreover the envelope was typed, which is normally a good, or at any rate neutral sign. But, since the Grandson's missive, I've developed an instinct about these things, and this envelope undoubtedly had an aura of THE BLACK SPOT.

Dear Madam,

We note from our records that you have not consulted your doctor since...

At this Health Centre we like to see our patients, particularly those who are not in their first youth, at least once a year, so that we can spot any little problems that might be developing, and put your mind at rest as to whether you are in sound health.

Why don't you pop along some time soon for a consultation with Speckledy Head? Our surgery hours are as follows yes yes yes.

No appointment is necessary.

We look forward to seeing you.

Yes, yes

It was well thought-out, of course. The Grandson and his cronies do not do things by half. Notice the unfilled-in space in the first paragraph, which gives the impression that this was a round robin, carelessly sent. But for heaven's sake, I do know how to read. It is but a small step from being auntied to becoming a patient, a patient moreover who is in the particularly-those-who-are-not-in-their-first-youth category. Only a few weeks ago, I kept having to remind myself, I was simply *me*.

And then there is the style, the product of that self-same hatchery in which my bright-eyed and bushy-tailed boy-scout of a lawyer was germinated, syntactically and semantically speaking. Here is the identical oily incompetence, as like as peas in a pod. Let me DIY your house, since it's sure to be in a mess. Let us reassure you that your health is bad, in case you might be under the impression you are sound in wind and limb.

But the point is: Speckledy Head and Smelly Nurse are unwilling conspirators. Do-gooders. The type who would hobnob perfectly innocently with the likes of the Grandson. I can see what happened (you've always got to see what happened). The Grandson decides he needs to worry about my health. Particularly about my mental state. The Mental State is a small country, full of shadowy valleys but singularly lacking in high places; and riven by civil war. It adjoins the Land

178

Where Lost Things Go. The Grandson, pith helmet on head, butterfly net in hand, useful penknife in pocket, makes an exploratory expedition. He discovers anarchy. The rivers have turned blue, and meander. The natives talk mumbo–jumbo on account of ill–fitting false teeth. The ill–fitting false teeth have a tendency to burst into flame. It is, in short, a place ripe for a colonial master, who will set the house in order, who will do what is best, who will supply the qualities of leadership. Be prepared! as the Boy Scouts say. The Grandson finds exactly what he is looking for, as one usually does.

When he arrives home, he rings up Directory Enquiries. He is probably on hobnobbing terms with *them*, too. People like myself go through life without ringing Directory Enquiries even once. How do you find out their number?

Then the Grandson phones round until he comes across the practice responsible for me.

Ring ring

– Smelly Nurse speaking
– I'm ringing about my aunty. You know the sort of thing I mean. Mental state, and so forth.

[He winks concernedly down the phone. I've done something similar in my time. Not a wink, exactly, since women can't normally wink, for reasons of modesty. What we do is screw up our eyes, give a quick, forced smile, and put our head slightly to one side, as birds and dogs do when they are inspecting people. One directs such an attitude across the counter of a chemist's shop for example, when one is discussing Germoloids, one's old father, and so forth. Smelly Nurse of course has an ear for these messages. She can detect the tiny clang of winking eyelids even across miles of telephone wire.]

– Perhaps Speckledy Head ought to have a look at her?
– I'd be infernally grateful. It's just that I'm not quite sure she can manage her affairs, if you know what I mean.

(*I* know what you mean, even if she doesn't.)

179

– We'll try to make an appointment, straightaway.
– I'd be grateful if you'd um...

[I see him suddenly as a dreadful young man in a sports-jacket, clutching an embarrassed hat; the sort who appeared so often in those tedious plays which my generation went to see, plays in which nothing ever happened. The world had been destroyed once and was about to be destroyed again. All the men were dead. Then the leftovers stood on the stage and pretended to be on edge because they weren't sure whether their young ladies would marry them or not. As a matter of fact the Grandson is far more robust than those specimens. He hammers things. He has nails in his mouth. He makes up poetry while he is uncorking champagne. But, after all, those young men on the stage were also far more robust than they pretended to be. They had survived the Great War.]

– [Smelly Nurse can decipher an um as efficiently as she can hear a wink]: You would like us to approach her tactfully?
– You know how older people can take offence. At a certain point they recoil. The pressure of time makes their brains go dense. It might help if you'd apply some oil.
– I beg your pardon?
– Excuse me. I'd be most grateful if you don't let on that I um...
– Of course. After all, it's for her own good.

And so we have it: proof, if proof were ever needed, that art doesn't imitate life, nor even vice versa.

Little Olive goes to Anne's party.
Dot and Harry go to the Ball.
*I* go to the doctor's.

I went promptly, the next day. Possibly promptitude was part of the test. In any case, resistance was useless, so I might as well get the whole thing over with.
I'd not been to the surgery before. I don't go to doctors. It was a new, shabby building, with a dreadful patch of garden in front of it, containing some marigolds that might have been

bits of litter for all the good they were doing. You went into a sort of hallway, with a window set in the wall on the right-hand side, framing the receptionist for all the world as though she were an ancestral portrait. She was sitting in a sort of cubby-hole with orange lipstick on her lips. The lipstick was the precise colour of the failed marigolds in the front garden. There was a fissure in the glass to enable transactions to take place.

Through it the receptionist asked unpleasantly: 'What's your name?'

A faint orange cloud of nasty breath drifted through the fissure, like an after-echo.

'Watson,' I replied.

'What?'

'Son.'

'No, *your* name, not your son's.'

'I told you my name. Olive Watson.'

'For heaven's sake,' said the receptionist grumpily. 'Members of a family have separate files, you know. Your son will have *his* file and you will have *yours*.'

At a certain intellectual level argument seems hardly worthwhile, so I forebore to reply.

The receptionist got off whatever she was sitting on, and opened a filing-cabinet which shared her cubby-hole with her like an oblong and silent friend.

'What was your name again?' she asked, after she had riffled in it for a few moments.

'Watson. It still is. Olive Watson.'

'Your file's not here.'

'That's not my responsibility,' I replied, catching her tartness. Then I remembered that I was on trial, and tried to lighten the atmosphere: 'I have enough trouble with my teapot.'

'Have you been to the doctor recently?' she asked. 'If so it might still be in his consulting room.'

'I haven't been to this doctor ever,' I replied. 'That's why I was sent a letter.'

'Oh, you were sent a letter! Why didn't you say! In that case, it'll be over here.'

She dug a brown envelope out of a heap on one side of her

little desk. 'Here it is,' she said, peering at it critically, rather as an antique-dealer might inspect a crack in an old saucer. Then she looked at me as though I'd just that moment materialized. 'Go into the waiting-room,' she said coolly. 'Wait your turn.'

I nearly said: that is what one does in a waiting-room, but I thought better of it. In any case, it would have given a totally false air of confidence and competence; and waiting brought problems of its own.

When people are put at random in a room or on a bus they have a tendency to look like cartoon creatures. They are thinner or fatter than they ought to be. Their ears seem cauliflowerish. Their bulbous noses are about to drip. Brutal-looking women slap their children harder than they should. Silly-looking people simper. There is the sort of extremeness that comes with caging. Animals, in all probability, are far less animal-like in the wild than they appear to be in zoos. In the waiting-room there was one lugubrious-looking man who would periodically say wer-roit-dah!, a propos of nothing in particular. I thought at first he was clearing his throat. This was a place where people talked in completely inaudible whispers, but every other sound they made was inordinately loud. They coughed and sneezed deafeningly, and blew their noses like ships' foghorns. Even the breathing of some of them sounded like sawing or a bellows. But when this individual made his odd sound for a second time, I realized that no throat clearing was taking place. The sound lacked the rough scrape of a shovel on rubbish, real or imagined. Wer-roit-dah (now a third time) wasn't a noise as such at all, it was a statement. It was abstract, as though one might be clearing one's brain. By the fourth time I realized the poor wretch was in the grip of a compulsion. He was stuck with the word as a needle might stick on a cracked record. Imagine his inner struggles, his despairing attempts to keep wer-roit-dah at bay, to shove some verbal thumb in the dyke. Perhaps, knowing victory was impossible, he would try to ration himself. I won't say it again until I've counted to ten. One, two, three, and the word would sag mightily, like a storm cloud, four, five, did I say five?, wive, wah, the word would rumble round the edges, evilly and angrily, six, seven, and then, as necessary as a sneeze, wer-roit-dah! a plateau of relief that was exactly the dimensions of the utterance; then the build-up again, just once more, please, please, please: for only in saying it is there respite from the *need* to say it.

Wer-roit-dah! of course, was why the dismal-looking person in the waiting-room was going to see the doctor. Heavens, envisage such a consultation. Doctor, I'm suffering from a word. Perhaps he thinks he is consulting a Doctor of Letters, in which case I too have come to the right place.

When I'm nervous I try to be clever; and of course, as attempted cleverness will, it only made matters worse.

When the doctor was ready to see another patient a red light went on above the door which led to his consulting-room. The grunts and mooing would abruptly cease. The next victim would rise modestly to his or her feet. A brief brave smile would come to the lips, redolent perhaps of the Blitz. Then through the door. The light would go suddenly off, as though the creature liked to shut its red, predatory eye while it got on with gobbling. Then, almost timidly, the mutters, snorts, breathing, would start up again. A nose, more courageous than the rest, would blast at full volume, and the general sound would rise to its previous level.

No, not the Blitz. The French Revolution. First the little seamstress, then Sidney Carton, and so on.

I had been watching this sad process with half an eye, thinking meanwhile my thoughts about the man who couldn't stop saying wer-roit-dah! The quarter of my brain that was attached to the half an eye noted that it was a long time before my turn would arrive, and assumed therefore that I didn't have to pay attention. But at last a horrible realization dawned.

I had been so busy being clever that I had not been taking mental notes. I had not itemized the people in the room when I arrived; even worse, I'd not been keeping count of who had arrived after me. In amusing myself in that idiotic detestable way I have, with notions of doctors of letters and galloping clauses, I had failed to notice that each person knew exactly when it was his turn to have his head chopped off. On went the light, up stood the victim. There was no haggling; there were no embarrassing dead heats. How did they do it? Each one, however neanderthal, possessed, or bulbous-nosed, had a clear picture in his brain of the state of the room as he'd walked into it. It seemed impossible. Surely one of them could oblige with a mistake?

The only hope was that perhaps the light would look different when it was *your* light. Perhaps you simply knew.

That was a comforting notion. Unfortunately, however, I couldn't rely on it. And meanwhile I sat among the cacophony and imagined how it would be if I didn't know. All those faces which had never quite looked directly at me would look directly at me. I would feel old and fat. And, to make matters worse, justifiably so.

As my moment drew nearer, I began to take precautions. Each time the light went on I'd make a series of tiny adjustments. Grasp my handbag more firmly. Shift my bottom so that it wasn't so solid on the bench. There would be a brief interval when I teetered on the very verge of rising; not exactly on tiptoe, but on a kind of tiptoe of my rear. And then some other victim would get to his feet instead, and I would settle back as gently as I'd risen, my heart pounding within.

If it wasn't this light, it must be the next.

Or at least, surely to goodness, the next. I'd been here long enough. I'd been in the waiting-room so long that I could hardly remember what it was like *not* being in it.

It wasn't.

It wasn't.

It wasn't.

And then, at last, it was.

You *did* know.

Your light was different, just as your house is different, or your children, if you have them. I know that's comparing small things with great, but nevertheless the things that are yours have more in common with each other than they do with those that aren't. An object – pot of paint, half a pound of butter – on a shelf in a shop is at best studiedly indifferent, at worst surly and obstreperous. But an object you are going to *buy* reaches out its buttery arms to you, like a child who through some dreadful administrative muddle has been placed in an orphanage, and now sees its mother peering in through the window.

But then a funny thing happened, or rather an unfunny one.

184

When it was *my* light. I prepared myself for getting to my feet just as I had when it was somebody else's. But as I was about to rise, I sank. My legs went weak, for all the world as though I really *were* going to be beheaded.

I sat on the bench, trying to pull myself together, but there seemed to be altogether too much of me to pull. I felt as though part of me was somebody else, who refused to take orders. I found myself muttering at me, in disapproval.

The other patients began to look. They were embarrassed at doing so, so as their eyes approached they made their faces, and all the rest of them, recede. The room, like a dark wood, filled with eyes.

Then they began to send signals. The eyes went from me to the light and back again, no longer sinister but busy and helpful, like jelloid boy-scouts. I became aware that the bodies, to the rear of those eyes, had begun to shift about, by way of hinting that mine should do likewise. Then there was a voice, or rather, in accordance with waiting-room etiquette, a breathy whisper in my right ear: 'It's your turn, duck.'

There was a sympathetic imperative in the whisper that caught exactly the atmosphere of a queue for the guillotine and made my legs weaker than ever. The whisperer's breath was warm in my ear, and seemed to remain there, intensely irritating, after the whisper was finished. I moved my head to one side in order to shake it out.

'No, dear,' said the whisper again, 'I promise you it is.'

'Yes it is,' somebody else said.

It is it is, people said all round the room. Heads nodded, though the eyes now remained fixed on me, so that they looked like bearings on which the heads pivoted. And the more all this happened, the more I couldn't get up.

At that point, things took a turn for the worse; the receptionist came in. She had presumably been summoned from her cubby-hole in the hall by the doctor, who would be wondering what was going on. Or perhaps she'd heard the growing tide of *It ises* even from out there. She leaned down towards me. She was wearing sweet perfume that clashed peculiarly with her smelly breath.

Then Pelion upon Ossa, the worst thing to date: she was nice to me!

185

'I think it's you now,' she said, each gentle word carved out of halitosis. 'Would you like a hand up?' She smiled, took me by the elbow, and pulled me upright. It was her kindness that made me seem even more like a *heap* of something than her action did. I felt foolish by the pound. I took the only revenge I could, and forbore to say thank-you. And as I strode towards the doctor's door, I made sure I didn't give my fellow-victims the requisite Blitz (or seamstress) smile.

The doctor's room smelled as doctors' rooms always do: a combination of manly and medical. The manly wasn't tobacco or leather: but whatever it was was of that kind. And round the edges of it hung the sweet-sharp smell of medicaments.

The doctor, seated at his desk, was a small man with a white moustache. The top of his head was babyish, with a little bit of thin hair, and the splodgy freckles we all get with age. He had half-moon spectacles, with eyes as green as peas, and unkind.

'I was beginning to think I'd finished for the day,' he said, flummoxing me at once. His statement was a kind of joke; but you were intended to see that it wasn't a sincere joke, and to understand that he wasn't amused. While I was pondering on this paradox I became aware that the doctor was repeating himself, louder this time, possibly under the impression I was deaf. I say repeating, but all I caught was a word that sounded suspiciously like 'daisy'. Then he pressed a button on his desk. It obviously switched out the red light. Clonk into the basket went my head.

'I received a summons,' I said.

'A summons?' he asked. He raised his eyebrows and made his eyes look uncomprehending, except that they weren't uncomprehending at all; moreover, I was intended to *understand* that they weren't uncomprehending at all. Heavens, I thought, even his eyes are double negatives.

'Invitation,' I glossed.

'You're obviously a very special patient, if you were *invited*. I'd better handle you with kid gloves.' He smiled. 'Let me take a little looky.'

Looky?

Daisy?

He reached into my medical envelope and pulled out some documents. As he read them he made a tut-tutting sound.

'You haven't been to a doctor for years,' he said. 'The ink is turning brown.'

For that matter so is the top of your head, I thought darkly.

'I think the time has come,' the doctor went on, 'for a good going-over. Let's take our clothes off, shall we?'

We? I thought. 'We?' I asked.

He looked directly at me with those hard little peas of his, all but saying: if you don't play tiny-tot, I'll think of a nastier game for you, don't you worry.

'I'll call nurse in,' he said, 'to keep an eye on us. There's the screen, over there. Why don't you go and hide?'

I went behind the screen. When I arrived there, the first thing I did, with my usual crackling initiative, was to stand facing it as though it were a view, rather than the opposite of one. I wasn't thinking of anything, I felt terribly tired – I could imagine falling asleep standing up. I was snapped out of it by the sound, beyond the screen, of the nurse arriving, and talking to the doctor in a low inaudible voice. Like a Monday morning, the thought of my underclothes came into my head. Heavens, I wondered, have they been Let go? For the life of me I couldn't remember. Underclothes are hardly objects which command my attention: which of course was precisely the problem. The nuisance was that in spite of their name, underclothes are taken off last, which means that they are at the top of any given heap of clothing.

Immediately I'd identified the problem, the solution came to mind. I could craftily insert them in the bottom of my pile. But that in turn brought a new worry in its wake. I would be performing my sleight-of-hand, or rather of-drawers and -brassiere, at the *end* of the process: precisely the sort of time when some nosy nurse would choose to peer round the screen to see how I was doing. And that I'd been caught *in flagrante* concealing my disreputables, if it got back, would be music to the Grandson's ears.

All of which meant, of course, that I had to hurry. I took off my cardigan. So far so good, that was easy enough. There was a little table on which one obviously had to place one's clothes. I put my cardigan on it. I wondered whether to fold it but decided against. There is something very unfoldable about a cardigan, though as a matter of fact I've never been a natural folder of any kind.

Now for the dress. I don't understand why you don't seem to be able to get the sort of dress that buttons from top to bottom any more. While it's a nuisance undoing all the buttons, when you've finished you can unwrap yourself in one go, like taking the silver paper off a chocolate biscuit.

As it was, what a palaver! There was hardly room enough behind the screen for what went on.

What you have to do, I've realized over the years, is pretend someone is pulling your dress off for you. You bend in the middle so they can pull it over your head. It's rather like a tug o'war: you pull in the opposite direction, so as to give the tugger something to tug *at*. But of course, since the tugger is imaginary, your hands and arms have to behave as if they belonged to *him*, or perhaps more decorously, *her*, rather than to you. They creep over your shoulders and down your back as if they aren't yours at all. They grab hold of any material where they can find purchase and pull, and at last you feel your dress beginning to give, here and there, until it culminates in general movement. It's even worse than pulling the curtains because the corner the pull has to go round is *you*. But you can't straighten up because then your hands would have nowhere to start from: they can't come down at you from the sky!

Pulling at my dress made my eyeballs swell and shrink, like eyeballs drawn on a balloon.

To cut a long, too long, story short, in due course I was naked. Naked, I may say, is a strange thing to be with only a screen to protect you from other people in an alien room. It was midnight at ten in the morning, and I was Cinderella, dressed only in the rags and tatters of herself. Though a screen, I suppose, is a form of long-distance clothing, like its cousin, the curtain, or rather they are both in-between items, halfway between clothing and a wall. To be honest-to-goodness clothing the item has to protect you from yourself as well as from other people, and the screen lamentably failed to oblige. I regret to say, in my popped-forth state, there is a lot of me to need protecting from. I suddenly remembered an embarrassing moment when I was taken out to lunch by my very first editor. I was so nervous that I didn't feel like eating at all, but when the waitress offered me a plate of vegetables, I made myself take some. Then of course my editor took an amount so minute that it would not have satisfied a flea. I felt porcine. I felt even worse when I couldn't finish my helping and had to leave most of it on the plate. Fat and old, with all sorts of unnecessary *business* about me, I felt much the same now: as though redundancies of *me* were heaped up on my plate.

Worse still, what next? Should I tiptoe round the screen like some grotesque cabaret performer and endure the gawping of Speckledy Head and his nurse? Surely not.

'I'm ready,' I called, speculatively.

To my surprise an arm immediately appeared round the edge of the screen, clutching something white in its hand, rather as a dog might hold a newspaper in its mouth. As I stared the arm grew visibly annoyed, and began to waggle about, as if looking for me without being able to see. I took the white thing. The arm went away.

The thing was folded to such an extent that I didn't know what it was. How different in its sheer aloofness from my heap of apple-pie clothing, with the underclothes all ready to jump out and say boo to you. I opened it as one might open a flat box.

To my relief, it was a sort of coat. But when I put it on it turned out to be far too small. Also, there was no means of doing it up, so that it hung open at the front. Worst of all, it was made of something strange, which tore as I worked my shoulder into it. Paper! I was expected to wrap myself up in paper like something one has purchased in a grocer's shop!

'Are we ready nen?' Speckledy Head inquired from just beyond the screen.

'It doesn't fit,' I replied.

'Nurse, trotty,' riposted Head, full of glee. 'To the rescue.'

This time it wasn't simply the arm that came round, but everything, including a flashing set of orange lips. Heavens, I thought, they *have* to wear them here! Then I realized that the nurse was in fact the receptionist! She looked unabashed at the disguise, which was effected merely by the addition of a white coat, not a paper one in her case.

'Next time,' I advised, 'you should remember to remove your lips.'

She took no notice. 'It doesn't have to fit,' she said simply. As though that was his cue Speckledy Head also materialized on the hither side of the screen.

'Goody goody,' he said, in acknowledgement of the lack of fit, presumably. He nodded towards a bed that was positioned against the wall behind me. It looked depressingly like some sort of punishment bed, with a frame of enamelled metal, well-battered, and a very thin mattress. When I was a girl, bed was a frequent punishment for wrong-doing amongst my school-chums. My mother discussed the habit once, incredulously.

'Bed,' she said, plump as a pie, 'why, bed is *bliss*.'

'Sis,' Uncle Taylor put in, 'it is an eight year old with whom you are dealing.'

'Bliss,' my mother insisted. 'Sheer and utter.'

The bed wasn't high, but there was nevertheless a tiny set of steps on the floor near it.

'Up the wooden hills,' the doctor said. 'Make ourselves comfortable.'

Goaded beyond endurance I looked him in the eye and tried to say: 'Don't you mean comfortable-wumfortable?' but before I could get out the wumfortable, Smelly had taken my elbow and was guiding me, like an executioner on the stroke of eight, to the steps.

'Goody goody,' said Speckledy from my rear. At least he can't gawp at my *bottom*, I thought to myself.

Despite the steps it was unexpectedly difficult to get on to the bed. I tried to pull myself up with my arms, but to no avail: too short, as usual. They wouldn't raise my body any-where near high enough: in fact my feet barely left the top step.

'Can't we manage?' Speckledy asked. 'It's tricky, that bed. Why don't we turn around and try it bottom first?'

Why don't we? I turned round, only to remember, too late, that all my front was visible. There was nothing for it, how-ever. *Be* visible, I told it.

Speckledy took one armpit, Smelly the other, and they hoisted me up. My legs came loose, and I began to swing them round.

'Ooopsy,' said Speckledy on my behalf.

'Aah!' I cried.

'A bit stiff in the old joints,' Speckledy agreed.

It wasn't simply that. With your legs at one angle, as they swivel round to line up with the bed, and your body at another, you inevitably get to the point where you ought to break in two, stiff joints or no.

190

Then I was on the mattress.

The plastic with which it was covered felt horribly slidey, even under my paper coat. I suddenly wondered about the state of my feet, particularly the soles. Oh blow them.

'Now let's take a look at you,' Speckledy announced with the satisfaction of someone sharpening up his carving knife. 'Starting with the old tummy.'

He would start with the tummy. One does not, as a rule, inspect one's tummy, but now and then I give mine a passing glance, and recently I've noticed that some nasty brown grooves have appeared, going into the navel. Speckledy ran his hard green peas along them, as if they were faded sentences.

'I see,' he said.

'They've appeared in the last year or two,' I told him.

'I beg your pardon?'

'My grooves.'

'Your...? Oh, you mean the stretch marks. I think they go back a little further than that.'

For heaven's sake! I thought. Allow me to measure the vintage of my own grooves!

'It's the woman's lot,' he went on. He may even have said lotty-potty, lot-pot, wimminy-pimminy, I don't know, I was getting too upset to tell. He could take any word and twist it about so that it became silly, but his eyes never softened, and the effect was of prattling in Siberia.

'I can't think why. Don't *men* fold in the middle?'

'It's all right. Nursy told me all.'

'All *what*?'

It was exactly like those irritating moments in the cinema, when the soundtrack has gone askew, and lips flap in one direction and people talk, somehow, in quite another. The doctor opened and shut his mouth, but no words came out. Meanwhile inside my head I could hear exactly what he was saying.

'You've given birth to a son.'

Suddenly in the middle of all the shock and outrage, I thought of the children in my books.

'Oh yes,' I said. 'Quite a few. And daughters to boot.'

'My,' said Speckledy. 'We *have* been busy.'

191

# Chapter 12

## Drowning Dry

Something burst out of the dark rhododendrons, like a huge black bird. But then it caught the light from the house windows and I saw it wasn't a huge bird but a housekeeper. When she saw me, she patted her hat confusedly with her hand.

'Goodnight, missy,' she said, and hurried round the side of the house.

'Goodnight,' I replied wonderingly.

The horse I'd heard in the road snorted, and then apparently spoke.

'Is that you, Olive? Well I never. Climb aboard.'

It was Arthur, on a trap. I couldn't see him, but his voice suggested a welcoming fish-like patch of night-time. His arm came down and hoisted me up beside him on the driving-seat.

'Mattie and I have been for a little drive. Her ladyship wanted to take charge of festivities herself. Mattie *said* she thought it was ending at seven but I said no, no, eight, I'm sure Olive said eight. So as soon as the poor thing alights, out stream the multitudes.'

'Why did she hide in the bushes?' I asked.

'Can you suggest anywhere better to hide?' Arthur replied.

Before I could think of a reply, Arthur was in full flight: 'Isn't it extraordinary how well horses can see in the dark? I wonder if it *is* seeing, now I think about it. Perhaps they go by smell, like dogs. Their noses are big enough, for heaven's sake. Mattie was telling me about a cousin of hers who breaks horses in the Rocky Mountains. He was very nearly killed when one hoofed him on the top of the head. They can be vicious beasts when all's said and done, though not so dangerous as pigs.'

As I sat beside him my fright and shock faded away. Even so, I was surprised by what the sudden proximity drew out of me, as soon as Arthur paused for breath.

'I saw Uncle Taylor doing something *funny* once,' I said. 'A few months ago.'

'I've seen him do something funny more recently than that,' Arthur replied wittily.

'No. This was *really* funny. He was lying on the floor. He had hardly any clothes on. He only had his drawers on. There were two chairs on top of him. Mother was there. She was lying on the floor too. She had her clothes on. She was laughing her head off.'

'Good gracious,' said Arthur. 'That does seem to be *funny*, as you say. With hardly any clothes on? And Sis in attendance?'

'Yes,' I replied, my heart thumping. He understands it, I thought.

'Not even his walking-stick?'

'No.'

'I can't imagine.'

'He looked like a pile of sausages,' I said, trying to help him imagine.

'Did he?'

'Those thin ones,' I qualified hastily. 'Not the fat ones. The thin sausages that are all joined together with little tails.'

'A pile of thin sausages. Without a walking-stick.'

'He'd been thumping before. Mother was hanging out the washing, Uncle Taylor was thumping upstairs, and I was playing under the table in the dining-room. Then I heard a big crashing noise. I thought it was thunder. I went up to see what it was. At first I thought it was thundering under the table.'

'Thundering *under* the table!'

'Well, it was a nice day outside. I thought the woodwork was brown clouds. But it wasn't. It was Uncle Taylor.'

'Perhaps that's the strangest thing of all,' said Arthur musingly. 'The thought of Uncle Taylor thundering. He seems too thin to thunder, sausages or not. And another thing. How could Sis be in two places at once?'

'Perhaps she came in because *she* heard him thundering too. Or thumping.'

'What do *you* think he was doing?'

'I don't know.'

I already felt better, however. Getting it out into the open made it seem less sinister, particularly because Arthur, man of the world that he seemed, chaser of women, intimate of housekeepers, beheader of ducks, had no dark niche of his own all prepared to place my information in.

'I think he fell off the chairs,' I said, suddenly inspired.

'By the same token, he's a thin man to sit on *two* chairs. And then to top it all by falling off them both!'

'I think he was lying on them.'

We clopped on through the darkness, both trying to see it. Uncle Taylor had lain, almost undressed, across two chairs in his room, with a bed only a few feet away.

'Let's ask some questions, like Sherlock Holmes,' Arthur said. 'Why does one take one's clothes off?'

Because Speckledy Head tells you to, I might have replied, if I had only known.

'The reasons are,' Arthur went on, 'to sleep or to exercise.'

There was a slightly strained silence as a third alternative passed through both our minds. One could take one's clothes off in order to be rude. This indeed was the very possibility that had loomed in my imagination since I'd witnessed the scene, all those weeks before. Even in Edwardian England little boys and girls were acquainted with farmyard compulsions. It's true that we never learned about them at school. When I was old enough to receive lessons in biology, they concerned themselves solely with the eyeball and indigestion (as we insisted on calling it). But surely in the end one doesn't need to learn about the birds and the bees. In certain important respects one *is* a bird or a bee. Or one could have been, had one been so inclined.

'Since there was a bed to sleep in,' said Arthur firmly, scotching waywardness, 'that leaves us with exercise.'

We clopped on. The lights of the town were receding by now, as we began to climb up the lane that led to our house. A large drop of rain, cold and rather rubbery, hit me on the nose.

'Dash it!' said Arthur. 'Still,' he added after a short pause, 'with the rain coming on, I'm glad I took Mattie back to the house at seven, hordes of children or not. It would have been

194

a to-do if she'd arrived home sopping wet. You know what those people are like.'

'Oh yes,' I replied urbanely. 'Anne's father is an ogre.'

'By jove, I've never noticed.'

'He guards their Christmas tree. And tries to smack your bottom.'

'I've got it!' cried Arthur. 'I know what you do when you lie upon two chairs.'

'What?' I asked trembling, my urbanity swallowed up by the night.

Arthur laughed. I can still hear that combination of noises: the horse's clopping, the plinking of the firm ripe raindrops, and Arthur's loud but quite high-pitched ha ha ha.

'Uncle Taylor,' he got out finally, 'dear old Uncle Taylor, is learning to swim!'

It turned out that Uncle Taylor had announced his intention to learn to swim some time previously, though it was not a matter which had aroused any particular interest within the family. He claimed his medical man had advised it, on account of his (alleged) bad leg. Of course nobody had expected him to learn *dry*, though that could have been predicted if people had put their minds to it. In many respects he *lived* dry, after all.

Subsequently Arthur interrogated my mother on the subject. Apparently Uncle Taylor had stripped down to his drawers to allow freedom of movement, rested himself upon two chairs, and peered down at an instruction book that he had previously positioned on the floor.

Possibly, during the exercise, he had been overwhelmed by an imaginary breaker, and thrust down and down to the wooden bottom of the sea.

It was a great relief to be told all this. It set my mind at rest.

But one can have two minds, just as one can have two noses, and my nasty mind took no notice of the explanation whatever.

I know now what the problem was. Perhaps I've written all this down just to find out. Little girls and boys differ in all sorts of ways from grown-ups, and one of the most important is that they try to think logically. (Adults on the whole are too impetuous.) My syllogism was rooted in what I saw.

I saw (in my nasty mind's eye) Arthur chasing WOMEN.

Women in this sense of the word are plump red turkey-like creatures who utter high-pitched gleeful squawks. I also saw Uncle Taylor devoted to his sister. Possibly his imaginary bad leg prevented him from going further afield. Moreover he didn't own a yellow bicycle. And he never piloted our pony-and-trap. But his sister, apart from being his *sister*, was my mother. Ergo, I was jealous.

My nasty mind remained jealous even while my nice mind laughed in relief at Arthur's explanation. If Uncle Taylor was learning to swim it was so he could swim towards Mother.

After all, I'd seen the two of them on Uncle Taylor's bedroom floor, splashing about in my mother's laughter.

While we are on the subject of childish logic, here is an equation:

As Uncle Taylor was to my mother
So Harry was to me.

At least, that is what I feared.

The next stage in the saga of Uncle Taylor's swimming lessons must have occurred early in the spring of the year in which I was nine – that is to say, within a few months of my conversation with Arthur on the pony-and-trap. It was an even drier stage than its predecessor: in fact it didn't involve swimming at all.

All I remember is the shouting.

I was in my bedroom, lying upon my bed with a book. There was a fire in the grate. Suddenly I heard a booming voice. It didn't sound like an ordinary person shouting, it sounded large and deep, as if a giant were talking. Then I realized that it was my father's voice. I had never thought of him in that light before: he was such a small, quiet, preoccupied man. His voice penetrated the house, firm and definite and devastating. Anger is a volatile emotion as a rule: it doesn't trust itself. You go high to convince yourself you are angry; you subside as soon as your concentration diminishes for a moment. But there must be a boiling point in anger, or perhaps it would be better to say absolute zero, a state of stable ferocity, and my father had reached it now. His voice didn't go up or down, it simply went on and on, with a deep compelling

196

clarity (even though, from my bedroom, I couldn't make out a word he was saying).

At last he stopped and my Uncle Taylor's voice began. I can't hear the sound of it, any more than I can of my father's: I simply remember remembering. It was high-pitched, scrabbling, desperate, very unlike anything I'd heard before, yet not surprising, not if you thought of him limping for so long all alone on my private beach, or lying beneath overturned chairs in his bedroom.

Then my father resumed. I remember thinking, though it must have been a much later memory, of a butterfly broken upon a wheel. Despairing squeaks and what Uncle Taylor would call expostulations sprang up in the cracks between my father's awful sentences.

When at last the dialogue ended I continued to lie stiffly upon my bed as one does in a bath after the water has gone cold, not daring to move. Though my father had never sounded more gigantic than he had while breaking Uncle Taylor upon his wheel, the next time I saw him he seemed to have shrunk. Smallness was always his giant destiny.

I got gleamings of what had taken place during that conversation over the course of time, but it was not until many years had passed that I discovered the whole story. By then the great Man Engine catastrophe had taken place, the failing mine had been sold for a song, and Uncle Taylor had long ago vanished. My mother was dead; Harry was dead; Arthur was dead. My father was living with me in Shrewsbury, where I worked for a Shropshire newspaper and was just beginning my career as a writer of children's books.

My father sat by our fire, stiffly, legs apart in that rather horrid old man's style (brought about by piles, probably, or arthritis) and told me what had happened, from the very beginning.


He'd been the manager of a coal mine in Yorkshire, and my mother was the owner's young widow. When they married they sold up, like a pair of fools, and bought a tin-mine in Cornwall. My mother's brother, Uncle Taylor, just returned from a post in colonial administration somewhere in Africa, persuaded them to do it. Perhaps my father was eager because he didn't want the sensation of stepping into dead men's shoes. Uncle Taylor handled the finances; my father was the manager; and shortly afterwards Arthur moved down from Yorkshire where he'd been a mine engineer, and took over that department.

The mine was a dead duck. *But it prospered!*

Let us track Uncle Taylor through the heart of darkness.

It is very different from the wood in which Harry and Dot found the witch, or rather in which the witch found them. There is nothing rectangular about the jungle. I've seen something like it in my kitchen, not to mention my front garden. It is a place immune from the horrible man's petrol mower. Plants tangle. There are sickly flowers like butter going off. The canopy above wobbles and sways, pierced by shafts of green misty light. There are dim shadowy places with a faint glitter of eyes. Everywhere shrieks and trumpets and moans, as though one is in the waiting-room of some monstrous doctor. Things out of Charles Darwin swing and scuttle. Insects zing, or bumble about, or even flap. Birds cry as if in pain. Somewhere in the distance throbs a drum.

And in the middle of it all is Uncle Taylor. His bright monocle punctures the morass. He is being paddled down a river by painted natives. The river is sludgy, and slimy, and chockful of things with teeth. Uncle Taylor is precise and neat and pernickety as usual, like a latinate word in a paragraph of expletives. His 'bad' leg is propped up on the side of the canoe. His silver-topped cane rests on the hollowed-out floor. He is doing some calculations in a small ledger on his 'good' knee, converting this gibbering anarchy into the pounds, shillings and pence of Empire. Every few hours he is paddled into a settlement. The people become progressively more primitive. I see ladies like black barrels, scrawny men with broken teeth. As Uncle Taylor proceeds up-river I picture him coming across natives with bones through their noses or terribly long necks, though that may be old-fashioned of me. And what about pygmies? Were there really such things? Little dwarves with blow-pipes? One could almost as readily imagine dragons.

Finally, Uncle Taylor comes to the last staging-post.

We know what he finds there. Haggard and Kipling and Conrad all agree. When the light is dimmest and most green, the screechings are at their most hellish, the plants slash like cutlasses or assegais, in the last hut at the furthest bend of the river, what you find is inevitably a white man (or woman).

Man in this case.

A Frenchman called Charles Hautbois.

He has a proposition to make. He has a tin-mine.

To be honest I don't know whether M. Hautbois' tin-mine was in the jungle at all. Do you get mines in the jungle? Perhaps he and Uncle Taylor met in rocky terrain somewhere, or in a desert. I don't even know whether the mine was in British Africa, or French Africa or Belgian Africa. What I do know is that Charles Hautbois had an arrangement to sell the tin to Germany at an enormous profit, but for some reason regulations prevented him from dealing direct. He was enlisting the help of various people to act as middlemen, and Uncle Taylor, with his mining connections and his genius for figures, became one of them.

So it didn't matter that our tin-mine in Cornwall was a dead duck. Uncle Taylor was exporting African tin to Germany, as if it were the product of our own mine, and making us a sound profit from doing so. The books, however, for Father's benefit (not to mention the Revenue men) suggested that it was the little giant's labours which were reaping their just reward. My father was a practical man, and a moral one. Or perhaps I should say, a rather childish one. He believed in cause and effect.

In 1908 the scheme collapsed. Tension and rivalry between Britain and Germany reached such a point that the government passed the Export Restriction in Tin and Other Metals Act. My father recited its name as if, twenty years later, it was still a dreadful curse. The British were no longer to provide the tin which Germany might use for its armaments (or for whatever foul purpose the Kaiser could evolve). Uncle Taylor's little scheme had outlived its usefulness, and as he limped by the sea during that hot summer when I spied upon him from my position outside the Hole, he must have been only too aware that within a few months the short-fall in his books would become obvious, and he would have to tell my father how the mine had been making its money.

When he finally did so, my father was devastated. He had

been living a lie without even knowing it. His life was fiction.

There were practical problems to be faced, to wit survival. Here Arthur came up trumps. (I've no idea whether he was in on Uncle Taylor's scheme: my father didn't say. In any case it was surprisingly irrelevant. Arthur couldn't be corrupted by what he knew or did. He was a man enthusiastic about umbrellas and raincoats and he seemed well waterproofed in this respect also. Which goes to show that innocence is not merely a lack of something but a quality in its own right.)

Arthur worked like a slave. He made the mine more efficient. He installed a Man Engine. This is a kind of lift which saved the men from having to climb down and up that eternal ladder with each shift. It consists of a continuous belt, with little platforms at man-sized intervals. You step on one as it travels past you, and down (or up) you go, with men on similar platforms in a long line above and below you. If you saw them winding up to the surface of our tin-mine, you might think it was the end of a production line for human beings, freshly forged in the bowels of earth (though I suppose that's a somewhat unfortunate mixed metaphor).

Then the war came along, and helped Arthur's efforts. Tin was in demand. Soon it was in short supply. Even a mine where the tin had been in short supply to *start* with could make a profit.

After the war, the bottom fell out of tin. Everyone knows that. In our case, the bottom fell out literally.

One evening in 1919, the returning dayshift reported that they had heard unfamiliar clankings and groanings from the Man Engine on their way to the surface. Arthur joined the night gang on the descent, to check. While they were in motion some part of the contraption broke and the whole conveyor belt dropped down into the darkness. Twenty-nine men, including Arthur, were killed.

Think of them, one on top of the other, standing upright in the dark, falling to their deaths. Most were men not long back from the front, Arthur included. Arthur had won a medal. He had been proof against bullets as well as rainwater and wickedness. My own experience of that hellish night was confined to standing in our front garden, and listening to distant shouts in the darkness. I asked if I could go and be of help to the injured. There weren't any injured, I was told.

200

Later, towards dawn, my father came back and drank a cup of tea by the fire. He was shaking. He had little to say, but at one moment he took his eyes off the flames and looked at me and I knew, and he knew that I knew, that he was recalling what he'd said to me in my childhood about the Knocker.

Long before then, though, one day in the late spring of 1909, my brother Harry and myself went off to play on our 'private' beach. We trotted across the field to the edge of the cliff and then down the footpath. But on the way down we caught sight of Uncle Taylor standing on the beach as if he owned it, exactly as he had been that day, in the previous year, when I emerged from the Hole.

Harry and I tiptoed down the incline till we reached the ledge, then lay down flat so that we could watch Uncle Taylor's perambulations.

He was doing what he'd done before: walking without a stick and pretending to limp.

It was one of those silver days, when the sun never quite breaks through the clouds, and even the shingle on the beach seems to glitter. Uncle Taylor still walks there in my mind's eye, following the silver lip of the water, crunch-crunch crunch-crunch crunch-crunch. He is silvery too, in a white linen jacket and a pale hat with a soft brim. After a while he stopped walking and stood staring at the sea. I knew just the sort of thing he would have been thinking. He was picturesque and intricate and poetic. He was imagining drifting, like a feather wafting from side to side in a still room, down the long stairs of the ocean.

He took off his hat. His thin hair lifted in the breeze, like waterweed in a current. He bent down and placed his hat on the beach. Then he took off his jacket. He folded it neatly, and positioned it beside the hat. Next his little boots. Finally his trousers. Then he stood in vest and drawers, more silvery than ever, facing the sea like a tiny lion tamer facing an unimaginable lion. Harry's eyes were bulging.

'I saw him do this before,' I said complacently. I meant both things, I suppose: be dressed in his underclothes, and stand on our beach; but of course they had not been simultaneous.

201

'Let's throw stones at him,' Harry whispered. 'Then we can hide in the Hole.'

I thought this a good idea as well, but before we had time to act Uncle Taylor was on the move. Very elaborately, as if he didn't want his feet to quite reach the shingle, he took the necessary steps to get him to the margin of the sea. Once there he poked the water with his foot, as though to see if it were awake. Then, all of a sudden, he strode in.

At least his *legs* strode, quite manfully. His top half swayed and waggled in protest. As he got a little deeper even his legs had to become more tentative, accommodating the larger rocks that lay below the tideline as one's jaws accommodate a large ungiving toffee. A water stain began to creep up his drawers, like ink up blotting-paper. His arms flapped in a vain attempt to fly away. Then he lurched forward, half falling half diving, and began to swim.

For a few moments he swam nicely. In fact from where we were lying on the ledge he looked like a stick-man in an illustration, demonstrating how-to-swim on a great silver page. He had obviously memorized his textbook well. But after a few strokes he slowed and then stopped. He floated face down in the water for a moment; I leapt off the ledge on to the beach and rushed towards the sea. As I crashed through the water towards him his arms and legs began to flail. He wasn't swimming this time, simply panicking.

Afterwards Harry asked me how I *knew*. He felt ashamed because he had not gone to the rescue himself. It was really almost a matter of etiquette: children *don't* go to the aid of adults. He assumed that Uncle Taylor was doing whatever he was doing in the water for reasons of his own. And of course he was correct. But the moment I saw Uncle Taylor stop moving his arms and legs I realized one important thing about that scene I'd witnessed in his bedroom. Arthur had been wrong. I had been wrong too.

Uncle Taylor had not been learning to swim; and his destination was not my mother.

The important part of the exercise had been the very part that had attracted my attention in the first place: his falling off the chairs. Uncle Taylor had been learning to *drown*. Dry.

I suppose the good weather of the previous summer had given him the idea. Limping along the shingle in the sunlight, staring at the blue sea, knowing that his ruse would shortly be discovered, that he would lose everything, his role in the mine, my mother, self-respect. But of course he wouldn't want to let himself drown, like an overlooked baby, in an inch or two of water. He would want to do it *properly*, in due order. First learn to swim.

I wasn't at all sure what to do when I got to him. I was a good swimmer myself, considering my age, but I'd never rescued anyone. He was scrabbling so hard at the water that it was difficult to tell whether he was trying to get in or out. Perhaps he didn't know himself. I grasped him by one white shoulder. His head flicked round, he saw me, and – I swear it – he blushed. His face was already red from the coldness of the water, but it went distinctly redder.

'Hello, Dot,' he gasped. He often called me Dot for some reason of his own.

I gave him a shorewards tug, and began to go under myself. Nevertheless it was enough to start him in the right direction, and I was able to let go and concentrate on keeping myself afloat.

'Well,' he said, as we stumbled back on shore, 'that was most refreshing, in its way.'

'It's very cold,' I said, shivering so much each word was shaken into its separate letters.

'I daresay. Perhaps a little early in the season. And Olive, I hope you don't mind my saying, but it's customary to take one's clothes off first.'

'I was rescuing you.'

'Oh, you needn't have bothered. It's just that I'm not quite up to the mark with *steering*. As I was swimming out I thought to myself, heavens, how does one go about swimming *in*? So it was very helpful of you. Most grateful.' He blushed again, at his fib.

Harry was standing nearby, following our conversation in astonishment. He looked as though he'd like to bolt for it at any moment. It was almost as though Uncle Taylor and I were adults together, talking over adult concerns, and he was still a child.

Of course Uncle Taylor didn't stay rescued for long. He left home shortly afterwards, and was never heard of again. (At least not until the Grandson hove into view.) He drowned in the world at large, which I suppose was the sort of drowning he was practised in. It's the way to drown *dry*, after all.

# Chapter 12

## Dot and Harry search for the Princess.
## Guess Who They find Instead?

Harry went off to look for his Princess. Dot went with him. Or rather, somewhat behind him. As you know, Harry was not so much a person, more a trick of the light; and light moves very fast, so it's hard to keep up!

First of all Harry went to see all the young ladies of the town. He thought one of them might be the Princess in disguise. It didn't matter if the young lady was fat or thin or pimply or squinty; it didn't even matter if the young lady was old. He knew the Princess had magic about her, so that her disguise would be very convincing. He tested all the young ladies alike.

Remember: the Princess had left something behind her when she vanished. Her handkerchief. It had fluttered out of her grasp at the very moment midnight struck.

You can't, of course, try a handkerchief on, as you can, say, a glass slipper. But you can blow your nose in it. So that's what Harry asked each young lady to do.

You would hardly believe some of the noises they made! There was one dear young lady with the tiniest nose you ever saw. When she inserted it in the handkerchief Dot expected a mouse-like squeak. Oh no. OOMPAH! It was a terrible noise, it nearly blasted your ears off. Another nose, confessedly a bigger one this time, went waaaaaaaaaAAAaaaaaaaaaa as if it was imitating a railway-train rushing past. Yet another made the noise you normally get by blowing through your lips and making them vibrate together: Blllllllllrrrr. There was one particularly ferocious-looking nose, and Dot waited in some trepidation for this one to have its turn. It was pock-marked and bristly and before it blew it rocked gently from one nostril to the other, as boxers on the television rock from foot to foot before they begin to fight. And when it finally blew! Well, if Dot had been wearing a wig it would have shot off her head. It sounded like the great complicated crash an orchestra often makes when it starts (or ends) something. In short, it blew a full chord.

There were of course more modest noses. One made delicate trickling sounds, like a mountain stream. Another plipped and plopped like a tap with a faulty washer. One ordinary-looking nose emitted a strange low-pitched hum.

Of course, people don't look at their most attractive when they are blowing their noses. And at the end of the process many of the noses in question were quite red and shiny. They *glared* at you, if you know what I mean. But between ourselves I'm not sure their owners minded. People don't *always* want to marry Prince Charming, you know, and in any case it wasn't Prince Charming, it was only Harry. And Harry didn't want to marry *them*, for that matter, unless they should turn out to be the Princess. He had never heard her blow *her* nose, but he knew he would recognize it. You can always tell when it's your beloved's nose. It would make a faint sibilant sound, like a breeze in an elm tree.

No such sound was forthcoming, and finally Harry had to conclude that none of the noses in the locality would fit his handkerchief. He would have to go further afield.

The first place to try was the sea.

All sorts of strange creatures live underwater, as you know: big ones, little ones, ugly ones and pretty ones (much as they do on land), and Harry thought it possible that the Princess was one of them. A mermaid, in other words. She'd been wearing a long ball-gown so there was no knowing whether the lower half of her was a fish or not. It's true that a pair of glass slippers peeped out from the bottom of her dress, but she could have been wearing those on her tail. Mermaids are supposed to be very beautiful and so was the Princess (though of course that may have been coincidence).

So off went Dot and Harry to the beach.

It was one of those silvery days when the sun never quite

breaks through the clouds, and even the shingle on the beach seems to glitter. Harry was silvery too, as he paced along by the silver lip of the sea. Then he stopped to gaze; and suddenly he danced into the water.

Harry swam beautifully. He was like a speck of light, a sparkle, upon the sleepy wavelets. He flickered and twinkled and flipped and glittered amongst the other points and prickles and slivers of light that played on the surface of that magic sea. It was delightful to watch him.

But after a while, Dot began to worry. She was finding it harder and harder to pick Harry out from the other specks, flecks, and beams with whom he was cavorting. In fact, she realized that at any moment he might become part of a general dazzle. Then she would have lost him, just as she had in the witch's wood.

There was nothing for it but to dive in herself.

Sploosh!

There is a moment before the sploosh, when you see the surface of the water at a crazy angle dropping down on you from what ought to be the sky. It's a long moment, and one has time to think about things like: will the water be cold? I wonder how deep it is? Did I remember to leave a note for the milkman? What Dot thought during that moment was: heavens, I've still got my clothes on.

She should have taken at least some of them off and left them on the beach. A vest and drawers would have been clothing enough to wear – the Atlantic Ocean is very informal. But when you're halfway to a sploosh you have to travel the other half. Passengers may not alight.

So sploosh! (See above.)

It wasn't the first time she'd found herself fully clothed in the drink, as you may remember. But it's one thing having a fish-pond on the wrong side of your dress; it's quite another to have the sea! However there was no point in worrying about it now; and Dot's mother loved mangling in any case.

Dot was an excellent swimmer, and soon she was far out in the water. In fact she had almost caught up with her brother when suddenly he seemed to flicker and go out.

He'd dived under the surface, of course, to seek his Princess.

Dot put her face to the water and watched.

207

It's another world down there. The air is delightfully thick, so that you can flap your fins and fly, and if you let yourself fall you fall so sleepily! Harry was drifting, like a feather wafting from side to side in a still room, down the long stairs of the ocean. Down and down he went until he was a little glimmering patch of light on the sea-bed. Immediately he started hurrying to and fro, in search of his beloved.

It was busy on the bottom, and noisy too. Some cheeky and unkempt sea-urchins rushed about, pulling each other's hair and squealing. A dogfish began to bark and chased a dear little catfish, who scuttled over the floor of the water (it's comforting, somehow, to remember that water always has a floor) until she came to a big sea-weed, which she began to climb. She sat in its branches, miaowing piteously. Each of her miaows was in a little bubble, as though she were a cat in a cartoon.

Not far off a group of fish and chips sat and read yesterday's newspapers. Some small tins of pilchards clunked about on the gravel. A watery-looking cod blew its nose quite hard (but not, I hasten to say, in the least like a Princess). In a quiet corner two or three goldfish were counting their treasure. Beyond that there was a table, at which some greedy jellyfish were gobbling jelly. There were other dishes set out too, in lovely shells; octopies, sea-cucumbers and sardines. Dot averted her gaze: the meal was too reminiscent of witch cuisine. The inhabitants of the sea came in all shapes and sizes: from shrimps and minnows and tiddlers, to something huge that was very like a whale. Most of the fish were neat and tidy, with a well-buttoned and waistcoated look about them. Above the throng flying fish flapped by. Higher still fluttered a few pious angel-fish. They were so near Dot she could hear the tiny music of their harps.

There were sea-people too, men and women with long green hair, eyes of pearl, bones of coral made, and big bulging handfuls of fish fingers. Some of them were galloping about on sea-horses. Others skated. A few squidged and slithered with soles tied to their feet instead of boots. They were as red as lobsters, and seemed distinctly crabby. None of them remotely resembled the Princess.

After this disappointment there was nothing for it but for

Harry to go to Africa. You are always hearing about princesses being discovered *there*.

Being in the African jungle is rather like being underwater, as a matter of fact. The canopy above you wobbles and sways, pierced by shafts of green misty light. Plants tangle. There are shadowy places with a faint glitter of eyes. But the noises are different. There are shrieks, trumpets and moans: insects zing and bumble. Some are so big they flap. Birds cry as if in pain.

Dot and Harry were paddled upriver in a canoe. Dot captured. Small tribal chieftain with speckled head and bone through his nose master of ceremonies.

'Tie her to poley.'

The tribe shuffle round with their cauliflower ears and whatnot, chanting, just like those beasts in the waiting-room who kept saying 'It is' at me. Poor Dot was frightened out of her wits.

Harry meanwhile had gone on up the river. He had been listening to rumours and intimations: a phrase muttered in tribal dialect, a little unaccountable remark throbbed from the distance on native drums, a pssst! here, and a say no more! there. He could pull what he needed to know out of the air, probably because he wasn't much more than air himself. And what these hints and innuendoes amounted to was that where the light was at its dimmest and most green, the screechings at their most hellish, where the plants slash like cutlasses or assegais, in the last hut at the furthest bend of the river, lived . . . a white princess! So off he went, in case she was *his* Princess.

But she wasn't. She wasn't a princess at all. In real life she was a nurse (so-called) who had escaped to Africa from a humble doctor's surgery in Shrewsbury. Her disguise was a grass skirt (and grass bodice), but she had forgotten to remove her lipstick. Though the natives wore war-paint, it was usually in tasteful colours: malarial white, yellowfever yellow, swamp green, despairing blue. But this nurse's lips were orange. They reminded one of the brickwork on cheap housing estates, of traffic lights changing; they weren't in the least *jungly*. Nor of course were they in the least like those of a real princess. Harry's Princess's lips were like a sweet rose-bud: indeed, when you looked at her you had the odd sensation that she

209

must have a mouth *inside* her mouth, out of which the rosebud was poking, and so on, I suppose, rosebud mouth within rosebud mouth, like a factory line of sweetly smiling dolls. I am afraid that the nurse's mouth was a long way from being a rosebud.

Just to make sure, Harry put a pea on her seat at the very moment the nurse sat herself down. Needless to say she didn't notice a thing (and when she got up again the pea was squashed flat). Harry didn't even *bother* to ask her to blow her nose. It wasn't worth the trouble.

But his visit wasn't entirely wasted. It turned out that Speckledy's tribe worshipped the nurse as a goddess. She was the first white person they'd ever seen. When Dot had come along, she was the second (or rather, the second-and-a-halfth, since she was sitting behind Harry in the canoe. Harry was white enough, but he wasn't properly a person). So naturally Speckledy and the other tribal elders had calculated that the white goddess would like to have Dot as a sort of present. The way you send gods presents, at least when you (and they) live in the African jungle, is by sacrifice. There is no postal service apparently. You set fire to the person, animal or goods, and convert whoever or whatever it is to smoke. The smoke wafts to the god's abode. It's really, I suppose, like a primitive form of television transmission. Perhaps the god has a sort of box in his or her dwelling-place, with which to convert the smoke back into a person again. The nurse needless to say had no such box, but luckily Harry was able to persuade her to go over to Speckledy's tribe and tell them she'd collect the victim in person.

When they arrived poor Dot was in a fix! She was still tied to poley, as it was called in Speckledy's pidgin English, but now a heap of brushwood had been placed at her feet. It was getting to be horribly like that business in the witch's cottage, but without the advantage of a modern oven. All Dot could see were the villagers shuffling around her pyre in a cloud of dust their feet had kicked up. They looked horribly ugly, as people do when they are going to kill you. Occasionally she could glimpse Speckledy through the fog, clutching a burning brand. He was still muttering things that end in y.

Then Dot looked down and to her horror she saw a little

yellow flame licking up through the brushwood. The torch must have been applied already! The dreaded cookery had begun.

The flame rose higher and higher until it was standing side by side with Dot. But it wasn't hot at all, it was just pleasantly warm. Perhaps being burned to death isn't as bad as you might imagine, Dot thought: possibly it's received a lot of unfavourable publicity. If it *is* as bad as you imagine, how on earth are those it happens to able to *bear* it? Wouldn't it be nice if each of the people who has ever been afire at the stake felt they were in the middle of a golden rose!

Dot's rose, as a matter of fact, had only one petal. Then of course she understood that it was not a flame at all, it was Harry!

'It's all right, Dot,' Harry said. 'Nurse has come to the rescue.'

And sure enough, beyond the natives, through the blur of scudded dust, there was the nurse, whispering in Speckledy's ear; and Speckledy's head was nodding sagely up and down, as though the bone through his nose were writing a succession of ticks. And before she knew what was happening the shuffling tribesmen had shuffled off, a little ladder had been placed in position, and Speckledy and the nurse were helping her down off poley.

She was rather stiff. You'd be a little stiff if you'd been left bound to a stake for an hour or two, even if, like Dot, you were lucky enough not to be set ablaze.

'Aaagh!' she cried, as her creaky legs found the ladder.

'Ooopsy,' said Speckledy, on her behalf.

Dot and Harry wondered where to go next. They'd been round the houses of the young ladies who lived in their village; they'd explored the kingdom under the sea; and they'd travelled to Darkest Africa. These were all *real* places, even if some of them were a bit unlikely. Perhaps it was time to go somewhere UNREAL for a change. After all, if a princess vanishes at midnight it seems very possible that the place she has vanished *to* is not a real place at all.

They decided to return to the wood under the dining-room table.

You can imagine how frightened they felt, as they walked

between those upright, wooden trees. It was all so different from the African jungle, so still, and regular, and empty. Naturally the memory of their captivity in the witch's cottage weighed on their minds, with those endless, terrible meals, and Dot could not shake out of her head the image of the witch cooking in her own oven, with her mouth open to speak or shout and her teeth melting into long soft points like cooking toffee. It was a relief to arrive at the tree of light and bask in its warmth for a while.

But when they left its shelter the wood seemed even worse, as it had for Dot the last time she ventured beyond the tree. Once again she had the sense of recently stifled movement, of sounds that had just that moment dissolved into the chilly, still air, of eyes that you could not see. And once again the cottage came as a surprise, even though she was expecting it.

It looked exactly as it had before, and yet it looked completely different. You know how you feel when you are very hungry and you are presented with a delicious meal, with all the things you like best, roast this, baked that, boiled something else, plus all the trimmings. And you know too how it is when you are feeling very full and slightly sick and you are presented with that self-same meal? Well, that was the sort of change that had or rather hadn't occurred with the witch's cottage.

The red roof looked like clotted blood.

The white walls were like frozen snow.

The green shutters were the colour of slime.

The black windows were like dead eyes.

The blue roses looked furious.

The glass flowers were sharp as razors.

The yellow of the yellow knocker was vile.

The cottage was deserted, thank goodness. Nevertheless, Dot and Harry crept quietly round it, just in case you could indeed wake the dead, despite what people said. Then they continued onwards, into a part of the wood they hadn't explored last time.

As they left the cottage behind them their spirits lifted, and so, they realized, did the light. Gradually its colour shifted from the grey-mauve of Sunday afternoons, to grey-blue, to blue-blue to yellow-blue to yellow-green, and before they knew what had happened, Dot and Harry found themselves

212

walking the sun-flecked paths of a woodland glade. As soon as
she understood this, Dot understood something else too. The
trees were no longer severe and rectoid. They were bulbous and
grainy and twisted; their leaves glowed and sparkled and celeb-
rated the air. They were like *real* trees; or to put it another
way, they were very unlike the legs of a dining-room suite.

'Perhaps they were seeded by the great tree of light,'
suggested Dot.

'Perhaps they were,' agreed Harry.

It was strange to think of the tree's small bright seeds, its
sparks, drifting on their own breeze through the still and
breezeless woods, until at last they'd found some open soil in
which to grow.

Dot and Harry found it delightful to walk between these
trees. They were so human after the miserable-looking ones
in the witch's part of the wood. Their faces didn't look as if
they'd been squashed in a mangle: you know, the way maths
mistresses' faces look when you can't do a sum. And their big
knobby arms almost came down to give you a hug.

After a while those nice trees became more widely scattered
and Dot and Harry found themselves in a gently sloping pas-
ture. A herd of naughts were grazing peacefully here: huge
juicy ones, far bigger than Uncle Taylor's, for this was the
sort of place where naughts and other aery animals of that sort
thrive. It occurred to Dot to take a good look at Harry and
sure enough he'd become much more solid again, almost as
he had been in the witch's cottage.

The meadow led down to a little river, with a wooden
bridge over it, and beyond that was another field, in the middle
of which stood a tall, rather crumbling, tower. It was exactly
the sort of tower in which you would imprison a princess if
you had one on your hands and didn't know what else to do
with her. In fact even from where they were standing Dot
and Harry thought they could make out a blonde glitter drifting from the window, as if fine-spun hair were catching the
sunshine while it folded and refolded on the breeze.

Harry pointed excitedly.

'Come on, then!' cried Dot, and rushed down the grassy
slope towards the bridge.

Bonk bonk bonk went her feet on the planking. Then suddenly, over the edge of the bridge, poked a nose. Poked two noses, in fact.

'Ooo's that knockin' on moy bridge?' a beastly voice said. 'You'll knock down the 'ole 'arse.'

It was the brother of that nasty troll who guarded the Christmas-tree at the Princess's ball. But this one guarded the bridge, which he regarded as the roof of his house. He had a horrible life, which suited him. It's one thing living underwater altogether, as fishes do, and other sea-people; it's quite another living half-in, half-out, like this troll. His armchairs always had a puddle in the middle of them, so that you got a cold slithery feeling when you sat down. His cooker was always going out. His slippers went slip slop as he walked. His life was untidy and damp, and it's not surprising that he had a very bad temper indeed. He glared at poor Dot, who scuttled back to the meadow.

'What can we do?' she asked Harry. 'I'm sure he'll eat us.'

'You always think people want to eat you,' Harry replied unconcernedly. 'I'll go first if you like.'

And with that he skipped on to the bridge.

'Fee fi fo fum,' said the troll. 'I smell the blood of an Englishman. No, I don't,' he went on, sniffing Harry with his other nose. 'This boy an't got no blood at all, as far as I can make art. Blow me.'

And while the troll was still scratching his big damp silly head, Harry tootled carelessly across the bridge and on to the field on the other side. And while the troll was *still* scratching that same big damp silly head, Dot trotted rapidly across the bridge to join him.

'Now *she's* give me the slip,' the troll said. 'Watch her go.' As he stared he reflectively picked all his four nostrils at once. Then he went back down under the bridge to eat a horribly wet egg sandwich.

Dot and Harry continued across the field to the tower. When they arrived they realized that what they'd seen hadn't been blonde hair at the window but merely the yellow reflection of the sun on the pane. Nevertheless the tower still looked promising enough. There was no door, for a start, and the one window must have been twenty feet off the ground. The stonework was grey and grim and mossy.

'Princess, Princess,' called Harry, 'let down your hair.'

There was a pause.

Slowly the window slid up. It wasn't possible, from where Dot and Harry stood, to see who was inside. But suddenly a great black stream of hair began to descend the tower wall. It flowed around the outcropping stonework like a night-time river: and as its moving surfaces caught the sun it almost seemed to sparkle like running water.

'But Harry!' cried Dot, as she saw her brother run towards it with his arms outstretched. 'It's black!'

For a moment Harry was stopped in his tracks. Then he said: 'Perhaps it's a wig. Her hair wasn't this long anyway. Or she may have dyed it.'

And with no more to-do he clutched hold of a handful of the dangling hair, and began to climb. Dot was still worried. The hair looked unpleasantly familiar, but she didn't want to be left behind in the field, so she grasped it in turn, and like a pair of salmon the two children climbed the great black waterfall towards the window at the top.

It's a horrible swaying sensation, wending your way up crumbling towers by means of tufts of hair, and you keep wondering if it's not going to pop pop pop out by the roots. But at last Harry arrived at the top, with Dot close on his heels.

She glanced down at the field sloping towards the stream. There was no sign of the troll on the bridge. Hopefully he was snoozing in his wet armchair. Beyond in the meadow grazed the naughts, quite tiny from here. The hair blew in the breeze and the whole landscape moved round. Oh dear! Dot turned back, just in time to see a face appear at the window.

It was a grinning toothless face with cunning eyes, hanging like a balloon against the dimness of the room behind.

It was the witch.

She had lost her teeth of course – Dot had seen them melt. And she had grown old, as though the oven in which she'd been baked had been the oven of time. Perhaps her hair wasn't real: it ought to be shrivelled or at least grey to match the rest of her. On the other hand she did look wicked enough to have the blackness of night streaming from her brain, as her hair streamed from her head, so who knows?

'Welcome,' the witch said, in a cracked old voice. She

reached out her claw-like hands to grab Harry. But at that moment, to her great and immediate fury, Harry let go of her hair. All Dot saw was the flash of his pale form in the air like the flash of a white bird's wing, and he was gone, far far away, in search of his lost Princess.

'Oh well,' said the witch grumpily, turning her attention to Dot, 'she will have to do instead, one supposes.'

# Chapter 13
## Kissing Goodbye

My mother regarded me in the same light: I would *have to do instead*. I suppose that's not the sort of thing a dutiful daughter should think. I could write: my mother was more loving towards me over the next few years. But that isn't how I thought about it, even at the time. I thought, now Uncle Taylor's gone she has to make do with me. There was my brother Harry too of course, but somehow he always seemed to be minding his own business. Perhaps he was serving a sort of apprenticeship – the dead have to be proficient at minding their own business. My mother would often take me in her arms in those days, and though this was something I can even now remember wanting when I was small, I no longer wanted it then. In fact, her embraces frightened me. She seemed voluminous, oppressive. There was an insistent blindness in her movements, as if she were forcing herself to mistake me for Uncle Taylor. I wanted to struggle to escape like a small animal in a trap but I didn't dare. I had to concede her caresses.

Part of the trouble was that she was growing ugly. Poor, poor woman, she was being baked in the oven of disease. I don't believe she grew fatter but her flesh somehow became more loose, which gave you the impression, when she was hugging, that it was attacking you from all sides.

Hark! Or rather look! At who is talking. But I don't embrace people, there is that to say in my defence. And of course my wretched physique has taken a lifetime to reach this point. My body crept up on me, as it were (except those aspects which *popped forth*). In my mother's case the transformation took perhaps two years. Her person transmogrified from generosity to redundancy. In my heart of hearts I feared I was responsible for the alteration. I had been privy to her secrets: I had watched her and Uncle Taylor upon the bedroom floor. Perhaps I recoiled inwardly from her love because I knew I didn't deserve it. It's hard to analyse your own recoil, you're facing in the wrong direction.

Naturally, my mother began to drink more than ever. The habit was still furtive but it was no longer fun. When she sang she sang in a strident, aggressive voice. The household staff had orders to confiscate her bottles, but she always seemed to be able to lay claim to a fresh one, pulling it out of her sleeve like a cunning but incoherent magician. What I remember most about that time, however, is the way she would sit still for hours at a stretch, her head resting in her hands as if it were too heavy to support itself.

Finally, she was sent away on a 'cure'.

I don't know how long she was gone. Children aren't very good at measuring time. When she came back everything was different. She had lost weight; indeed, had become painfully thin. She no longer seemed subversive – no, that's not the word, she no longer seemed *naughty*. She was quiet, brave, adult. My father treated her with tenderness now. I don't know how he'd treated her before but it hadn't exactly been with tenderness. I think he'd been decent enough, but he'd averted his gaze when he could. He'd stared at the fire. Now he behaved as if she were precious but inaccessible. I can see him, in my mind's eye, stroking her hair, her shoulder, but doing so as if he could never quite reach her. He told me years later, in Shrewsbury, that a growth on the brain had been diagnosed while she was on the 'cure'. Her alcoholism had not been an illness in its own right but a desperate attempt to escape from an enemy which must have seemed to have established a stronghold at the very centre of her being. Nothing one makes up could be as frightening and horrible as that. Books, no matter how hard one tries, even children's books, fall short of the terrors of life.

She grew worse and worse. It wasn't so much that her behaviour became erratic, as that for long periods she ceased to behave altogether. When she felt animated, she would hide: crouch in cupboards, steal away to the greenhouse or the vegetable garden, sometimes even wander away down the

218

country lanes; anywhere to escape the pursuit of that horde of rogue cells. Occasionally, when the trouble eased, she mangled, as in the old days. But for much of the time she was still. Her speech was always slurred; her voice went quieter and quieter, as if she had a perpetual sore throat. Her eyes became wild. Her hands developed a tremor. Her complexion became blotchy. At last she was taken away to hospital.

Before she went she asked to see Harry and me. We went nervously up to her bedroom, as if we were going to a headmistress's study. We went in one at a time, Harry first. I suppose her horizons had diminished to the extent that she could only cope with her experiences in turn. Harry and I hadn't been told what was wrong with her. I don't think, however, that we still attributed her illness to the demon drink. We knew that it was simply a demon.

Harry walked stiffly, schoolboyishly, in, to his first introduction to death.

When he came out he was transformed. Tears were streaming down his cheeks. I thought: how odd. When a child goes into his mother's bedroom he normally comes out with his hair brushed, though ours had never been that sort of mother to any great degree. Anyhow, it was my turn.

Mother looked dreadful, frightening. She stiffly peered at me without raising her head, as though there were something wrong with her neck. When her hand came towards me, with the rest of her motionless, it was as though it came of its own volition. It resembled a claw.

She drew me towards her. When she spoke her adam's apple moved disproportionately. Her voice was weak and fragmenting; there was something terribly wrong with her mouth.

'Olive,' she said. 'I've got to go away again for a time. While I'm gone, I want you to remember something.' Her eyes, in contrast with her voice, were steady and firm, though there were little exposed veins in the whites, like tiny red worms. She went on, in her dreadful croaking whisper: 'You'll become a very boring person if you're always as good as gold.'

I looked down at her, puzzled, trying to understand what she meant. When you are a child, it doesn't occur to you what *kind* of a child you are. You are simply you. Certainly it hadn't crossed my mind that I might be *good*.

219

The claw pulled me closer. We were almost head to head. I waited for her to say something more but she didn't, and finally I realized I was expected to kiss her. I did so. It was a horrid kiss, like losing your footing. Her soft lips seemed to absorb and contain mine. I tried to pull away but found they resisted. It was like trying to pull your foot off the plughole in the bath when it won't come. I made a little squeak and pulled harder, trembling with revulsion. Finally I came free. Her eyes looked at me coolly, appraisingly. I could have wept. I felt as if I'd failed some test. I wanted to kiss her again, to prove I could. Was that what she meant, with her warning against being as 'good as gold'? To kiss, no matter how far down it seemed to take you, no matter how like quicksand it felt, no matter how much your lips were swamped? To surrender to a kiss?

I don't know, I didn't have the chance to find out. I never kissed her again. But if I put my mind to it I can feel that horrid sucking kiss on my lips to this day. It was only later that it crossed my mind that she hadn't been wearing teeth.

It came as no surprise that the Great War broke out within a year or two of my mother's death. Things had inevitably wound down to that point.

I took refuge in my friendship with Anne. We were inseparable in those early days of the war, moony girls. We would talk for hour after hour. Girls of fourteen and fifteen at that time had very little hold on the world, or worlds, belonging to the rest of society. They were neither children nor adults. There was no group to whom their opinions and feelings really mattered. I suppose this difficulty has been eased a little since the invention of the teenager. But in those days Anne and I had to convince each other of our importance, which we did to our mutual satisfaction. Harry was away at school. He would come home each vacation looking much taller and older than before; and make Anne and me realize we were taller and older too, as though he were a walking calendar. His principal friendships were elsewhere, of course, which ironically meant that he was more visible in the household during his holidays than he had ever been when a child. The only young man he went about with locally was a farmer's son called Robert, a slow-talking red-faced lad who seems to me now to belong to a different historical period from the rest of us, a time when you could talk about peasants and yeomen and so forth.

There came a period when Harry began to associate with Anne and myself also. He would knock on my door on the pretext of looking for a book (he never seemed embarrassed at repeating the same excuse, just as, when he was little, he would always claim he needed to go to the lavatory when he tired of the games we played together). I remember him standing in my bedroom by the little fire, sheepish but obstinate, while Anne and I sat side by side on the bed, arrested in mid-flow and baffled as to what to talk to him about. It's dreadfully hard to have to switch from pubescent babble to a considered conversation with a member of the opposite sex, even when the one in question is your own brother. I suppose the problem was that he didn't feel like my brother any more. There was too much of the young man about him, and a foreignness in his behaviour which derived, I imagine, from being at boarding school. Anne and I resented his incursions but were oddly thrilled by them at the same time – his presence made us see ourselves in a new light.

One day, early in 1916, Anne and I were sitting in my bedroom as usual. Outside it was a bleak January morning, with the lawns nipped white and the bare trees very black against the puddingy sky. But I'd poked up the little fire the general had made, and it was flaming cheerfully. I can remember thinking how cosy we were, even if there was a war on somewhere. Also we were having an interesting conversation. I was telling Anne that Robert had come round the night before, to take his leave of Harry and the rest of us. He was going off to the front.

'It was terribly sad,' I said gleefully, 'terribly terribly sad.'

'Was it?' asked Anne.

'Terribly. Horridly. I couldn't help thinking, I couldn't stop myself. You know.'

'What?'

'That perhaps we'd never see him again in this world. That he might get killed at the front, once and for all.'

'Lordy,' whispered Anne.

'I'm sure he'll be very very brave. He's always been a very brave sort of boy. Do you remember those boys at Miss Bowker's? That beastly crowd? Tad and Bowman?'

221

'Oh yes,' said Anne, pleased to reminisce. 'Tad, Bowman and the Terror.'

'And Pig,' I said.

'Yes. Poor little Pig used to tag on with them.'

'Robert rescued me once, when I fell into their clutches. He just waded in and rescued me. He had to fight them all at once. That's what I'm afraid of. I'm afraid he'll do something fearfully brave at the front and get himself killed for his pains.'

'Yes,' said Anne. We both thought about it, luxuriously.

'Pig's dead,' Anne said suddenly.

'Is he?' I asked, shocked.

'I saw it in the newspaper.'

'Heavens,' I said. For a moment the mood was broken. Then I intoned, in a deep portentous voice: 'The Pig is Dead.' We both squealed with laughter.

'Not like that, silly!' gasped Anne.

'No,' I agreed, ' "It is with deep regret that we announce the death of Private Pig, of the Porker Fusiliers." '

'Poor Private Pig,' Anne said.

'It is the Pig's lot,' I pointed out.

'His name was Prescott.'

'I know. Pig Prescott. To his friends.'

'Oh Olive. Anyway, you're *try*-ing to change the subject. Which was Robert. And his bravery.'

'I don't suppose Pig was very brave,' I said.

'That is *not* the point. What you must tell me is: whether or not?'

'Whether or not what?'

'Olive, do not pretend you don't know.'

'But I don't know.'

'Whether or not you kissed him farewell, silly!'

I looked at Anne in astonishment, my face glowing. Anne looked back at me, in equal astonishment. 'You didn't know, did you?' she asked finally.

'I do not know *what* you are talking about, *Miss* Anne.'

'Tee hee,' Anne said. 'She didn't know.'

'I certainly did not. And nor did Robert, I'm quite sure. And if we didn't know, who did?'

'I did,' Anne replied, perfectly unruffled. 'Why do you think he's been round here so often?'

222

'To see Harry, of course. Harry is his friend, if you haven't realized.'

'Olive, dear, I've watched him go quite spoony while he looked at you. And oh, those eyes. He has lovely eyes. So *big*.'

'Moo-cow's eyes,' I explained.

'Misting over as he gazes at his beloved. Oh Olive, you should have given him a little kiss.'

'Oh yes,' I said, 'with my father in the room, and Harry. "Goodbye lad," says Father, giving him a manly handshake. "Good luck." "Here's a big smacking kiss," says daughter. "I'll shoot the scoundrel," says Harry. And a wonderful evening was had by all.'

'What you should have done,' said Anne, quite po-faced despite my frivolity, 'was say you needed some air, and would walk down the driveway with him. Then by the gate he could have put his arms round you and done the deed. His face would have descended on your face like the moon.'

'The moon does *not* descend on people's faces.'

'Robert's face would,' she said breathily.

'I really find this conversation perfectly beastly. And extraordinarily boring.'

'I think a soldier is entitled to a girl's kiss before he goes off to die in battle.'

'He is not going to die.'

'You said he would.'

'I said he *might*. And that was before we got on to the subject of kissing. Now I think he *won't*, if you must know.'

There was a knock on the door, and in came Harry.

'What book do you want to borrow this time?' I asked, rather tartly.

'I just wanted a bit of a chinwag,' Harry said. 'I went off for a walk, but it's rotten out. Cold as charity. Hello, Anne. I didn't know you were here.' He went over to my fire and warmed his hands. 'I keep thinking about Robert, on his way. Lucky devil.' He didn't sound sincere, and after a pause he said, 'I've been meaning to say, did you know old Pig Prescott bought it?'

'We were just talking about him,' said Anne.

'I don't know why I said old,' Harry said. 'He was a year younger than me.'

223

'But that's different,' I put in. 'He left school when he was fourteen. You don't leave till the summer.'

'What difference does that make?'

'All the difference in the world. Heavens, Harry, you're still at *school*. You will be till the *summer*. And then there's the mine. The country has got to have tin. Father will need you. With Arthur gone it's all he can do to manage.'

'There you are,' said Harry. 'If Arthur can go –'

'Excuse me a moment,' I said impatiently, and left the room. It was an argument I'd had with Harry before, and in any case I wanted to use the lavatory. I must have come back more quickly than they anticipated. When I pushed open my door, I saw Harry and Anne standing together in front of the fireplace. She was folded in his arms and he was kissing her deeply, deeply.

I tiptoed away, across the landing, down the stairs, into the sea of cabbage at the bottom, along the hall, through the front door and round the side of the house to the back garden. I hardly breathed, I was so scared of being seen – as if it had been me doing something furtive. I always seemed to be the catcher, never the caught. I scurried across the frosty lawns towards the vegetable garden.

I pushed open the creaky door. Here, as always, the sun was shining, a winter sun, of course, but that only made it all the whiter. The frosty green eyeballs of Brussels sprouts glittered in its light. The winter cabbages bloomed like sturdy blue roses. Our cat dozed on the soil. She had one eye open, as though absent-mindedly, to check on intruders and spot arriving birds. Luckily Mr Tremaine must have been pointing his pointed buttocks to the sky in some other part of the gardens, or perhaps he was having his cup of tea with Cook. I leaned against the door and tried to collect my wits.

I don't know how long I stood there. Long enough to become very bored. I'm always impressed when people explain to me that they've been thinking about their lives, because when I try to do the same I invariably find I have only one thought in my head. It's as ungiving and immovable as if it were a wardrobe that had been placed there. In this case the thought was: Anne isn't my friend, she's Harry's sweetheart.

She couldn't be both at once, it seemed to me, because she'd not confided in me about her feelings for Harry. Her behaviour had been deceptive, horrid: letting him kiss her while I was in the lavatory.

One can imagine that an hour or two of coping with that one thought is not likely to hone the mind. I was sedentary standing up, like the vegetables whose garden it was. They only had one thought too. Each Brussels sprout thought: I am a brussels sprout; and because it could think nothing else, a brussels sprout it remained. Thus we create our own heaven or hell or sprouthood. And the winter cabbage said to itself: I am a winter cabbage. And Olive: I am a girl whose best friend has been stolen by her brother. Whose brother has been stolen by her best friend. Whose best friend loves her brother instead. I was jealous, and jealousy was all there was of me.

At last, cold and bored, I trudged back to my room. Harry was lounging in my easy-chair by the fire, reading one of my books.

'Where on earth did you get to?' he asked peevishly. 'You went off to the toilet, I *presume*, and never came back.'

'Where's Anne?'

'She must have become tired of waiting. She went home. You look perished.'

'I went out for some fresh air.'

'Come to the fire and warm yourself.'

The switch to solicitude disarmed me completely. He sounded so like a *brother*. I suddenly wanted to weep.

'I've been waiting for you because I wanted to ask your advice,' he went on.

'Yes?' I asked, my heart sinking again. It's about Anne, I thought.

'Olive, I've decided to sign up. Leave school. Just go. This war's been going on for a year and a half now, it's about time.'

I was thrown into inner turmoil. 'I see,' I said cautiously. 'You don't seem to need my advice, from what you say.' I gazed down at him on my chair. He was rumpling his hair, his forehead screwed up almost testily. His legs were ridiculously lanky and long, like a spider's.

'I want to know,' he said, 'whether I'm being silly.'

Suddenly I remembered Anne's words: I think a soldier is entitled to a girl's kiss before he goes off to die in battle. And as I remembered a great wave of relief swept over me. Yes, I must write it down. I must have it in black and white. Or blue and white as it happens. Black and blue would probably be more appropriate. As I remembered, I suddenly felt *joy*. I was a child (because in my own defence I *was* still a child, not quite sixteen) who was used to loss, and this suddenly felt like pure gain. Anne had been doing no more than simply giving Harry his going-to-war kiss.

I felt as though I had been given back my best friend, and my brother.

I must repeat. My mother was dead. My father was a very small, nay, diminutive, giant. I felt the need to cling on to what I had.

'You're not being silly,' I said. 'There's nothing silly about going to war.'

I was a writer already. I took refuge in playing with words.

I went with Harry to Plymouth station. Mr Tremaine drove us in Arthur's lovely yellow motorcar. Father didn't come. He and Harry had had a terrible row. I had heard their colliding voices just as, many years previously, I'd heard my father's bitter harangue to Uncle Taylor, and Uncle Taylor's responding squawks. When I say heard, of course, I mean heard the sounds. I was in my bedroom once again, and couldn't pick up the individual words. Nor did I want to; I already felt I had implicated myself enough. I should have told him NO, I kept thinking to myself. I should have said you mustn't mustn't mustn't mustn't go to war. I knew what that war was like, we all did. The trenches were the bowges of hell. He'd said he needed my advice: that's what my advice should have been. It might just have been possible to convince him then. It was too late now, I knew that. Harry had always been one for going his own way.

We said very little on the drive. I sat, trying to marshal my teeming thoughts. There was so much I wanted to tell him, but whenever I got to the verge of utterance a dreadful inertia would develop, as though my words had stumbled into mud, and could go no further. I wanted to tell him not to die. I wanted to tell him that despite that sensation of relief I'd experienced when he told me of his plans, I didn't really want

226

him to go to war. Above all, I wanted to tell him that if my friend Anne meant so much to him I would relinquish her. There was no need to go all the way to the front and do battle. But I said none of it. Harry kept singing some little song, half under his breath, which grated on my nerves, a tuneless evocation of a tune. Even at the time the thought went through my head that it was his swansong.

Dot knew that Harry would come back; to rescue her and to seek his Princess. The witch knew also, and began her preparations. Soon the gentle meadow that sloped down to the river had become a battlefield, complete with a mighty army. Everything that had a little magic in it was under the witch's command. Let us watch her troops as they march to the front.

Well, Brussels sprouts don't exactly march: they roll. They rolled to various hidey-holes, under hedges, on the river bank, behind trees, from which they peeped out with their little green eyes. They were the witch's spies.

Here comes the Boiled Egg, and his squadron of soldiers. How like a general he is, so important and well-fed! His soldiers, as befits mere privates, are spindly and weak at the knee. I'm afraid to say they even appear to be a little bit yellow. Their names are Tad, Bowman, Terror, and Pig. If you remember, we've met them before.

Now, what next? Do you see those giants? You might not, unless your eyes are as big as saucers. They are very hard to fit in. As a matter of fact the giants have a dog of their own with eyes as big as saucers. There it is, snapping around their ankles.

Flobber flobber flobber.

That's a funny noise! What on earth can be making it? Oh my goodness, look! The toads have crept out of the toad-bowls, and are following the giants. They flobber as they walk with their fat damp flabby feet. In fact they are so fat they look as if they could explode at any moment. When a battle has been going for some time there's a lot of mud about, and plenty of dank holes, so a battlefield's a place well-suited to toads. The troll will be quite at home too: he is used to sludge and wet and goo. He's over guarding his bridge, as usual, his noses quivering for the first whiff of approaching Englishmen.

And now something very horrible indeed is coming this way. It's the Knocker! As you will remember, this ghastly creature lives in the depths of tin-mines on a somewhat restricted diet of Cornish pasty corners; varied only by the occasional miner. I can't describe what he looks like because since he is never seen he doesn't look like anything. And don't tell me that since he is being seen *now* he must look like something. The point is, he wasn't seen, and didn't look like, *before*, and he hasn't changed in the meantime. Indeed I'm not sure he *is* a he. Insofar as he's like anything, he's more like an It.

And now the battlefield is filling with troops so fast that my writing and your reading won't be able to keep up. That Knocker creature has dragged along the tin-mine's Man Engine with him. He thinks it's a wonderful device, a contribution to eating convenience on a par with the fish-finger and the sliced loaf. He winds the handle. Out pops a man. Again: another. On and on. The field is filling up.

And to make matters worse, the witch has herded all the naughts from the far meadow beyond the stream to her battlefield. And every time a naught ambles towards one of the witch's troops, hey presto!, there are ten men where one had stood before. Or ten creatures. Or ten things.

As she watched the grazing naughts from her prison in the tower, a horrid thought came into Dot's mind. Perhaps, before long, people would start dying on this battlefield. And when a naught chanced to approach a corpse, hey presto!, ten corpses would appear. Dot remembered how the naughts had begun to multiply out of control when she and Harry had tried to play naughts and crosses at Uncle Taylor's farm. But the field below the tower wasn't a field for growing crops, it was a field for growing dead bodies. It was a battlefield. Here everything would be horribly topsy-turvy. The naughts would make the *crosses* multiply out of control.

Choo! choo! Dear me, what next? Gracious, winding over the landscape was a railway train. Choo! choo! it went. It was a very long train. It had come from its depot on Uncle Taylor's numbers farm. Do you remember it? Dot and Harry played on it once. It was train number

228

Now of course, the train wasn't carrying children, it was full of troops. Though, sad to say, it is sometimes very hard to tell the difference.

Dot realized that however brave Harry might be, however agile, indeed, however *invisible*, he would never survive if he pitted himself against the witch's terrible army. There were so many people to shoot at him that somebody would be bound to hit, even if they weren't aiming at *anything*. Wars are so big nowadays that you don't have to aim any longer. You just kill in a general way.

Harry must be stopped from coming at all costs. One way that would stop him would be to convince him that his Princess was to be found elsewhere. If only Dot knew where, though, so she could send him off in the right direction! Then, at last, he might have the chance to live happily ever after.

Just as she thought that thought, Dot had an inspiration. She found herself remembering the Princess's palace again, perhaps because it is always in palaces that people live happily ever after, lucky things. But of course the Princess's palace wasn't a *posh* palace. Indeed it was rather a humble palace. It was a palace where the butler was required to put a lick of paint on the ballroom doors before the guests arrived. And if a court is short of money what is the most sensible thing to economize on? Why, princesses, of course. Nothing and nobody is a bigger drain on a palace's resources than a princess. And it's not as if you can ask them to double up as painters and decorators, as you can do with butlers, even grumpy ones. Princesses are well known for being hopeless at doing *any*thing except being princesses. I once watched a princess trying to make a cup of tea, and you ought to have seen the mess she made of it. She couldn't find the tea. She couldn't find the teapot. She declared that the water had gone rancid. She didn't bring the water to the boil. She poured the tea out before it had had time to sit. She was quite hopeless. Between you and me I think people like that are more trouble than they are worth. But of course *we* can't look at a princess with the eyes of True Love, as Harry did.

But if you can't afford to have a princess around the palace for twenty-four hours a day, eating chocolates, buying jewels,

229

blowing her nose musically in a lace handkerchief, and if you know that she'd be a terror with a paintbrush or a steaming kettle in her hand, then the only solution is to switch her off for part of the time, as you switch off the light when you're leaving a room. In other words, turn her into a *part-time* princess. Have her on duty from, say, twelve noon to midnight (princesses are rarely available before twelve noon in any case). Surely that was the most likely explanation for her disappearance during the Christmas Eve Ball? It had happened at exactly midnight, after all.

This would explain why Harry could not find his heart's desire under the sea, or in the African jungle. His heart's desire was exactly where he had discovered it in the first place. She was still at home.

If Harry could be told all this, it would prevent him from going to war, and the certainty of being killed. But how could Dot tell him?

There was no telephone in the witch's tower, naturally. There wasn't even any writing paper. Dot searched frantically for something to write on but to no avail. And then it occurred to her that she did have one white thing: the handkerchief. She had been the one to carry it during the hunt for the Princess. (Invisible people tend to draw attention to themselves if they try to carry things.)

There were of course no pens or pencils in the witch's tower, to match the absence of writing paper. There were things to prick yourself with, though, like nails, hatpins, thorns, and so forth, so Dot decided to write her letter in blood. That at least would suggest that what she had to say came straight from the heart.

It took a long time. Writing in blood is far from easy, and there was a lot to say. Dot's finger was like a leaky pen, and her blood kept blotting and clotting and smearing on the handkerchief. But the message was clear enough: don't do battle for your Princess, she's been at home all along. Poor Dot. Writing that message was rather noble of her, don't you think?

Dot took the handkerchief to the window of her tower. Down below, the witch's army was still assembling itself: nasty things were scurrying this way and that, monotonous rows of men were marching into position like mechanical dolls. The witch stood just outside her tower. Her black hair streamed in the breeze as though night-time had chosen to break out exactly where she stood.

Dot opened the window and held the handkerchief in the air. It flapped like a flag. She brought it back in and blew her nose in it one last time, by way of farewell. Then she held it in the air again. It flapped, as if it was saying farewell too. Then she let go, and watched it float away on the light blue breeze. It would scurry through the sky until it reached her brother, she knew. He wasn't magic like the witch, but he was magic enough for *that*.

When her handkerchief was out of sight, Dot felt she had lost her final contact with her previous world. She wept.

The station was milling with men in uniform, going off to rejoin their regiments. Harry's civilian clothes made him look like a little boy on the first day of school.

'There's no need for you to wait, Sis,' he said. 'There's nothing worse than hanging about on a railway station.'

'All right,' I said.

He gave me a quick kiss on the cheek. I wanted to say something about Anne but I could not. I felt I needed to blow my nose and took out my handkerchief, but as I raised it to my face I realized that it was the lacy handkerchief Anne had given me at her Christmas party, years before.

Harry had been following my actions, amusedly.

'That's not much use,' he said.

'Take it,' I said suddenly, and thrust it into his hand. 'It'll remind you.'

He examined it. I think he was quite touched. 'I'll think of you,' he said. 'There's your little o.'

'It'll remind you of Anne,' I went on. His head gave that little jump which heads give when they are surprised. 'She gave it to me.'

He seemed pleased. He put it in his pocket and patted it. 'I'll think of you both,' he said.

I felt immediately horrid and guilty. A handkerchief seemed such a worthless thing to give when so much was being taken.

We continued with our clumsy farewells a few moments

231

longer, and then, thankfully, I left. But as I approached the station exit, I stopped and looked back. Harry was just stepping on to the train, but he sensed me looking at him and glanced towards me. So we looked at each other for the last time, over our respective shoulders. I began to cry.

As the women of Europe sent their menfolk to die, they looked back at them over their shoulders, and cried till the tears ran down into the cracks in their bottoms.

# Chapter 8

## Returns Yet Again

## (In More Ways Than One)

No excuses necessary.

It has been a day, a day. A Saturday to boot.

Though I have spent very little of my adult life reporting to a place of work, I still have a Saturday morning feeling once a week. As I get that purple rain-charged Sunday afternoon feeling also, be it the bluest and most sunny Sunday afternoon imaginable.

But today I did something I have not done for I don't know how long, Saturday or not Saturday. I slept right through the approach of the milkman. I had been working hard on Dot the night before, and when I went to bed I slept like a log. The chiming of the bottles entered my dream, but this time it stayed there, so I didn't follow it back to wakefulness. Perhaps I really mistook it for the tolling of bells and thought, in so far as I thought at all, of churches and then of Sundays. Though I don't lie abed on Sundays any more than I do on Saturdays, I would be more likely to, if likelihood rather than the actual fact were the criterion. On Saturdays I tend to get out of my bed with a dreadfully senile, slow-motion version of alacrity. Saturdays are yellow, even when the sun isn't shining. On Saturdays I think what fun it would be to read the newspaper, though I don't take one. How nice it would be to go for a jolly long walk before lunch, despite the fact that I rarely do. I hardly ever even go for a jolly short one, except to buy provender. The last time I went for a walk for its own sake, for an altruistic or disinterested walk, was when I went in pursuit of the milkman's dropped bottle, and that walk

233

perhaps had a necessity of its own. Mostly I simply open my front door a crack and drop my *eye* into the outside world, as one might dip one's toe into bath-water. Somehow or other the world never seems quite the right temperature. Ultimately, I suspect one's timidity about one's bath is caused by its undue wetness rather than its temperature; by the same or opposite token the world outside seems uncompromisingly *hard*. At my age, at least.

But this Saturday I slept. I incorporated the chiming into my dream, and then the banshee whine of the float. No doubt these two external effects had a deleterious influence on the quality of my dreaming, because I awoke to fear, dwarfish fear. There was banging somewhere in the house. I was in that long-ago wood again, with the dwarves at work somewhere nearby, and the witch queen approaching through the forest glades, carrying that apple which was half green and half red – 'Like life!' I exclaimed on my pillow, where my divorced head lay like an apple also, but wholly pink. I cackled victoriously as best I might. I suppose I was trying to prove my superiority to the apple and the other components of the dream by seeing them as symbolic. But I didn't convince myself, as I often fail to do. My heart thumped at the prospect of imminent thunder, and then there was a sudden crash and the banging stopped.

It wasn't a crash of thunder, it was the crash of a dropped bottle, but inexplicably near. Far far nearer than before, streets nearer, as near almost as the proffered apple. The realization that I was out of the world of dwarves and witches and back in the realm of common or garden milkmen did nothing at all to alleviate my fear. I felt rather as though some monstrous dream milkman were lurching towards me through the woods, with great white bulbous bottles instead of fingers, so that he looked like a milk-bottle variety of neanderthal man. It was as though I hadn't woken up at all but rather that my dream had escaped into the woken-up world.

The banging had stopped, as banging seems to have to do after a crash. I hoisted me up from the depths of the bed. I was shaking all over. I swung my legs over the side of the bed. One foot shook its way into a slipper. I put my dressing-gown on until it was shaking too. Then I hurried off to the front door.

234

Though the banging and crashing had ceased the front door wasn't silent. There was a curious noise coming from outside. It sounded for all the world like something sniffing. Something with enormous nostrils, a troll perhaps. It's odd how a homely detail like a sniff can make things worse, not better. When I was a girl there was a huge chemist in a tiny chemist's shop in the local village, who squeaked. He was a strange being in all sorts of ways, but a pillar of the community. In fact he played the organ in church on Sundays, sometimes rather tipsily according to my mother, who should have known (not that she went to church very often). But when children came into his shop he had a tendency to squeak, as if despite his gigantic form he'd been given the vocal chords of a mouse. Probably he did it to make himself seem less alarming, though the effect was the opposite: he became the Squeaking Man, and a terror to us all.

The sniffs tinkled. What was being sniffed was the broken glass.

I put my shaky hand to the knob and opened the door.

The milkman was out there, sweeping up a bottle with his little broom. I'd known this would be the case, and yet I'd been frightened because I'd expected my dream-milkman. Instead it was the workaday one, grizzled, serious, busy. Sniff sniff went his little straw broom. Tinkle tinkle went the heaping glass.

'Damn and blast it,' he said conversationally, without looking up. 'I was knocking at your door. I must have forgotten the bottle in my other hand. Forgot what I was doing. Bingo, down she drops.'

'You seem to be making a habit of dropping bottles lately,' I said, perhaps more hostilely than I ought, but I needed some revenge for his previous manifestation. I was still shaking.

'I beg your pardon,' he replied, ceasing to sweep. 'I don't know when I last dropped a bottle.'

'I do,' I told him. 'No, I don't. But it wasn't very long ago.'

He gave a last testy sweep. 'I don't think I ever *have* dropped a bottle down this road.'

'I didn't say this road.'

'For heaven's sake,' he said. 'Have you got a dustpan?'

With a certain amount of presence of mind, I replied: 'Don't worry about that, I'll dispose of it later.' The last thing I wanted

235

was him hopping about on my doorstep while I undertook a dustpan hunt.

'Thank you,' he replied.

'Perhaps you would be kind enough to tell me what you were doing knocking on my door in the first place. It's not pay-day, as far as I know.'

It was then that he delivered his bombshell. 'Oh,' he said, 'it's just I didn't see you in your usual place. By the window. So I thought I'd just knock to see if you were all right.'

I stared at him, pole-axed. He tucked his broom under his arm as if he didn't have a care in the world.

'I must say,' I managed to splutter out, 'that it's hardly your business whether I'm all right or not all right. It's your business to deliver me my milk. Which you seem to have done this morning with too much, too much...' I looked down at the dropped bottle. As usual just when I was about to win an argument I'd lost my grip on a vital word. 'Alacrity,' I said finally. It was probably wasted on him in any case.

'I'll be off then,' he said, as if that were the logical outcome of the discussion.

'I wouldn't mind a bottle of milk before you leave. I don't think that one is in any condition.' I pointed at the milk-soaked shards which looked like a heap of unwanted diamonds, recklessly left.

'I've left yours there,' he said, pointing in turn to a bottle that sat plump as pie on my doorstep. I hadn't noticed it, typically. 'The one I dropped wasn't yours.'

'Thank you very much for being so thoughtful as to drop other *people's*,' I riposted as tartly as I could.

He went off. I had the feeling that somehow or other he had had essentially the last word, despite my efforts. Damn my damned dustpan. I'll dig it out later. I picked up my bottle of milk and went in to breakfast.

Which was uneventful. I had a boiled egg and soldiers. Nothing exploded. Very little went missing. When I had finished I felt ahead of myself. I could go to my desk and do some more Dot. I decided not to clear away. That could be reserved for unsatisfactory days. I experienced an onset of minor hubris, rather as you can experience an onset of minor arthritis, at least according to an advertisement that was wrapped around my vegetables. Saturday had hurdled its initial obstacles, and was proving to be a satisfactory Saturday after all.

I rose from my dishevelled table. I walked over to the kitchen door. Up down up down. I was limping! For a second I really believed there was something wrong with one of my legs, though I wasn't sure which. How can you tell, impromptu, whether one leg has grown, or the other shrunk? At least, in the absence of pain? I went, as though by a limp of the mind, from hubris to O me miserum. I thought: I've inherited Uncle Taylor's bad leg after all. And then I took the trouble to look down and realized I was still wearing my one slipper. I had eaten breakfast in my spying-on-the-milkman attire!

Obviously over-sleeping had put me out. And then the wretched milkman deciding to knock upon my door. Silly little man, perhaps he *liked* to be spied on. Little did he know, when he knocked his knock, that he was casting a sort of spell upon me, like a reverse fairy godmother, that would keep me in my nightie and my solitary slipper for another hour.

I hurried into the hall on the way to my bedroom. As luck would have it, at the very moment that I glanced in passing at my front door, a letter poked like a sudden tongue through the letterbox, and flopped on to the floor. I stopped in my tracks. I wouldn't be able to dress in peace of mind knowing it was down here waiting for me. I diddle dumpling-ed over to it and picked it up. The envelope was brown and business-like, and my address was typed, so at least it didn't emanate from the Grandson. Or did it? My heart plummetted as I made out what was printed on the top left hand corner of the envelope: Shrewsbury Area Health Authority.

I began to open it there and then, with fumbling hands. Then I realized that was silly. At my age I ought to be able to make some sort of effort to accommodate life's slings and arrows. I could sit at my chaotic kitchen table at the very least. So back I went to the eyesocket of my boiled egg, the crumbs of my soldiers, and all the other casualties. So much for not tidying up, I thought. A letter sliding, as from a butler's silver tray, on to a refined and shiny surface, that would be a letter with which one could deal! When hubris is extinguished by the all too real realities of my existence, it has a tendency to pop up again, phoenix-like, in that other realm of Later, where my boiled eggs will have been disposed of, and my kitchen table will be just-so.

Tum-ti-tum
Tum
Tum

Dear... *Miss Watson*
We are writing to inform you that the result of your recent medical examination was... NEGATIVE.
Please consult your doctor promptly in case of further health problems.

Yours sincerely

*Scrawl* (no doubt Speck and Pong,
Licensed Practitioners)

When, all those years ago, we got the telegram about Harry saying We regret to inform you, *I* had to open it. Cook brought it in at breakfast. She gave it to Father. She was not weeping for once, but her eyes were filled to the brim with tears, to more than the brim, as if only a frail meniscus held her bawling in check. Father held the small telegram in his big hands as if he didn't know what it was. No, that's simply not correct. He knew exactly what it was so he had decided not to know *any*thing. His eyes were as blank and bland as a newborn kitten's. He looked at that telegram as an occupant of the Garden of Eden might look at a telegram that had for some strange reason been delivered there. Perhaps that marked the beginning of my impatience with him.

'For heaven's sake, Daddy,' I said. 'Don't sit there like that. Open it.'

He continued to sit there like that. I knew exactly what the problem was. If he so much as moved, his final argument with Harry would come back, his refusal to go to the station, his very forethought in fearing such a telegram as this. It would be as though the telegram had crystallized out of his own fears and anticipation. As if he were after all responsible, precisely because he had worried about this eventuality. As if by saying

238

it, he had made it happen (as writers do). As if he had laid a curse. So he sat there, pretending he didn't know what a telegram was. And finally I snatched it out of his big clumsy incoherent hand and read it myself. It didn't say anything interesting, just words. It was nothing to do with Harry, who was a person. That's what happens when you are dead. You stop being a person, and become, if you become anything, simply words.

The word *I* had become was Negative. Hardly even a word. More like a dull little box to store something away in. What was being stored away in it in this case was my health. My rude health could struggle away in the darkness until it was worn out, like a rabbit in a sack. Negative. How outrageous of them, how impertinent, how utterly shameless. It was one of those big fibs that came true simply because the fibber is in a position of authority, so that what he says, *goes*.

In this case, I was perfectly healthy until I went for my check-up, and then Speckledy and Pong, egged on by the Grandson, applied a word as in the old days we used to apply a cold compress, and sucked the healthy juices out of me, leaving me, fat and popped-forth as I am, a mere husk. If you can metamorphose into words when you die (here lies *Olive Watson*), then, by the same token, words can kill you. I sometimes think I began to die in 1916, when I read the words of that telegram. (And perhaps I had killed too, when Harry asked me for a word, and I gave him the wrong one.) And now along comes the Grandson, his mouth full of nails, bludgeoning me with his *Negative*.

I had just about arrived at this glum conclusion when the banging resumed.

Dutifully, I felt shocked, all over again. I sat in place, Speckledy's word clasped in my hand, with my ears staring, as it were, at the resumed din. Surely not the milkman again? What excuse could he use this time? That he was worried that I hadn't put my clothes on yet? Or done the washing up? Was *he* in the pay of the Grandson also? It wasn't so far-fetched. Grandson rings up dairy, I'm a lawyer, open sesame, can I speak to the milkman who delivers my beloved Aunty's milk, rather worried about the old dear, her health is somewhat negative, perhaps you could keep an eye on her for me, harass her to oblivion, break some bottles in her vicinity?

After a few moments I realized I *was* being silly after all. For one thing, the knocking wasn't thunderous, as previously, but a regular and doom-loaded bang bang bang. And for another, no milkman would go back unnecessarily to the scene of a dropped bottle, Grandson or no Grandson. He'd done his hostile duty for today.

No, it would be the horrible man. I hadn't seen him for a week or two, it was about time. In fact, it wasn't beyond the bounds of possibility that the Grandson had got in touch with him, too. What could be more natural, assuming a ruthless, greedy, and utterly machiavellian sensibility, than to sneak around to my neighbour and pry into my eccentricities? To what extent has the old girl been Letting Go? Rejected chicken in favour of pilchards. Refused offer of lawn. Doesn't allow me in. And then, after these preliminaries, the enquiry would reach a more intimate plane. She needs to be protected from herself. Her health is, well, pretty negative I'm afraid. We'll be doing the ancient thing a favour, in the long run. What I need to know is, you know, the whereabouts of her, what do they call it, her soft underbelly.

Alas and alack, the whereabouts of my soft underbelly are an ill-kept secret. Here on the kitchen table is my soft underbelly. There in my short curtains is my soft underbelly. Below in my one slipper is my soft underbelly. Outside in my unkempt lawn is my soft underbelly. Over at the Health Centre, in my negative report, is my soft underbelly. Deep in the past, in my alleged and non-existent offspring, is my soft and stretch-marked underbelly. (Not the Kingdom of Later, this one, but of Once Upon a Time, a world in which all sorts of things didn't happen, including my being a mother. In Once Upon a Time I'm no doubt surrounded by unreal children, though in the real world I have brought no one to birth, except those fictional children in my books, and of course they inhabit the Kingdom of Once Upon a Time in any case.)

I am all soft underbelly, except where I have Achilles' heels. Nowadays even my belly is a soft underbelly.

What a masterplan! The milkman attacks from one flank, the horrible man from another, Speckledy and Pong gallop down the middle. I've lived in a century of wars, I know what

240

that strategy is called: a pincer movement. And wielding the pincers is the Grandson, standing aloof from the battlefield as a good general should, pacing up and down, perhaps, with his hands behind his back. And what is to be extracted with his pincers is *me*.

I rose to my feet and headed for the door. The milkman's attack hadn't been wholly successful: he had dropped his bottle. Possibly the horrible man would show a similar tendency towards fiasco. Let us say I am a witch, and this is my cottage. One would expect a witch's dwelling to be shrouded in a spell, as gothic houses are shrouded in fog. A spell to stop people coming in, or going out, or surviving. In my case, surely the spell could involve a tendency towards fiasco. A spell must catch something of the qualities of the caster of the spell. As a stick bends in water, so perhaps do the most level-headed intentions as they approach my abode.

To bolster up these tracings of optimism, I pictured the horrible man preparing for the fray. There he would be, in his spick and span, his *spanking*, little house, washing his breakfast dishes to a point beyond mere spotlessness, till they became breakfast dishes in the sky, before the Fall, breakfast dishes of the mind. Then he puts a deep patina on his breakfast table. Polish away, horrible man! Can you see the blank disk of your face in it yet? Or perhaps the blank disk of the table in your face? And finally he puts on those spectacles with his nose and moustache attached, makes the quick fluttery adjustments to his hair and clothing that fastidious people do, and sets off on his sortie. Revolving in his mind the battle plan for today. What is it to be: chicken? Or mail? Whichever it is, I'm ready for you, horrible man!

I opened the door. There was the Grandson, fist upraised.

'I'm sorry,' I said, in a voice that brooked no nonsense, 'I am not the slightest bit interested in chicken today, fishy or not fishy. And I've already received quite enough mail for one morning, thank you very much.'

Why? I ask myself now, hours later, why, why? I had *seen* the Grandson, I knew who I was talking to.

Probably the only fully satisfactory explanation is that I was under my spell myself. I am a witch born without immunity to my own black magic.

241

I feel ashamed to admit what went through my mind. I saw the Grandson while I was still thinking about the horrible man's false features, and because I superimposed one over the other in my mind, I assumed, for a crucial, idiotic second, that that is what must have happened *in reality*. I thought that the horrible man, in an access of cunning, had put on a different pair of spectacles this morning, one with the Grandson's face on them. I'll tell you where my soft underbelly is, it's in my brain! Lord have mercy on me, the Grandson doesn't even *wear* spectacles.

'I beg your pardon,' I went on. The Grandson remained in his knocking posture, fist raised, face gormless. 'I thought you were the horrible man,' I explained.

'I hope not, Aunty,' he replied.

I was in a position, as so often, of maximum disadvantage. The only way of alleviating it was to give him my blobby eye, as I call it. This is when I stare at someone with great intensity with my right eye (which happens to be the more powerful of the two), and screw up my left as though in the face of strong sunlight. The effect, I like to believe, is that the left transfers its rays to the right, cranking the latter to burning-glass power. I've never quite decided whether this is a mere impression I like to give, or a genuine phenomenon. I gave my editor the blobby eye when he turned my last book down in 1956. He didn't rescind his decision, but he looked upset.

'Are you all right, Aunty?' the Grandson asked. 'You look upset.'

I blobbed for a second or two longer, focusing my gaze just below his eye-level, in hopes that the effect would be to drag *his* gaze down and put him in a position of slight disadvantage. If you're the taller one of a pair and don't catch someone's eye you look as if you don't live up to your height. If you're smaller, and do ditto, then it looks (I fondly imagine) as if you're not prepared to go all the way up just to please the opposition. But as with anything else, to blob successfully you have to have an appropriate blobbee. The Grandson, big, robust, rudely-fashioned, was not, I suspect, sufficiently nuanced for an exchange of rays.

'What about you?' I finally threw back at him, 'with your fist in the air? You remind me of that poem. I'm a little teapot,

242

short and stout, here's my handle, here's my spout. Except that in your case, I suppose you're a big teapot.'

'I'm sorry,' he said, lowering his spout, 'you took me by surprise.'

'I don't see why. When you knock at somebody's door, there's always a possibility that somebody might answer it.'

'Talking about doors,' the Grandson said eagerly, his big face suffusing with a boy-scout glow, 'I could give this one a dollop, if you like. I might not be a saint, but I'm handy enough with paint.' Suddenly his face darkened again. 'I'm sorry, you know me. I like to rhyme.' He looked strangely as if he were about to burst into tears.

'I suggest Tinker Bell climbs down from your back, and you come in,' I said, trying not to sound too hospitable.

'Tinker Bell?' He furrowed his brows.

'You know. What's her name?' I knew perfectly well, but you don't always feel like spitting these things out. 'The nubile wife.'

'Maggie's not with me.'

Oddly, given that I couldn't bear the woman, I felt quite put out. 'I hope my disgusting kitchen didn't put her off,' I said in a loaded tone.

'Oh no, it's not that. Do you mind if I come in, Aunty?'

'I've just told you to.'

'Did you? To tell you the truth, I'm not taking things in very well at the moment. I don't seem to be able to concentrate.'

'Perhaps you're becoming negative,' I said. 'Possibly it runs in the family.'

He looked gormless again. 'You can imagine what effect it has on your briefs,' he said dolefully, 'when you can't concentrate.'

'Oh lordy,' I responded, triggered by the word briefs, 'I haven't got round to putting my clothes on yet. Never mind. Come in as I am.' I withdrew from the door, to allow him to get in. 'We'll sit in the front room,' I said firmly. 'Where we sat last time.'

'I'd love a cup of coffee,' the Grandson replied, branching off to the kitchen on his own initiative.

'I note,' I said, following him in, 'the lack of champagne.

243

But I suppose, given the negative state of my health, that it wouldn't be the right thing.' I stared at my former egg while I said this. It looked poignantly back towards me, like the Duke of Gloucester in *King Lear*. Exchanging gazes with the Grandson hadn't proved particularly fruitful to date. If the truth be told, I was frightened to look at him as we approached the nub of the matter. 'But you know all about that, don't you?'

'All about what?'

'The negative state of my health. The letter arrived this morning. Why don't you sit down?'

He sat down. To my surprise he sat down in the place I had occupied to eat my breakfast, facing the table and the shell of my egg. This meant of course that he had his back to me. Perhaps he didn't want to catch my eye, any more than I wanted to catch his.

'What letter?' he asked absently. Equally absently his hand travelled across my table, and dived into my bag of bread. 'I hope you don't mind,' he went on, pulling a slice out, 'I haven't had any breakfast.'

'The letter from Speckledy and Pong,' I replied.

'Speckledy and Pong who? I can't seem to see the butter.'

'It's over there. Speckledy and Pong. By the tea-caddy. The letter about the negative state of my health. The letter you've been waiting for. I wouldn't bother with the butter, if I were you. It's off.'

'The letter I've been waiting for?' He sniffed the hideous blossom of my butter. 'It smells fine to me.' He began to spread some on his slice of bread.

'There is really no need to be coy. It only arrived this morning and here you are. It's my marching orders, isn't it. My *call up*.'

The Grandson took a neat semi-circular bite out of the bread and butter. 'It's not the least bit rancid,' he said. He turned a sad, bovine, slowly-chewing head towards me, looking up at my face over his seated shoulder. 'Did you say Speckledy and Pong?'

'Yes, I did.'

'What did you mean?'

'The letter's right in front of you. Why don't you read it for yourself?' He remained looking up at me. His arm, as though it were a butler's arm, came round to the front of his head and inserted the bread and butter into his mouth. He chewed, blankly. 'I can't think it contains any surprises,' I concluded in a dark tone of voice.

He turned back to the table, put the remains of the bread and butter down, and picked the letter up. 'It's from the Shrewsbury Area Health Authority,' he said. He seemed never to lose his zest for stating the obvious. 'It says your medical examination was negative.'

'If you hoped to be convincing you should have expressed more surprise. You might even have gone so far as slight shock.'

He looked round at me again. 'I don't know what you mean by convincing. It says negative in black and white.'

'As you jolly well made sure it would.'

'I'm pleased, of course I am, but when I first met you you looked to me like the picture of rude health.'

'Oh yes,' I said sarcastically. 'So much so that you invoked Speckledy and Pong, and made sure I was given the thumb's down.'

'I think we're at cross-purposes, Aunty,' he said in pat lawyer fashion. 'I've no idea who these people Speckledy and Pong might be. Naturally I'm pleased that —'

'There you are. You're pleased that I'm negative.'

'Aunty, negative means that there's nothing wrong with you.' His arm came round and gave him another bite of bread and butter, as though by way of a concluding flourish.

I stared at him in amazement. For a while I was dumbfounded. I felt very conscious of the coldness of my bare left foot, for some reason. 'Are you saying that negative means positive?' I finally managed to ask.

'If you want to look at it like that, I suppose it does. It means you're fine.'

'If I'm so fine, what in heaven's name are *you* doing here?'

'I didn't come here about you, I came here about me. About...' His voice broke, and I realized he'd suddenly come to the brink of tears again. 'About Maggie. She's all I've got, Aunty. Except you. That's why I've come. She's gone.' He was still seated bang in front of the detritus of my breakfast, his head resting on his own shoulder, to look back and up at me. His thick goldfish lips looked oddly poignant, particularly when, even *in extremis*, they parted to admit the last portion

245

of his bread and rancid butter. The simple practicality of his lips brought to mind Arthur's ducks of so long ago, extending their necks so conveniently to be beheaded. 'She went,' the Grandson continued. 'You know what she's like, Aunty. *You* appreciated her. What was it you called her? Tinker Bell. You understood. She's a magical person, Aunty. She's far far too good for me. I knew she was. I always thought she'd go. She liked *you*, of course. She said to me, if you were half as much, if you were one bit as much, as, as your Aunty is, you'd be worth having. She said she was going away to think about us. She didn't know whether she'd come back. The thing is, Aunty, I don't know what to do.'

'You could go after her, I suppose,' I said. He looked somewhat disappointedly up at me. His fish-lips opened and closed as though he were lip-reading, trying to gloss my text and find hope in it somewhere. 'Search high and low.'

'That's what I was wondering, Aunty.'

'Or you could just go home and wait for her.'

'Do you think she'll come back?'

'Sometimes people come back. If you wait long enough.'

And then the Grandson did something dreadful. He suddenly skewed his chair around and leapt from it. But instead of landing on his feet he flopped on to his knees and held me tight. I looked down at him, utterly non-plussed. He looked like Arthur. He was Uncle Taylor's grandson. His giant but abruptly foreshortened size recalled my little father. He was lost and forlorn like Harry. It was as though my family had returned from the Land Where Lost Things Go to embrace me – round my knobby and unprepossessing knees, more's the pity, enfolded as they were in my beastly nightie, and culminating floorwards in a solitary slipper with a pom-pom on the top. Only my mother was missing. O heavens, I thought, from his point of view my mother is *me*.

I felt repelled by him, as you do by somebody you've misjudged. Nevertheless, I patted him somewhat amateurishly on the head. I'm at a rather late stage of my existence to be called upon to be maternal.

At last he went off: back to the chimaera or reality of his Tinker Bell. After he'd gone I felt suddenly very depressed, and I wept.

# Chapter 14
## The Following Morning

The following morning Dot felt much better.